The Tattered Cloak
and Other Novels

The
Tattered
Cloak

and Other Novels

Nina Berberova

Translated from the Russian
by Marian Schwartz

ALFRED A. KNOPF ❧ NEW YORK 1991

THIS IS A BORZOI BOOK PUBLISHED BY
ALFRED A. KNOPF, INC,

Copyright © 1990, 1991 by Marian Schwartz
All rights reserved under International and Pan-American
Copyright Conventions.
Published in the United States by Alfred A. Knopf, Inc., New York.
Distributed by Random House, Inc., New York.

These translations published in Great Britian in two separate volumes as
Three Novels: The Resurrection of Mozart; *The Waiter and the Slut*; *Astashev in Paris*;
and *Three Novels: Volume II: In Memory of Schliemann*; *The Black Death*;
The Tattered Cloak by Chatto & Windus Ltd., London, in 1990 and 1991.
Originally published in France in six volumes as *La Résurrection de Mozart*; *Le
Laquais et la Putain*; *Astachev a Paris*; *La Mémoire de Schliemann*; *Le Mal Noir*; *De
Cape et de Larmes* by Actes Sud, Arles, in 1986, 1988, 1989, 1990, and 1991.
Copyright © 1986, 1988, 1989, 1990, 1991 by Actes Sud

ISBN 0-679-40281-0
LC 90-53565

Manufactured in the United States of America

FIRST EDITION

Contents

The Tattered Cloak
and Other Novels

The Resurrection of Mozart

I

IN THE EARLY DAYS of June 1940, just at the time
when the French army was beginning its final and irrevocable retreat after the breach at Sedan, on a quiet warm
evening, a group of four women and five men were sitting
in a garden under the trees, about thirty miles from Paris.
They were in fact talking about Sedan, talking of how
the last few days had restored to that name which, like
crinoline, had long since gone out of fashion, the ominous
connotations it had had before; this town, which none
of them had ever seen, and which had died in the time
of their grandfathers, seemed to have been resurrected
in order to relive the tragic events that were destined for
it alone.

The silence was so complete that when they stopped
talking and returned to their own private thoughts, they
could hear through the open windows the clock ticking
in the large old house. The sky was green, clear, and
lovely, and the stars were just beginning to shine, so few
and far-flung that they failed to form any definite pattern.
The old trees—acacias, limes—neither breathed nor

trembled, as if standing stock-still were a safeguard against something that was invisible to men but somehow immanent in the summer evening. The hosts and their guests had just finished supper; the table had not yet been cleared. Some wineglasses were still on the table. Slowly, the green light of the darkening sky transformed the faces of the seated company, which were now obscured by shadows. They were talking about war and about the omens of war. A young woman, a guest who had driven out from town with her husband and sister, restraining her brassy voice, remarked that she had seen a meteor a fortnight before.

"It was about this time of day. The sky was just as hazy. At first it looked like a falling star, but it was so long and it was so bright."

"You probably wouldn't even have noticed it a year ago," said another guest, smiling. This was Chabarov, a bald, robust man with a drooping black mustache and wearing a bright blue shirt. He was a groundsman at a château about eight miles away and had just arrived on his bicycle.

"A year ago," said Vassily Georgievich Sushkov, the host, a tall man, taller than anyone else at the table, grayhaired but not yet old, with a sharp and furtive look in his eye. "Yes, it was exactly a year ago today that Nevelsky died. He knew a lot of this was coming. He predicted so much of it."

"Well, he couldn't have picked a better time to die. At least he doesn't have to see what we see. If he were resurrected he'd either spit in disgust or break down and cry."

Facing the hostess, at the opposite end of the table,

sat a Frenchman brought along by Chabarov but whom no one else really knew. Simply, and without any fussy apology, he asked them to translate what they were all saying.

"Monsieur Daunou, we were talking about the dead, and what they would say if they were resurrected and saw what's going on now," replied Maria Leonidovna Sushkova.

Daunou took his black pipe out of his mouth, furrowed his brow, and smiled.

"Is it worth waking the dead?" he said, looking his hostess straight in the eye. "I suppose I might well invite Napoleon to come and have a look at our times, but I'd certainly spare my parents the pleasure."

Suddenly everyone started talking at once.

"Resurrect them for your sake or for theirs? I don't understand," Manyura Krein, who had come from Paris, asked with a lively expression, not addressing anyone in particular and no longer trying to conceal her loud voice. She had a full mouth of her very own white teeth, which gave the impression of being false. "If it were for their sake, then of course you'd resurrect Napoleon and Bismarck and Queen Victoria, and maybe even Julius Caesar. But if I could bring someone from the past back to life for my sake, just for mine, then that's an entirely different thing. That calls for some thought. Such a large choice, so many temptations . . . still, silly as it sounds, I think I'd resurrect Pushkin."

"A charming, fun-loving, marvelous man," said Maria Leonidovna Sushkova. "What a joy it would be to see him alive."

"Or maybe Taglioni?" continued Manyura Krein.

"I'd lock her up at home so I could look at her whenever I wanted."

"And then take her to America," put in Chabarov, "and let the impresarios tear her to shreds."

"Come on, if you're going to resurrect anyone, then don't resurrect Taglioni," said Fyodor Egorovich Krein with barely repressed irritation. He was Manyura's husband, twice her age, and a friend of Sushkov's. "There's no need to be frivolous. I would make the best of the occasion. I would drag Tolstoy back into God's world. Wasn't it you, dear sir, who denied the role of the individual in history? You who declared that there would be no more wars? And wasn't it you who took a skeptical view of vaccination? No, don't try to wriggle out of it now. Just have a look at the result." It was evident that Fyodor Egorovich had scores to settle with Tolstoy and that he had an entire text prepared should they happen to meet in the next life.

"*Avec Taglioni on pourrait faire fortune,*" Chabarov repeated his thought in French.

"And I, gentlemen," piped in Sushkov's mother, who wore heavy violet powder and reeked of some unpleasant perfume, "and I, gentlemen, would resurrect Uncle Lyosha. Wouldn't he be surprised?"

No one knew who Uncle Lyosha was, so no one said anything for a minute or two. Little by little the conversation had drawn everyone in, taking them far from that evening, that garden, and into the past, the recent or the very distant past, as if someone had already made a firm promise to wave a magic wand and fulfill everyone's wish, so that now the only problem was in making a choice, and it was a difficult choice because no one wanted to miscalculate, especially the women.

"No one but Mozart will do for me, though. Yes, it has to be Mozart," Maria Leonidovna thought. "There's no one else I want, and it would be useless anyway."

She had decided not out of any morbid love of music, as can happen with women who have reached a certain age and who are generally thought of as "cultured," but merely because she connected that name in her mind with her earliest childhood, and because it lived on as something pure, transparent, and eternal that might take the place of happiness. Maria Leonidovna smoked avidly and waited for someone else to say something. She didn't feel like talking herself. It was Magdalena, Manyura Krein's sister, a young woman of thirty, full-figured and pale, with unusually rounded shoulders, who spoke up. The sight of her always brought to mind those undeniable statistics about how in Europe so many millions of young women had been left single because there weren't enough husbands to go round.

"No, I wouldn't resurrect a single famous man," said Magdalena, with a certain disdain for men of renown. "I'd much prefer an ordinary mortal. An idealistic youth from the early nineteenth century, a follower of Hegel, a reader of Schiller; or a courtier to one of the French kings."

She shrugged her heavy shoulders and looked around. But already it was nearly dark, and one could barely make out the faces round the table. But the stars were now quite visible overhead, and the sky seemed familiar again.

Chabarov didn't say anything for a long while. Finally he made a muffled nasal sound, drummed his fingers on the table, opened his mouth, but suddenly hesitated, said nothing, and sank back into his thoughts.

The ninth person present, who had been silent until then, was Kiryusha, Sushkov's nineteen-year-old son and Maria Leonidovna's stepson. In the family he was considered a little backward. Slowly he unglued his thick, wide lips and, gazing trustfully at his stepmother with his blue and very round eyes, asked if it was possible to resurrect two people at the same time.

God alone knows what was going through his dreamy mind at that point. He seemed to think that everything had already been decided by the others and that only the details remained to be settled.

"*Mais c'est un vrai petit jeu*," noted Daunou with a sad laugh, and immediately everyone seemed to move and smile once more, as if returning from far away. "Everyone has their own private passion, and everyone is being terribly serious about it."

Maria Leonidovna just nodded at him. "Mozart, of course, only Mozart will do," she repeated to herself. "And it's a good thing I'm not young anymore and don't have any physical interest in seeing him. We could sit up till dawn, and he could play our piano and we'd talk. And everyone would come to see him and listen to him— the neighbors' gardener and his wife, the postman, the shopkeeper and his family, the stationmaster. . . . What a joy it would be! And tomorrow there'd be no post, no trains, nothing at all. Everything would be topsy-turvy. And there wouldn't be any war. No, there would be war all the same."

She lit another cigarette. For a moment the match illuminated her thin, slightly worn face and her delicate, beautiful hands. Everything about her, except her face, was feminine, youthful, and sleek, particularly her light and silent walk. Everyone noticed when Maria Leonidovna suddenly got up and walked out under the trees, and then came back to the table, and they could see the lit end of her cigarette in the darkness of the advancing night.

A chill came up about then from the low-lying part of the garden, where two little stone bridges crossed the narrow loops of the flower-banked stream. Old Mrs. Sushkova, wrapped in a shawl, was dozing in her chair. Kiryusha was looking up blankly, and it was clear that like the trees and stars he was merely existing and not thinking. And suddenly, somewhere far off, perhaps twenty-five or thirty miles away to the east, where the sun rises in the summer, the sound of gunfire rumbled, burst out, and then disappeared. It was very much like thunder and yet completely different.

"Time we were on our way," everyone started saying immediately, and Manyura Krein, jangling her bracelets, ran into the house for her coat and bag.

They went through the dining room and big dark hallway and came out into the yard where the car was parked. Sushkov's mother was going back to Paris as well. She put on a hat with a big violet-colored flower; even her suitcase was a shade of violet. The motor idled a few moments, and then, cautiously spreading its black wings, the car backed up to the gates. Krein, sitting behind the steering wheel, waved once again to those left behind. Manyura, whose porcelain mouth alone was illuminated, smiled behind the glass and said something. The car started up, stopped, shifted into forward, and, as if it had hauled itself out, disappeared, leaving behind it a wake of invisible, acrid exhaust.

Chabarov went to find the bicycles.

"We'd be very happy to see you here any time," Sushkov told the Frenchman. "We're staying all summer, and on Sundays, as you see, our friends visit. You're always welcome."

"*Enchanté, monsieur,*" Daunou replied. "I have spent an unforgettable evening."

And following behind Chabarov he kissed Maria Leonidovna's hand.

The next day, as usual, Vassily Georgievich took the train into town, leaving Maria Leonidovna and Kiryusha to themselves. That Monday, at one o'clock in the afternoon, several dozen airplanes bombed Paris for the first time.

II

NEWS OF THE bombardment of Paris only came that evening. During the day you could hear the gunfire, but it was so far away that you couldn't tell whether it was in Paris or Pontoise, where it had been a few days before. In the evening the papers arrived, and all the people who lived in the little village, in the center of which stood a neglected church with a caved-in roof, came spilling out into the modest avenue of sturdy plane trees that led from the café to the *mairie*.

The village consisted almost entirely of old women. Of course they might have only been, as in any French village, about half the population, but they were the ones you saw most often. Seeing them out in the street, talking together or shopping or shaking out a rug or hanging out clothes, they seemed to make up nine-tenths of the inhabitants.

Some of them were no more than fifty, and they were still smart and cheerful, just turning gray, rosy-cheeked and sharp-eyed. Others were wrinkled and toothless, with swollen veins. Others, who could remember the invasion of the Germans in 1870, were hunched up and barely able to put one sore foot in front of the other, and they had darkened hands, long black nails, and lifeless faces. They were all much of a kind, talking to each other in the same way, and using the same words, wherever they met, be it on street corners, beneath the plane trees, or by their front gates. They all wore wide calico aprons that either tied at the back or buttoned in front. Some wore steel glasses on their noses and knit, rocking in a chair and holding the skein of wool under their left arms. Almost all of them were widows of men killed in the last war, and all without exception had seen either a son or a son-in-law set off for this war.

That evening, in the shady lane that ran alongside the fence to the Sushkovs' garden, the silence was broken. Kiryusha came to tell Maria Leonidovna that Paris had been bombed, buildings destroyed, warehouses burned, and more than a thousand killed or wounded. Maria

Leonidovna looked at Kiryusha, who was smiling broadly, and it saddened her that this human being, who was now completely grown, was still the same child she had first met twelve years before. There was a time—and lately she had thought of it often—when he had suddenly decided to learn the alphabet. A brief light had pierced the darkness of that sick brain. He had tried to learn the letters, but nothing ever came of it. It had all ended with Kiryusha's short and relatively happy affair with the girl who worked in the charcuterie. Relatively happy because after that he had started to get gradually worse.

Maria Leonidovna went through Paris in her mind. In that city, above all, was Vassily Georgievich, as well as their pretty, sunny, quiet apartment, which she loved so much. Then there were the Kreins, the Abramovs, the Snezhinskys, Edouard Zontag, Semyon Isaakovich Freiberg, Lenochka Mikhailova, and many many more who could have been wounded or killed. And when she thought about all those people living at various ends of the city, scattered across the old creased map of Paris that she kept in her mind, a flashing light lit up, here and there, and then went out.

"Yes. This had to happen," she told herself. "We were talking about it only yesterday. So why did he go? The Kreins could have stayed on, too. Yesterday we said . . . What else were we talking about yesterday? Oh, yes! 'You are God, Mozart, and of that fact yourself innocent.' One ought to aspire to something that combines everything beautiful, pure and eternal, like those clouds, not all these terrible things, all these murders and lies. Before the ultimate silence closes in on you, shouldn't you listen to what the stars are saying to each other?"

She went over to the little radio, brand-new, which Kiryusha was strictly forbidden to go near, and turned the knob. First a French voice spoke, then an English voice, then a German voice. All of it was crammed into that wooden box, separated only by invisible barriers. The voices all said the same thing. And suddenly it switched to music, singing, Spanish or maybe Italian, the voluptuous and carefree strumming of a guitar. But she picked up the word *amore*, and she turned the machine off and walked to the window, from which she could see the village road among the thick fields of oats, green and ash gray.

On Tuesday, Wednesday, and Thursday, soldiers were billeted on the village: heavy green trucks camouflaged with foliage as if decked out for a carnival and bearing numbers written in red lead paint brought in five hundred young, healthy, raucous soldiers and four officers wearing long overcoats and with tired, worried, feverish faces. A billeting officer appeared at Maria Leonidovna's door—the house the Sushkovs rented was by far the best in the village—and she immediately moved Kiryusha into the dining room, giving his room to the captain and the space in the annex to three sublieutenants.

The four officers slept in their clothes. The sentry— sometimes a short, swarthy, and yellow-eyed man or else a tall, erect, and big-faced one—came to wake them several times during the night. Vassily Georgievich called every day; his call came to the post office at the corner of their side street and the square. A little boy missing his front teeth ran to fetch Maria Leonidovna, and she ran after him in her silent, girlish way, wearing whatever she happened to have on, ran into the tiny single-windowed building, picked up the receiver, and listened to Vassily Georgievich say that everything was fine, that he had received the money, seen Edouard, was eating with the Snezhinskys, would arrive on Saturday.

"I have soldiers staying with me," she said, still out of breath from running. "I've given them Kiryusha's room. And the annex."

"Maybe I should come? You're not afraid?"

"Why should I be afraid? Good-bye."

And in fact, at that minute, she thought that she wasn't afraid in the least. In a way, it was even reassuring to have these polite, laconic men close at hand.

But at night she barely slept. She listened. From far away, in the dead of night, she caught the diffuse, persistent sound of a motorcycle. While the sound was on the far side of the woods, it was no more than a whisper, but as it got nearer it became louder and more focused, and then suddenly it was zooming down the lane and stopping at the house next door, where the sentry was posted. The motor was switched off, and then she could hear voices, steps. The gate banged. Someone was walking into the house, into her house, some stranger, and the old blind dog got up from its straw and went to sniff at his tracks in the gravel of the yard, growling. A light went on somewhere, she heard someone running through the house, through the annex. Something clinked, a door slammed. Kiryusha was asleep close by, in the dining room, whose door she left open. These night sounds didn't frighten her anymore. What frightened her was everything that was going on in the world that night.

She wasn't afraid of the quiet strangers either. They

left the third night, leaving the doors and the gate wide open, leaving the village in trucks camouflaged with fresh branches. She wasn't afraid of the sentries who came to see them or of the five hundred strong, half-sober soldiers quartered all over the village. She was afraid of the air, the warm June air, through which gunfire rolled across the horizon and submerged her, her house, and her garden, along with the summer clouds. And there was no question that this puff of wind, which was somehow just like time itself, would in the end bring something terrible and ruinous, such as death itself. Just as, looking at the calendar, no one doubted any longer that in five, ten, or fifteen days something dreadful was going to happen, so, feeling that faint breeze on her face day and night, she could say with assurance that it would bring to these parts murder, occupation, devastation, and darkness.

For the air, over the last few days, had been warm, clear, and fragrant. Kiryusha worked in the garden, watering the flowers in front of the house every evening and looking after the neighbors' ducklings. Maria Leonidovna, wearing a bright cotton print dress, and a scarf around her head, went to clean out the annex, where she found a bag of cartridges that had been left behind and two unsealed letters, which she threw away without reading. There were cigarette butts in the cup by the washstand, and a charred newspaper lay on the floor. She made up Kiryusha's bed in his room and when the woman from next door came over to do the housework, told her to wash all the floors in the house.

On the same day, toward evening, fugitives from Soissons arrived at the neighbors': two fat, pale women, an old man, and some children. A mattress was laid out on the roof of their filthy car, and to the amazed questioning of the villagers the new arrivals explained that this was what everybody was doing now, that this was what would protect you from bullets. The old man was carried into the house by his hands and feet: he was unconscious.

Before night other fugitives arrived to stay in the sky-blue, toylike house opposite the church. People said that some of the soldiers were still there, and were spending the night at the other end of the village. There seemed to be a stranger who had come from far away by foot or by car hiding in every house for the night. There were no lights, all was dark, but voices could be heard everywhere from behind the shutters; the café was full of shouting and singing. Under the plane trees the old ladies, who had stayed longer than was normal, spoke in low voices.

Maria Leonidovna locked the front door, hung the curtains over the windows, cleared away the remains of supper, and, as she always did, sat in the next room and talked with Kiryusha while he got ready for bed. From time to time he exclaimed happily:

"I cleaned my teeth! I took off my left shoe!"

And if you didn't know it was a nineteen-year-old man in there—who ate enormous meals, snored loudly in his sleep, and couldn't read—you would think it was a ten-year-old boy going to bed and, for a joke, talking in a bass voice.

After she had turned out the lights in the dining room and Kiryusha's room and went to her own, she stood for a long time by the open window and looked out at where, in the daytime, she could see the road and the oat fields. Tomorrow Vassily Georgievich was due to return. The idea was pleasant and consoling. But today Maria Leonidovna had barely given a thought to her husband; in fact she hadn't stopped thinking about Mozart.

Or rather, not about Mozart himself. Right now, as a new crescent moon appeared on the edge of this anxious but subdued night, her thoughts took on a special clarity. All day long, or rather, over the last few days and this evening, she had been asking herself the same question, and there was no answer to it: Why was it that horror, cruelty, and affliction made themselves felt so easily, became concrete and weighed all the more heavily, whereas everything sublime, gentle, unexpected, and full of charm cast a frail shadow across the heart and thoughts, so one couldn't touch it or look at it closely or feel its shape and weight?

"Except for love, of course," she thought, standing by the window. "Only love gives that kind of joy. But what about someone who doesn't want to love anymore, who can no longer love? I have no one to love; it's too late for me. I have a husband, I don't need anyone else."

And all of a sudden she thought she heard the latch on the gate click, and she distinctly heard someone come into the yard, take two steps, and stop.

"Who's there?" she asked quietly.

The darkness was not yet total, and the faint, blurred shadow of a man lay on the whitish gravel in the yard. The shadow moved and the gravel crunched. The man must have been able to see Maria Leonidovna clearly as she stood in the open window, to the right of the front door. The door, as Maria Leonidovna recalled, was locked. But the man, who was slowly and purposefully walking across the yard, made no response. She could hardly see him. He walked up the porch stairs, stopped three paces away from Maria Leonidovna, put out his hand, and the door opened. And when he had already walked into the house she wanted to scream. But, as in a dream, she was unable to produce any sound.

He was pale and thin, with a long nose and tangled hair. Everything he had on, from his shoes to his hat, seemed to have been borrowed from someone else. His dusty hands were so slender and frail that he couldn't have used them even if he had wanted to. His face was weary, youthful, but it wasn't a boy's face. She could tell that he looked younger than he was, but that in fact he could be over thirty.

"Forgive me for frightening you," he said in French, but with a slight foreign accent. "Could I spend the night here somewhere?"

By the light of the lamp illuminating the spacious entryway Maria Leonidovna looked at him, standing silently and barely able to control herself. But the moment he uttered those first words and looked at her with his long, hesitant look, her fear passed, and she asked:

"Who are you?"

But he dropped his eyes.

"Where are you from?"

He shivered slightly, and his fingers clutched the upturned collar of his ample jacket, which might have been covering an otherwise naked body.

"Oh, from far, far away . . . and I'm so tired. I'd like to lie down somewhere, if that's all right."

"A fugitive," she decided, "and maybe he's a Frenchman from some out-of-the-way province. Judging by his age, he could be a soldier; by his clothes, a fugitive? Maybe a spy?"

She led him to the annex, thinking all the time that he might strike her from behind, but at the same time knowing he wouldn't. By the time they had entered the bedroom, she had lost all fear of him. He didn't even look around, but silently walked over to the bed, sat down on it, and closed his eyes. Between his shoe and trouser leg she saw a thin, bare ankle.

"Do you want to eat?" she asked, closing the shutters on the low, folding windows from inside. "It's the war, we're not supposed to show any light on the outside."

"What did you say?" he asked, shuddering a little.

"I asked whether you'd like to eat something."

"No, thank you. I had a bite to eat in your local restaurant. They were all full up, though, and couldn't give me a place to stay."

She realized it was time she went.

"Are you alone?" she spoke again, rearranging something on the table as she passed.

"What do you mean 'alone'?"

"I mean, did you come here—to the village—with friends or what?"

He raised his eyes.

"I came alone, just as I am, without any luggage," he said, smiling but not revealing his teeth. "And I'm not a soldier, I'm a civilian. A musician."

She took another look at his hands, said good-night,

and, having shown him where to turn off the light, walked out of the room.

That time she gave two turns to the lock in the door and suddenly, feeling a strangely animal weariness, went straight to bed and fell asleep. In the morning, as always, she got up early. Kiryusha was already in the garden bawling out some song, and in the annex all was quiet.

III

JUST BEFORE LUNCH she wondered, anxiously, if something had happened: the shutters and door were still closed. "Can he still be asleep?" she thought. At four o'clock Vassily Georgievich was due to arrive, and a little before then she went again to see whether her lodger was up. She half opened the door to the tiny entryway, and then the door of the room. The man was sleeping, breathing evenly. He had not removed any of his clothes, not even his shoes. He lay on his back on the wide mattress, the pillow on one side. Maria Leonidovna closed the door again.

Vassily Georgievich was late getting back; the train coming from Paris had stopped for a long time at some bridge. Sushkov had carried a large suitcase from the station to the house, practically a trunk, on his broad, strong shoulder. It was full of things gathered up from their Paris apartment, without which Vassily Georgievich could not imagine either his own or his wife's existence. There were his winter coat, Maria's old squirrel coat, warm underwear which he always wore during the winter, an album of photographs of Prague (he had lived in Czechoslovakia for a long time), expensive binoculars in their case, a pound of dried figs, which he liked to keep in reserve, a handsomely bound edition of Montesquieu's *Lettres Persanes*, and Maria Leonidovna's ball gown, sewn for a charity ball the year before at which she had sold champagne. Maria Leonidovna was surprised to see warm underwear and heavy coats in June. But Sushkov assured her that they might be cut off from Paris or could be forced to escape, and then they wouldn't know what was going to happen.

"Escape from here? Yes, of course, we'll have to escape if everyone else does. Those fugitives from Soissons are packing up their things again, and the old man is being carried out of the house to the car." She took up the newspaper her husband had brought but learned nothing from it. Vassily Georgievich spoke to her sensibly and gently. Sometimes he argued with himself, sometimes he told her what Snezhinsky and Freiberg thought about what was going on. And everything he said was accurate, fair, intelligent.

"So, your officers have gone, have they?" he asked her. "It must have been worrying for you."

"They're gone, but since yesterday there's been a"— she wanted to say "fellow" but couldn't—"man sleeping, staying in the annex. He's still asleep. He must have come the seventy-five miles on foot."

"My God, you've been staying here alone with my

idiot and you're not afraid to let in strangers," he exclaimed, never mincing words when it concerned Kiryusha. And catching her hand, scratching himself on her sharp nails, he kissed it several times.

Toward the end of the day Kiryusha told them in his incoherent way that the man staying in the annex had gone. An hour later Maria Leonidovna heard him return and lock himself in again.

"That man came back. He must be sleeping again. Don't you go bothering him," she told Kiryusha.

All the next day was the same: the visitor either lay or sat by the window and neither moved nor spoke. It was as if he were waiting for something. Or else he walked to the village for a little while, walked down the lane, across the square, down the avenue of plane trees, bought himself something to eat, and came back quietly.

Strange thoughts occurred to Maria Leonidovna. Sometimes she thought that the man was bound to be arrested. Why hadn't he told her his name? Why was he wearing clothes that didn't belong to him? If he wasn't a spy, then he was a deserter. Maybe he was Russian? In many years of living abroad, Maria Leonidovna had grown used to the fact that there were no half-mad Frenchmen. Did he have a passport or had he thrown everything away, lost it? Had he run out of the house in his underwear and then received clothes from good-hearted people on the way? But perhaps there was nothing wrong, and he was just a lonely musician who had been turned out from where he sawed away at his fiddle or gave lessons to young ladies or composed just for himself, dreaming of world acclaim.

But these thoughts came and went, and life went on without interruption. This Sunday was nothing at all like the last, when they had sat in the garden over the samovar with the Kreins. No one came from town. Chabarov and Daunou arrived at five o'clock on bicycles. The three men sat in Vassily Georgievich's study for a long time and talked, about the war, of course, but in a different way than they had the week before: they were talking about their hopes. Daunou talked about his own hopes, about how they could still put a stop to this insane, iron advance at the Seine and the Marne. Each time Maria Leonidovna looked in on them she had the feeling that the Frenchman wanted to tell her something. He got up and spoke to her in particular, and for some reason she found that unpleasant. He gave her the impression (only her, though) of being a hysteric, and when she left the room she was afraid of running into him later in the dining room, the yard, the garden.

She couldn't have explained her feeling, but Daunou's serious, determined, overly expressive face was before her all the time. She started to make tea, and he came out into the dining room, closing the door behind him as if in despair, and Maria Leonidovna felt that he was about to tell her something she would remember the rest of her life.

"*Nous sommes perdus, madame,*" he said quietly, looking into her face with his small eyes of indeterminate color. "Even the Emperor Napoleon himself, whom I wanted to resurrect last Sunday, couldn't do anything now. I'm telling only you this. You make your own decision about where and when you should leave. *Paris est sacrifié.*"

He turned white. His face contorted. But he coughed awkwardly, and everything fell into place again. She was left, frozen, holding the porcelain sugar bowl.

"There will not be a battle on the Loire. The Maginot Line will be taken from the west. Nothing at all is going to happen. It's all over. They'll go all the way to Bordeaux, to the Pyrénées. And then we'll sue for peace."

At that moment Vassily Georgievich and Chabarov walked out into the dining room, and everyone sat down at the table.

She believed Daunou, but not completely, and for that reason when she and Vassily Georgievich were alone again she was unable to convince him that everything would be as Daunou had said. She said, "You know, I think it would be best if you didn't go back to Paris again. Let's pack up tomorrow and move to the South, all three of us, Tuesday at the latest. We can spend a month or two in Provence, until things calm down. Like everyone else."

He listened to her thoughtfully, but couldn't agree.

"What would they say about me at the office? They'd call me a coward. Tomorrow I'm going to Paris, and I give you my word of honor, I'll be back on Wednesday. Even if all's well, I'll be back. Haven't we seen plenty in our time? For them this is terrible, but we've seen a lot worse. . . . 'Nothing happens at a pace like that, a pace like that,' " he sang brightly.

The next day she was left alone again with Kiryusha. The traveler was still in the annex.

He continued to get up late, sit by the window, and look out at the yard, at the trees, at the sky. Sitting erect, his hands placed on the windowsill, he looked and listened with a sad and equal attention both to the birds moving about in the lilac bushes and to the distant gunfire and the human talk beyond the gates and in the house. Once or twice he got up, put on his faded, outsize hat, or picked it up, and went out, softly shutting the gate. He walked through the village, taking a good look at what was going on, since every day the people got more and more worried, agitated, and grim. In the evenings he sat for a long time, no longer at the window but on the threshold to the annex, his eyes half-closed, his hand lazily resting on the head of the old dog, who came to sit next to him.

Night fell; the moon glimmered. There was something menacing about the clear sky, the quiet fields, the roads running to and fro, this summer, this world where fate had compelled him to live. When he rested his head on his hand, it seemed he was trying to remember something and that was why he was so quiet, that he couldn't do it. Where was he from? And where should he go, and did he have to go any farther? And what was life, this pulse, this breathing, this waiting, what was this ecstasy, this grief, this war? He was so weak, but he had a powerful harmony in his heart, a melody in his head. Why was he here among all this, among the now incessant noise of the gunfire, among these preparations for departure in village families, where they led out horses, tied up cows, where they sewed up gold into the lining of clothes? He had nothing. Not even a pack. No family, no lover to sew him a shirt, cook him soup, rumple and warm his bed. All he had was music. That's how he had grown up, that's how it had been since he was a child. Feet to carry him, hands to fend off people, and music, and that was it. But there was no point coming, no, no point coming into a world where he would always go unrecognized and unheard, where he was weaker than a shadow, poorer than a bird, as guileless as the simplest flower of the field.

When Kiryusha saw that the dog was sitting beside him and wasn't afraid, he came and sat as well, not daring to sit on the porch, but close by, on a stone. And so all three of them sat for a long time, in silence, until it got dark, and then Kiryusha, taking a deep breath, let out a long, idiotic laugh and went into the house.

IV

ON WEDNESDAY MORNING Vassily Georgievich did not come back. There had been no telephone communication with Paris for two days, and Maria Leonidovna had absolutely no idea what to think. People were saying that there weren't any trains, that the papers hadn't come out, that travel across Paris was impossible, and that people had been deserting Paris for two days. The entire village was packing up and leaving. Those who only the night before had criticized people fleeing in fear were themselves loading things onto carts, cars, and prams. A swarm of little boys and girls sped around on bicycles. Three rows of small trucks and cars filed down the main road, which passed less than a mile from the village.

During the day rumors had been flying around, the gunfire went on constantly, growing ever nearer, and silver airplanes sailed high in the sky. Several cars, trying to take a shortcut, wound up on the avenue of plane trees and couldn't figure out how to get out, so they looped back and returned to the main road, nosing into the endless chain and continuing southward.

There were artillery, gypsy caravans, trucks loaded with ledgers (and on them sat pale bookkeepers, evacuating the bank, the foundation of the state); people on foot, on bicycles, broken-rank cavalrymen on light horses interspersed with Percherons harnessed to long wagons carrying sewing machines, kitchen utensils, furniture, barrels. And high above all the goods and chattels were perched old women, deathly pale and bareheaded; some old women sat in cars, while others went on foot, alone or supported by the arm. Troops hauled decrepit cannons, and an empty van surmounted by a magnificent red cross followed behind a sports car out of which leaned a lop-eared dog that looked like a soft toy. Then came the wounded, some of them sitting despondently, holding on to their own leg or arm, a stump that dripped blood on the road. Others vomited air and saliva. People carried hay, unthreshed wheat, factory lathes, tanks of oil. And this odd stream could be seen all the way to the horizon, living and yet already dead.

Up until nightfall Maria Leonidovna cleaned and packed, fully aware that Vassily Georgievich couldn't come by train, just as they couldn't leave by train. From the house she could see the main road, and since morning she had watched the relentless, slowly flowing, sometimes pausing, river of fugitives. The thought that she might be left alone after everyone was gone worried her, and above all the thought that Vassily Georgievich might not return. She was worried as well about Kiryusha, who in the rising panic had suddenly become grotesquely incoherent. In the middle of the day she saw her silent guest a few times, and even greeted him from a distance. She resolved to have a chat with him, find out about him, maybe help him out, and that decision preoccupied her for a few minutes. The evening came, she prepared supper, and just as they were sitting down she heard the sound of a motor, a comforting, familiar sound. Two cars drove into the Sushkovs' yard: in one sat the three Kreins; in the other, Edouard Zontag, Vassily Georgievich, and old Mrs. Sushkova. Both cars had left Paris the previous evening. They had been on the road all night and all day.

Manyura Krein broke down in tears when she walked into the house. "This is too much! Simply too much!" she said with her large mouth. "This is not to be endured. Children are being led along on foot, old people are hobbling on crutches. I'll never forget this as long as I live."

But Maria Leonidovna scarcely got to hug her because she had to say hello to Zontag and to Magdalena and follow her husband into the next room and listen to his agitated story about how yesterday afternoon he had realized that she was right, that they should have left on Sunday, that now they might not make it.

"Kiryusha's not too good," she told him, since even today she considered that that was the most important thing.

Edouard Zontag had long-standing business ties with Vassily Georgievich, and relations between them, for some reason only they understood, were rather strained. He kept aloof, apparently looking on the Kreins as relatives of Maria Leonidovna, and smoked a fat cigar. He was short and used to say that the shorter the man, the fatter the cigar he smoked.

An omelette, cold meat, salad, cheese, an apple tart, just appeared on the table, all at once, and they launched into it haphazardly and greedily, letting the abundance of that house fill them with contentment, fully aware that tomorrow it would all be gone. They drank a lot and talked a lot. They discussed how and when the decision had been made to surrender Paris, the bombing of its northern and western suburbs, and especially how everyone had dropped everything and fled, not only those who had been preparing for it but also those who had had no desire whatsoever to budge; how that night, in total darkness, it took them five hours to get from their apartment to the city limits. How they had been surrounded by thousands upon thousands of others like themselves, how the engine died on them, the radiator boiled over, and they took turns sleeping.

Then they had a conference: What time tomorrow should they go and which road was best? They bent over the map for a long time, sketched something, drew it out, and then drank again and even had another bite to eat, especially the men. In the yard an old lady slaughtered two hens, and Manyura cleaned them on the big kitchen table, lowered her fingers, covered in rings, with varnished nails, down into it, and drew out something slippery.

Magdalena and Maria Leonidovna, sitting on their heels by the linen closet, looked for one more pillowcase for Edouard. The men were trying to decide whether or not to drive over to pick up Chabarov, and old Mrs. Sushkova wanted to express her opinion too, but no one was listening to her.

She went to her room, that is, to Kiryusha's room, where she was supposed to spend the night, and it immediately began to reek of her perfume in there. Room was found for the Kreins in the house, but Edouard Zontag had to be put in the annex.

"Wait for me, I'll be back in a minute," said Maria Leonidovna, and she ran across the yard.

She knocked on the door. He was lying on the bed but not sleeping, and when she came in he raised himself and slowly lowered his long legs in their torn shoes and ran his hand over his hair, as if he wanted to smooth it, comb it, give it some semblance of order. She started speaking softly, scarcely glancing in his direction.

"Excuse me, but something's come up. We have a full house. People didn't sleep last night, and there's nowhere to put them. Please, we have a small shed by the garage. Move over there. I feel bad disturbing you, but you understand, there's nothing else I can do. And then, in any case, we'll be leaving early tomorrow morning and you'll have to leave too because we'll be locking up and taking the keys with us. You won't be able to stay."

He stood up and in the semidark (a cold bleak light fell from the entryway where a small lamp was lit) started pacing around the room, evidently at a loss how best to answer her.

"Tomorrow morning? Then why move to the shed? I'll leave tonight."

She couldn't help feeling glad that he'd said this.

"I feel that I'm chasing you away, practically in the middle of the night. Please stay. There's a folding bed in there. And tomorrow morning——"

"No, I'll go right now. After all, everyone else seems to be leaving, don't they?"

"Yes, if they haven't already."

"So I think I'd better go as well. Thank you for letting me spend so many days with you. Really, I'm most grateful to you. There are many people who wouldn't have done it, you know. I'll remember it for a long time, a very long time."

He turned out to have a thick stick, which he must have cut in the forest the day before. His eyes met Maria Leonidovna's, and his look confused her.

"Wait a moment, I'll bring you something." She turned around and lightly stepped out.

"That's not necessary. I don't need anything," he shouted firmly. "Don't worry, please. Good-bye."

In the yard the men were tying something to the roof of the Kreins' car. She ran into the house, pulled fifty francs out of her purse, wrapped the remains of the roast beef and two rolls in a napkin, and went back to the annex. The little lamp was still burning inside the door, but there was no one there now. He had left quietly, so that no one would notice, and very quickly. In the room it was as if he had never even stayed there; not a single object was out of place.

She looked around, as if he might still be standing

somewhere in a corner. She walked out, went back in again, and then walked to the gate and opened it. Someone was walking alone down the lane—already quite a distance away. She watched him for a moment, and suddenly, for no reason, tears came to her eyes, and she couldn't see anything.

"He's leaving, he's leaving," she said very quietly but distinctly, the way people sometimes utter a meaningless word, and burst into tears. And without understanding what was wrong, or why she had suddenly been overcome by such weakness, she closed the gate gently and went into the house.

In the morning a life began that had nothing to do either with the departed guest or with Maria Leonidovna's secret thoughts. They loaded up the cars so that the spare tire bumped along behind them on the ground. They locked up the house and sat Kiryusha between his father and grandmother—that day he had exhibited the early signs of rebellion, and they were trying to conceal it. Edouard Zontag, in good form after a night's sleep, was worried that they hadn't taken enough gas. He took one more long look at the map before setting off. In the first car rode the Kreins and Maria Leonidovna. Manyura rattled on incessantly.

They drove through the deserted village slowly, with difficulty, the spare tire constantly bumping against the road. When they reached the forest, they started taking country lanes heading in the direction of Blois. They stopped by the château where Chabarov worked as a groundsman. The iron gates were wide open, and horses, still saddled, grazed on the English lawn between young cedars. A French squadron had been stationed there since the previous day. Soldiers were lying on the grass in front of the house, and on the ground floor a vast hall, with two rows of windows, and its candelabra, mirrors, and bronzes, could be glimpsed through the broken panes.

Chabarov came out wearing corduroy trousers and a matching jacket. The lower half of his face was covered with gray whiskers. Without even saying good-morning, he said that he couldn't leave, that he had to stay behind: the night before Daunou (who lived in a nearby hamlet) had been found dead. He had shot himself, and since there was no one left in the area to bury him, Chabarov had decided to bury the body in his garden.

"If these brave lads," he said gloomily, pointing to the soldiers, "stay until evening and I manage to dig a suitable hole, then they'll be my witnesses, and that's the best I can hope for. But if they set off before then I'll have to wait for the new authorities to get here. There's no civilian population left."

Everyone became very quiet as they said good-bye. Krein even got out of the car to embrace him. A minute later both cars drove off downhill, heavy with their loads, following each other closely.

That day, the sound of gunfire came from the other direction, from the northwest. In the sky, with a noise that had not been heard before, like a wail, swooped two German fighter planes.

The Waiter and the Slut

I

SHE WAS THE DAUGHTER of a Petersburg bu-
reaucrat who had risen to the rank of full councillor of
state—a distrustful, unhealthy and discontented man with
a long, thin face. Her mother was so like the wives of
other Petersburg bureaucrats that after she died Tania,
who was nearly fifteen, was unable to distinguish in her
memory between her and all the other ladies who used
to visit, pinch Tania's little chin, and chat—shrieking
with laughter and toying with their lorgnettes—about
their servants, the shops, their charity committees.

A governess was brought into the house, but she
didn't get on, as she couldn't control Lila, the eldest, who
used to be met after school by a naval cadet. Tania and
Lila taught her to drink Madeira and curse in Russian,
and they assured her that the downstairs lodger was madly
in love with her. One day when everyone was out, the
governess surreptitiously packed her things, put them in
a cab, and departed, having left His Excellency a note
saying she just couldn't take it any longer.

That was a year before the Revolution. Her father

was assigned to Siberia, so all three of them moved to Irkutsk. The fourth in their party was Ella Martynovna, their mother's old governess, a dry old stick whose once flirtatious eyes had now grown dim. The sideboards, the grand piano, the two Shishkin copies, and the French rugs traveled with them too. And in Irkutsk, in their enormous official apartment, among new faces and new amusements, their haphazard life started up all over again.

Ella Martynovna was cool toward Tania's father. However, he struck up an affair almost immediately with the vice-governor's wife—although it was more than an affair, and soon became a nerve-racking and interminable romance. The vice-governor's wife, who was old and fat, and the chevalier of the Order of Stanislas met in the secluded lanes of the municipal garden or on the edge of town, on the banks of the deserted Angara. Sometimes they chose a moonlit night and, if it wasn't too damp, sat on the grass or on a dead tree stump. They played at youth, at Maupassant, at the forbidden, and the whole town laughed behind their backs at his frock coat and her pince-nez.

At the same time, in a smoky *shashlik* restaurant, a clarinet was wailing, and a bold, wasp-waisted Circassian woman was dancing the *lezginka*. And Lila, crossing her legs high (while an Armenian acquaintance held her closely), pulled on a cigarette, choked on the smoke, squinted, lifted her little finger from her wet glass, and then slipped into the toilets to make her eyes even blacker and give herself yet another spray of perfume.

On those nights Tania would sit at home and brood. She thought about what dream she might build for herself.

What should she be? Her life was just about to start and she had to prepare for it, not miss her chance, not make mistakes. Get married as quickly as possible? Become a diva? Or a writer, setting down the story of her inner life? Ella Martynovna moistened her long gnarled finger and read Tania's cards, and it always came out the same: someone tried to ruin her, someone envied her, someone stood in her way, but she overcame all those obstacles to be joined in holy matrimony to a dark man with a large fortune.

Another departure. This time with no sideboards and no Shishkins. Departure for Japan. Escape. From whom? Among others, from the vice-governor's wife, but chiefly from the Bolsheviks. Tsarist bank notes were sewn into corsets—one for Tania, one for Lila, and one for Ella Martynovna. And in their corsets crackling with bank notes and in their heavy frock coats weighed down on one side, it was the four of them again, as if they were the closest of families, unable to live apart. They were going to Nagasaki, they were running away. On the ship, to the courteous murmurings of the Japanese, Lila vomited blood and had to go below and lie down. Late at night Tania stood on the deck amid bags and boxes, pinned to the railing by an elderly engineer's kiss, and suddenly understood—without Lila she felt a hundred times happier, freer, and easier. Without Lila everyone liked her. It was just that there was no life for her when Lila was at her side.

Lila was beautiful, but when they arrived in Japan Tania noticed that her vitality began to seep away, and even her face—regular, pale, long—grew stern and bored.

In the mornings Lila did a lot of praying, and the medallion she wore held a portrait of the Tsar. By spring she had given in altogether, and no longer dressed up, or allowed herself to be kissed. She tied her hair up at the nape in a severe bun and was fond of saying that even a life dedicated to prayer would not be enough to absolve Russia.

"I congratulate you!" her sister exclaimed.

Tania had small, well-spaced teeth and soft, extraordinarily soft skin—even as an adolescent she had had no blemishes on her body. She had freckles and a broad nose beneath her narrow, heavy-lidded eyes, and the oval shape of her broad face was off-center. She was short, with a large bust. Her hands were big and strong, and her walk was lopsided. But within a few months Tania had men swarming around her, men who told each other candidly that she had a special way of giving her entire body when you kissed her. Now no one was paying any attention to Lila, and there was a persistent rumor going around that she was going to be thirty soon.

But among the men who brayed with laughter at weak jokes and ate too much, who sang Tania love songs, and seized her in their arms, there was one by the name of Alexei Ivanovich. Alexei Ivanovich had trained for counterintelligence and so knew Japanese, and he was now working in a Japanese bank, a meek man and painfully fastidious about using other people's forks and glasses. He had large, fixed, almost blue eyes and a silly black mustache that looked as if it had been drawn on. He came and went with the others. But one day Ella Martynovna said, "The king of clubs has confessed to the king of diamonds that Taniusha is divine but he's really in love with Lilisha." In fact, for some reason Alexei Ivanovich had imagined that the girl with the tragic knot of hair and the unhealthy complexion whom he had twice glimpsed in the hallway was precisely the celestial vision that he had been waiting for all his life. The next day Lila, after having powdered her cartilaginous nose, pinned a porcelain bird to her breast, and came out to the guests. She nodded her head, twisted her long bony hands, coughed in a particularly significant way, and a month later Alexei Ivanovich proposed.

For the first time, Tania lost her head. She couldn't sleep at night. She threw her arms over her head, grabbed the headboard, and arched her whole body until she was numb. It was inconceivable to her, incredible, that anyone could prefer Lila to her. Whether or not she liked Alexei Ivanovich she didn't know, he was the only one among all the men who visited them who hadn't tried to kiss her and fondle her, who hadn't whispered obscenities to her, who, in short, had paid her absolutely no attention. The thought that someone had slipped through her fingers, that life was beginning with a defeat, was intolerable to her. The black mustache and the fixed eyes were transformed for her into an unexpected temptation.

She went to see him at about nine o'clock one Saturday morning. He had just dressed and was still walking around the room in his bare feet (this turned out later to be a habit).

"So good to see you, Tatiana Arkadievna. I'm flattered. To what do I owe this pleasure?"

Smiling, he drew up the armchair for her with his

large white hands. In her fur coat and fur cap, she looked in astonishment at his clean bare feet.

"I came on a bet," she said, still not knowing how she was going to get through this. "I had a little bet with myself."

He laughed out loud. "With yourself . . ." he echoed, utterly oblivious to how upset she was.

"Look," she said in a low voice, and she flung her coat open.

Her stockings stopped at wide satin garters (bought the day before), and above them came the rumpled flounces of her beribboned drawers—and that was it. There was nothing else on Tania's body; her soft, extraordinarily soft skin had a blue shade to it, and the nipples and shadows under her breasts were orange-colored. She sat without moving for several moments, her legs pressed firmly together and one stocking pulled up higher than the other. Then suddenly she made a single movement. She couldn't remember quite where she had got it from—whether it was Maupassant again or just Krinitsky, or even the nameless author of a book she'd devoured back in Petersburg. But the essential part came from herself: by her moans and spasms she showed Alexei Ivanovich the kind of passion she had learned in her dreams.

It always seemed to Alexei Ivanovich that life meant proceeding as cautiously as possible and, principally, watching his step—to keep from falling into some trap. Death was one of those traps, and everything that changed life unexpectedly, untowardly, was a trap—the Revolution he pictured as a hole into which his brother and father had fallen and which he himself had skirted. But there were further unknown traps where the foot could slip.

The next day his passion for Tania seemed to him to be one of these terrifying abysses into which he had fallen with a dreadful crash, barefoot, his face contorted, his shirt ripped, hurtling down God knows how many steps on his knees and cracking his head on a stoop he couldn't see—this was his headboard, against which he banged his forehead until he nearly passed out from pain, fury, and happiness. A week later he had regained his meekness, his smile, and the mica-like glint in his large eyes. He married Tania and took her to Shanghai. There was a lost look to his face, and his trembling body seemed suddenly much thinner.

She was pleased with her husband and Shanghai and the fact that she had left home, and her nine years with Alexei Ivanovich—during which she had a brief affair with an American and an unhappy romance with a married Russian, produced a stillborn daughter, and visited her father once—passed peacefully, for she never thought about the present, and if she thought at all, it was about the future. The years passed utterly without trace. There was nothing in Japan which could remind her of her youth. Her father was paralyzed, and Lila was working as a translator in an export office. She had grown old and ugly. Ella Martynovna was no longer among the living. At the end of the ninth year Tania decided she wanted to go to Paris, where many other people seemed to be going, and Alexei Ivanovich decided that he wanted to go to Paris too—in any case, he always wanted the same things as she did. He had thought it all out very carefully (which demanded a considerable effort), and quit his job. So they left—to look for happiness, as Tania put it, calculating her chances, imagining the future. But it wasn't entirely clear just how she pictured that happiness, her own happiness in particular, her own and Alexei Ivanovich's Parisian happiness.

The trump card that Alexei Ivanovich hoped to play in Paris was his knowledge of Japanese, which he believed would stand them in good stead. But four months later, when their money ran out, he still didn't have a job, and they had nothing but complications with visas and passports and the French language, which neither of them knew, and Alexei Ivanovich began to have fits, during which he hurled and smashed everything within reach, cursed and swore, and became completely insomniac. Sleepless and barefoot he paced around the room of the small hotel in which they lived, and Tania beat her head against the pillows. Soon after, on a visit to some of his relatives (the host, a former hussar, was now a priest), he had his last fit.

It happened out in the suburbs. The house stood in the middle of a damp, narrow garden. The window was open, and flies flew at the lamp, burned themselves, and fell into the jam pot. It was all very much like Russia: a brass samovar stood on the edge of the table, and they poured boiling water into it from a kettle they heated on the stove. The priest's wife, with her pink nails and bleached blond hair, was telling stories about some grand people that no one had ever heard of. The guests were drinking tea, and one tiny slice of apple pie was left on the plate.

Suddenly Alexei Ivanovich interrupted his hostess and in a sobbing, powerful voice announced that he was hot. "Go and sit by the window," said the hussar priest. "The evening breeze will soothe your weary body." But Alexei Ivanovich jumped up and shouted that he wouldn't be tricked into going near that window. "Not on your life. You're not going to make me fall out!" Several of them gave him a troubled look, but in a flash he had torn off his jacket, vest, and trousers and had already pulled off one shoe before they seized him. His clear blue eyes were glittering, and he was now dressed only in white, but he grew meek again and smiled, smoothing his silly black mustache. However, he then began to beat them off so savagely that they had to call an ambulance. Two orderlies came and leapt on him, knocked him off his feet, piled on top of him, and dragged him down the road while, delirious, he shouted incomprehensibly.

A few days later he died in the hospital—swollen from beatings, his hair almost gray, his front teeth knocked out—in a ward for the dangerously insane. And Tania found herself alone in a cheap hotel room in Paris, where she had come to "look for happiness."

She was on her own now. Each new day began, gray like her life. She didn't want that kind of day or that kind of night, long, lifeless, passed in making calculations in her head: how much money was left, what could she buy for that much, and where could she find the kind of man she could hide behind, who would take care of everything, and pay for everything, and give her presents, and worship her, as it happened probably for everybody, as it had for two of her girlfriends from Petersburg that she'd run into here and for one from Shanghai, in short, for the women she thought she knew. The day began, and she started to visit shops, rarely buying anything but choosing, checking prices, digging through the stockings and gloves, begrudging the money, and in her dreams becoming so excited that her heart pounded as she pictured herself in this silk or that fur. She sifted through piles of lace and let buttons stream through her fingers, always hesitant and fearful of buying the wrong things, continuing to wear her worn red fox with the thick tail trailing off her shoulder and her dusty black hat with the black flower, which was supposed to signify mourning. She was thirty-two. Since her marriage and the dead baby she had put on weight, but her face was still just as fresh as ever. Even now, carelessly and vulgarly made up, it attracted notice.

Once in a while she visited her Nadias, Marusias, and Tatochkas, and one or another would give her something: a pair of laddered stockings, an old purse with a broken mirror. In the middle of a rapid and chaotic stream of chatter, one or another would reveal a corner of her life, and the wild abandon of passion, money, idleness, pampering, and happiness took Tania's breath away; she clutched at those crumbs, seized them and carried them back with her to her room where she spent the night trying to work out what life really was—not her life but theirs, where everything was so gay, solid, and calm. Then she went to see others who gave her nothing, who lived poorly and worked. Among them was Belova, a seamstress, and the topic of conversation at her place was always the same: What are the fashions? And how do you dress as cheaply and as well as possible? Tania's heart skipped a beat at hearing that one tiny mistake—a sleeve set in the wrong way or a badly cut collar—could ruin the appearance of a dress—and your whole fate with it. There was another, a tall, peroxided, bitter woman named Gulia who had tried her hand at dozens of professions. At one time she had gone to beauty school and been a model, but then syphilis and two miscarriages took the fight out of her and left her numb. Now she was a waitress in a restaurant where she broke the plates and cursed the customers.

Meanwhile Tania kept going to their houses, to the shops, through the streets, staring at the women she passed to the point of stupefaction, listening to their talk, which she didn't always understand, mentally trying on and fitting until she was utterly exhausted, spending sleepless nights sorting through all she'd seen and heard that day. Nadia told her: "My dear, first of all you have to learn to wash. You simply don't know how to wash." Belova swore that she had to dye her hair red and wear nothing but black. Another pleaded with her to lose weight. But all this revealed was their indifference, their contempt for her. Only Gulia never gave her advice, although doubtless she knew better than any of them what Tania should do.

So, a little at a time, without confiding in anyone, Tania began to transform herself, always keeping in mind that she had only enough money and skill to make herself one single outfit to go . . . where? To the Russian restaurant where they sang the "Charochka," and to another where they ate sturgeon and grouse, and, last, to a third, a bar where the music was Argentinean, not Russian, and where Tania—alone, at night, with her gentle face, large breasts, and her soft mouth—fiddled with her long nails, sipped something cold and alcoholic through a straw, and tried not to look around her.

But she was not allowed to enter the fashionable and well-reputed restaurant, either because she was alone or because you had to tip the maître d' for the privilege of an introduction. An arm stopped her at the door, and a velvety baritone asked her—in French, but with a Russian accent—to leave. She was so distraught that she lost her voice. Unable to control herself, she started to weep and walked out. While she was deciding how to get home, a high-spirited character in a cape and top hat called her *charmante* and kissed the air a couple of inches from her cheek.

A passing car splashed her with dirty water. It was too late to go anywhere else, as it was midnight, so she went home and, sitting on her bed, sobbed with rage. The mascara in her tears stained her dress, and she started to clean it with lighter fluid but ruined the whole thing in the process and felt like throwing herself out of the window. But her room was on the third floor (she always remembered that subsequently and never considered that solution again) and opened out over a courtyard which smelled so bad that she shut the window immediately.

The next day she went to a restaurant which had no music and no gypsies, but was simply very expensive. As she crossed the room she caught a glimpse of a menu on one table and saw that there was a hundred-franc minimum. Men who reminded her of her father—bald, bearded, chewing voraciously or already digesting—sat with their backs to the walls paying her no heed whatsoever. In despair she looked at a pop-eyed, middle-aged gentleman picking his teeth, realized that no one here had the slightest use for her, and said she just needed to use the phone.

She went out and knew there was only one place left for her to go: that noisy, rowdy gypsy bar which Tata had told her about. She went there. She was hungry. A band greeted her. She was seated in a corner, and solicitously relieved of her ermine-trimmed coat, her entire fortune. She could tell immediately that this was where she was going to find what she had been looking for, if only for the time being. It might not happen today, or even tomorrow, but it was going to happen, and it was going to happen here.

A violinist dressed as a Romanian and a singer dressed as a gypsy wailed over her head. A steamy smoky haze hung from the ceiling. Couples floated past her table. Setting down her white hand which held a long cigarette holder, and thrusting out her generous, tightly swathed breasts, her petaled face glowing in the restaurant's darkness, she sat and looked without seeing. And in her waiting, in her secret hunger which, over the last few weeks, had almost given her a pain deep down in her body, there was something which evoked the languor of a sweet young girl on a moonlit, jasmine-scented evening standing at the window of her parents' sleeping house. Her indefinable thirst was overwhelming, and, in the same way, the future ahead of her seemed misty, rose-colored, and terrifying.

Later, when she had put her coarse, degrading affair with the Romanian fiddler behind her, she remembered him not as a man, but as an animal. After a year and a half of shared life, eaten up by melancholy, jealousy, and fear of the next day, she left the hospital—where she had had an operation—thin, poor, with huge eyes burning with bitterness and lucidity (the fiddler was no longer there; he had joined up with a band and left for London), and she went back to the same bar, finally understanding that no one loved or adored anyone until death separated them; that there was no one to hide behind; and that what had happened to her had happened to all her Tatas and Nadias, but none of them ever let on; she understood that you had to lie and lie and lie some more, take everything you could from life and do your best to forget, drink, erase your mistake and the concession you had made to that black-eyed rat who had sold you a few times and then left you.

It was only once in a while now, in the morning, roused at dawn by the early noise in the stinking narrow courtyard, that she ran back over those months, bitterly, unrestrainedly, back to what at first had been a gypsy love song, like fire flowing through her veins, sung in a low voice straight to her heart, and which later had given off the smell of unchanged sheets, the stink of city sewers on a raw November day when some yellow and foul-smelling liquid runs down into the gutters, something you fear to step in and let your heel sink into. She would lie in this way for an hour or two immersed in these memories, avoiding any others, and then fall into a deep sleep. During the day she tried to retrieve that lost feeling, that long-gone frame of mind that had once led her—after Alexei Ivanovich's death—in search of something she couldn't give a name to but without which she couldn't imagine living in the world. This indispensable thing consisted of idleness and physical pleasure, in other words, in her private language, Parisian happiness.

But in the evenings she went back to the only place left in the world, there was nowhere else for her, that gypsy bar. And there were moments as she sat there in the smoky air, listening to the uproar of the music, when she forgot to shed her habitual expression of hurt, sadness, and suffering. The hand held out to her across the table—a short, sturdy, man's hand holding an open cigarette case—belonged to a man who liked in her precisely that weary and distraught face. She accepted a cigarette, took the cigarette case from him, and put it down on the tablecloth. Suddenly she squeezed that hand and, through her tears, smiled inquisitively.

"What could be better than a Russian woman!" exclaimed the man with an accent. "No, tell me, please, what could be more charming, more luxuriant, more magnificent than a Russian woman?" And with a drumroll and a wail the music seemed to echo that question just to please the customer.

Four years. Three times a week—in the afternoon—he came to "take a break" from the stock exchange, his wife, bridge, the unpaid bills, bounced checks, and crises—his whole hard, busy, masculine life. Each time he left her a hundred francs and said that only here, in this cheap, grimy, welcoming room, did he feel like a human being and not a brute. "Will he marry me?" she wondered sometimes. "Get a divorce? Leave his wife?" Sometimes she asked him to take her out. But what if someone saw them together and exposed them? That would wreck his life. No, he was careful, and as soon as he arrived demanded his dressing gown and slippers, told her to put the tea on, and unwrapped the pastries. "He's not going to marry me. He's never going to marry me," she told herself at night, staring with hatred at his red, tasseled dressing gown that hung behind the door, that gave off his smell in the room, that guarded his goods. How happy she had been that day when he had brought that smell of his to her, brought his pajamas and slippers. It was as if he had practically moved in; a little bit more and she would have had him completely in her power.

"Get a gun," Gulia said one day. "Just shake him up a little. Just imagine, what if a car ran over him? You'd be back where you started, like before. And you're getting older. . . ."

She didn't threaten him with a gun, and toward the end of the fourth year he disappeared. He had said he would be out of Paris for a week on business, but almost a month passed and he still hadn't come back. The home address she had for him turned out to be wrong. There wasn't any house with that number on that street. She had the phone number of his club, so she called, but they told her he hadn't been in for over six months.

She lost her head, scoured the town, felt like running to the police. She had practically no money left, she had borrowed in order to pay for her room, and she was alone again. "That pig didn't even give me enough to put

some aside," she thought. In anger and desperation, unwashed, her hair uncombed, she went to see Gulia.
"You're at home? You're not at work?" Gulia was sitting
by the window holding a kitten on her fat knees and
cross-stitching. They had let her go at the restaurant;
now she was taking in embroidery.

"You could too if you wanted," she said in her
husky voice, while ashes from her cigarette dropped on
the red embroidery wool and sky-blue canvas. "You could
make ninety centimes an hour. At least you wouldn't
starve to death."

"What about those other women?" Tania thought.
"The slim, chic, contented, happy women who work
somewhere as secretaries and salesgirls, sleep with their
bosses, go skiing, and buy all those smart clothes? Why
not me?" In the dark shopwindows she took a look at
herself, tear-stained, older now, with sagging breasts and
hips, walking her lopsided walk, gloveless. "They just
don't exist, that's all," she told herself. "For a month or
two maybe. Liars. They're all useless. Like me." Tears
streamed down her face, and she wiped them away.

Restaurants? She knew them all now. That gypsy
bar had closed, and another had opened in its place. The
smart restaurant they hadn't let her into that time was
the same as ever—Tatochka's lover had taken her there
once. She had eaten with Nadia a few times at the restaurant where the men had intimidated her so much
before: but the men, even if they weren't young and
reminded her of her father, were finally just like any other
men when you came right down to it, and a few of them
had even stared at Nadia and her.

But she couldn't go there wearing an old girdle and

with only a hundred francs in her purse. For a few more days she ran around town, stopped in to see Gulia a few more times, and started embroidering.

The first day she made nine francs; the second, eleven. She stayed in bed and cried nearly all of the third day, made four francs, and collapsed back into bed, her eyes all puffy. On the fourth day she bought half a lobster for seven fifty and ate it with mayonnaise. By the evening of the fourth day she was as good as drunk. It didn't even register with her when the landlady told her she shouldn't worry about paying for the room, she could take her time. On the fifth day she went to see Gulia on foot; she didn't have enough for the Métro, and she hadn't eaten. Gulia didn't have any work, but she did give her some coffee.

That same evening Tania borrowed a hundred and fifty francs from Nadia, a hundred-franc note and fifty in change, had dinner with her, listened to her stream of boastful lies, responded with the same, and in the morning, having spent three francs on food, started thinking what she should do. Her hands shook as she counted out the money. She had two plans, and one precluded the other.

The first was to buy a gun with the money, gorge herself, and then commit suicide. The second was to go to the hairdresser, get her hair done, have a pedicure, put on a becoming dress, and go somewhere to eat—but so that someone else was sure to pay for her and they would leave the restaurant together. She went over to the mirror and made the face she usually made when she looked at herself and that she never made at any other time. So, with all the will she could muster, she took herself in hand.

It was eight-fifteen. She was a little late. She never managed to get anywhere on time. She was wearing a black dress, and a black hat that showed her curled, upswept hair above its top; she had dyed it red recently, but the black roots were already starting to show at the temples. The collar of her seal-fur coat covered her fat white neck, and when she turned it back a warm perfumed column of air escaped and fogged up around her face. Her last intact pair of stockings formed a web over her feet; she wore her light, open shoes. She went to the mirror again and made that face—content, calm, the face she would have liked to have. She looked at herself for a long time. Beautiful. She could have done with a little dog, one more pretext for making friends. "Fool! Why didn't you get your Jew to give you a dog right at the beginning, when he was so kind?" Kind? Yes, he had been kind during the first and second years of their . . . love, shall we say, when he had given her the fur coat and put up with all her whims, her suspicions, her ugly face in tears. Later, when she started to reproach him for not marrying her and threatening to cling to him, he stopped being kind. And he was right. "I could have held back. It's my fault," she told herself quickly. "Oh, you stupid, hopeless fool!" She was alone with her reflection. She reached for the door to the creaky aspen cupboard, swung it open, and shut it. "He was kind, he was good, and he could have kept on being that way." She seemed to be reading from inside herself, but there was something else. "And now you're either going to take in embroidery or walk the streets." She covered the mirror with her hand to hide the expression of her mouth. "You're in deep water and you don't know how to swim," she read on, aloud. Just then she saw her contorted face again. Her confidence in herself, in the fact that what she was about to do was right, dissolved. Go to bed. Let yourself go. Buy half a bottle of brandy. Get drunk. . . . She dismissed those pitiful temptations, opened and closed her coat once more, and went out.

When Tania entered the restaurant, which was decorated with a pretentious severity, it was two-thirds empty: in the corner to the right an elderly couple; on the left a younger couple; and beyond them more faces, men's, not so young, she thought (all this she had to take in in a few seconds). Three men busy with their hors d'oeuvres and vodka were sitting at the back. The maître d' wanted to seat her near the young couple by the door, but she walked right past him and sat down at the table next to the three men. Two waiters ran up to her, but she kept her coat on. Immediately a menu flew into her hands, a place setting materialized out of thin air, and she was left with no choice but to unfold her napkin.

"He was kind. He could have been kind," she repeated to herself. She was drained after that long week. She remembered about her face, and smiled slightly to one side, but no one was looking at her. Meanwhile two more men (French, it seemed) came in and sat down across from her. But she felt she just couldn't cheer up, that she wanted to eat as quickly as possible and leave, that she needed to be left alone with her thoughts. "Think things through. Get a good night's rest. But what about tomorrow?" flashed through her mind. "Tomorrow I'll be like Gulia, or something else . . . I'll go to work. As a maid. Be a servant. These waiters running around here, they're servants." She began watching one of them, a tall, middle-aged, balding man in a short white jacket. His hairy hands were busy with something over her place setting. "He's brought the *selyanka*. He's serving the sturgeon."

"Mushrooms for the table on the left," a younger, pasty-faced waiter whispered to him as he hurried past, balancing clean glasses upside down between his fingers.

"Got it," the bald man whispered back voicelessly. He served Tania her soup and ran off somewhere, swaying. She nearly lost him among four others who looked exactly like him. Her gaze followed him and she felt troubled. He reappeared, sailing through the air carrying a narrow platter of marinated mushrooms. He uncorked a napkin-wrapped bottle of wine and rolled the cheese trolley to the far corner. "What does a man like that live for?" she asked herself. But the waiter kept flitting to and fro, carrying away dirty dishes. All of a sudden Tania saw him in the waiters' room close to her, greedily shoveling food from someone's plate into his mouth. She was disgusted.

"What does a man like that live for? My God, what for? But what am I living for? What does all of this mean?" she thought with pity for him and herself as well. "What do people live for at all?" She tried to think for a moment. "For pleasure. Yes, that's it. People live for pleasure. But what kind of pleasure is there in his life, or mine?"

"Didn't you like your sturgeon, madam?" he asked

respectfully, seeing that she hadn't finished her *selyanka*.

"N-no, I did."

With a deft motion of his hairy hands he whisked away the soup and something else and brought her a turkey wing on a silver oval platter. Standing very erect, he served it, moving only his wrists.

"Would you like a bottle of red wine?"

She ordered half a bottle of Nuits. One of the men sitting at the next table raised his wide-open, light brown eyes to her. For a moment he tried to recall something, to speak. "*Garçon!* A bottle of Nuits here too," he called out, finally realizing what it was he needed. Tania turned away.

"What does a man like that live for?" she repeated to herself. "Oh, my God, where is he? Here he is running and tottering with that gravy boat. What a tired old face he has. What a strange head. He must smoke a lot. He's smoked his teeth and heart out. But what am I living for? Why am I trying? Where does all this lead? Why will I die tomorrow and how? I've got to get ahold of myself. I'm not going to scheme or be jealous of anyone anymore. I've got to stop."

With inexplicable symmetry first the elderly and then the younger couple stood up. The little potbellied doorman with skinny bowed legs helped them on with their coats. They left. Her neighbors asked for the bill, snatched the slip of paper away from one another, and overturned the carafe; finally the leader with the light brown eyes paid. Tania held a piece of frozen peach in her mouth for a long time and watched—not their faces but what they left for a tip and how the bald waiter, his face indifferent now, bent at the waist, picked up the money, and thanked them, quickly pulling their chairs out for them.

Then he passed them on to the maître d', the maître d' to the doorman, and the doorman—by this time on the street—to the taxi driver. Meanwhile the waiter's face had become its old self again.

"Coffee, please," Tania said with only her lips.

There, that dinner was over, and she was going to pay for it herself. It was all very good. The place had certainly emptied out. There was the one with the pasty face and the other one, a little younger, hurrying by with a heap of napkins and once more with glasses, dirty ones this time, stems down. The Frenchmen were still there, it seemed, but now some ladies had joined them. She had missed them coming in: elegant, gay, lively. There they were, to have a good time. Here was the tall waiter again. He lit the flame under her café filter.

"Not many people here," said Tania. Even she didn't know why she said it. "It's nice when there aren't so many people."

"Quite. It's very nice."

He walked away. The spirit lamp was burning, heating the coffee. He came back just in time.

"Are there more people at lunch?" (Why am I asking this? I won't be coming back here anyway.)

"I should say so. Sometimes they're still here at three."

"It must be exhausting, isn't it?"

"You get used to it. I've been working here for over ten years."

"What did you do before?"

He had already gone to fetch the sugar tongs, though, limping just a little. She watched his hairy fingers again, and she imagined she could see his thin, sunken, very hairy gray chest through his short jacket.

"Before? When exactly?" Dancing in circles around her, he attempted a confused smile.

"Before. In Russia."

"I fought for my faith, my Tsar, and my fatherland," he said in a conspiratorial way.

She stirred her coffee and looked at him. He was standing to one side, at attention, as far as his round shoulders would permit.

"You're not from Petersburg, by any chance?"

"Indeed. Nikolaevsky Cavalry Academy."

Something like a long corridor was taking shape in her mind, but she couldn't see what was at the end of it.

"I knew Akhlestov and Zaune from Nikolaevsky Academy. They used to come around to see my older sister."

"I knew Akhlestov. He was four years below me."

So. Now she would give him a chance to move away, to gather up the dessert dishes, one by one, and take them out to the waiters' station until tomorrow, come back, stand by the cashier, his napkin pressed under his arm, running his eyes over the last customers. Others were still scurrying around near the door. If she had sat by the window it wouldn't have been him waiting on her but, say, that putrid blond with the translucent nostrils. He could move away now: everything was clear, a slim, fragile link had already formed between them, through Lila and the outsize, long dead Akhlestov, of whom Tania had been so afraid when she was a little girl and who had once seized her to do a little dance with her, crudely rumpling her dress.

He looked in her direction. No, she still hadn't asked for the bill. He walked past her.

"Tell me," she thought he wouldn't hear her murmur, but he did, and again he danced in circles around her, tilting his long head to one side. "Maybe you knew my sister, Lila Shabunina? I'm Tania Shabunina. That's my maiden name. I've been married. No? And the Vertyaevs? (What a funny name!) We were there a lot. There were the Filantievs, too. They used to have Christmas parties, I remember, with lots of children. All of them were older than me; there's six years between my sister and me. The Filantievs. They lived near Chernyshev Bridge. There were also the von Gogens. . . . My father served with Kirkilevich. You didn't know Kirkilevich? His daughter's married to Tsvetkov now. But from Nikolaevsky Academy, no. I do remember Okhotnikov from Konstantinovsky Artillery Academy. His father was a big shot."

He slipped an ashtray under her burning cigarette.

"Is that so," he replied mechanically. He bowed and scraped awkwardly and went to write out the bill. One of the round white chandeliers had been turned off, but Tania hadn't noticed.

"Listen," the cashier said to him, "your friend is holding us up. It's after ten."

He flicked the bill and ran quickly to the waiters'

station. He had a consuming, piercing need to be alone for a minute—solitude and quiet, and a chance to recall something, to reconstruct something. . . .

He opened the door to the small cloakroom, which was dark and smelled of cabbage and old clothes. Here on small hangers were the waiters' dark jackets. He recognized his own by the special light grain of the wool. He clutched at his empty sleeve, crushed it, and thought.

He wanted passionately to reconstruct, but he didn't know how to do it. He was one of those people who, when they hear the phrase "The windows of the house looked out on a garden," imagine an old house in the country that they once glimpsed somewhere and which has stood guard in their memory ever since. Whenever he heard the phrase "The train pulled slowly into the station," he saw the same black locomotive which had already come to a halt by a water tank half in ruins, a sign in Polish on the glass of a station door, and the whitish blue of the horizon, which had palled over the long years. Anything that didn't have its own fixed image in his memory simply wouldn't stick and had slipped away long ago. But just now something odd had happened to him. The words "Chernyshev Bridge" and "Christmas party" had swept across his brain like an avalanche, and what remained in the column of dust and the roar of Tania's words had frozen in place, touching his heart. A slender little girl wearing a red dress has snatched a shimmering spun-glass ornament from a branch of the Christmas tree and is crushing it to powder in her thin sweaty fingers. He is in his uniform; he has washed carefully, and on his golden curls he's wearing a three-cornered cotton cap tilted over one ear—also freshly laundered. The glass dust spills over the girl's hands and dress. Maybe this lady sitting here and smoking, powdering her nose, maybe she's the same girl? No, of course she isn't. Then maybe she's her sister? No, things don't happen like that. Then it's someone she must have known, or seen. The Filantievs. That was it. He couldn't remember anything else—or make any other associations. But that was enough: suddenly the sunny fragments of a child's summer day, when he snagged his jacket on the latch jumping out of the window, rushed, rolled, washed over him. Other days too—funny and sad, and multicolored, and so fast you couldn't hold them back. Tight white gloves on his little hands, and his long cadet's overcoat, and something proud and awesome which happened after he had joined the Corps. The wild and wonderful freedom of spring, and again the azure December weather, and that intersection near Exchange Bridge where for some reason he always imagined an ocean liner entering the Neva through the mists, bursting its banks, and growing and growing until it towered over the Peter and Paul Fortress; and something else: sobbing strident brass, the curl of regimental trumpets over his father's coffin. Sand and snow. And quiet. And in the black northern sky a comet he had glimpsed one night from a window. And something else, something . . . before everything exploded into life, war, promotions, boozing, marriage, escape. Before it all led him to this office, to the smoky gloom of the waiters' station, to customers' plates with mustard smeared around the rim, to lettuce that stuck to his fingers, to the half-empty glasses which he'd drained. He squeezed and crushed the sleeve of his coat on its wooden hanger. He tugged at it, expecting a bell to ring, a tocsin to sound all over the universe, and maybe people would come running to him. . . . But everything was quiet. The noises of footsteps and voices were muffled; all was quiet.

Then he opened the door and went back in.

She was sitting there as before, but now she was all alone in the half-darkened restaurant. Tablecloths were already being pulled off tables; the waiters were moving, gathering up chairs, crowding her out. The maître d', with his jacket off, was standing in front of the cash register, and the owner had turned up—a well-dressed Pole who pronounced his *r*'s like a Frenchman. There was a colored handkerchief in his breast pocket, and he was whistling as he went over the accounts. She was still sitting there. She could have left, but she couldn't. Or rather, he couldn't let her; she had something to say to him, she was going to remind him of something. What a marvelous, soft, fleeting beauty there was in her face, and how strange—her eyes, her fingers, her voice. She had said "Akhlestov." Who was Akhlestov? Maybe he was the one in '18 who . . . And now he had risen from the dead, risen and brought them together today, here.

He put Tania's bill in front of her.

"Allow me to introduce myself," he said. "Lieutenant Bologovsky."

She put a hundred-franc note down on the table, slapped it with her hand, and raised her face.

"Delighted to meet you."

He ran over to the cash register, got her change, and returned.

"Imagine meeting like this. Amazing. Did you leave long ago?" (Somehow he just had to. Still, could he possibly care whether it was ten, or fifteen, or however many years she'd been wandering around?)

"Oh, a long time ago!"

She took her change and left a tip. Wearing a frozen smile, he cocked his head in a signal to someone, and the pasty-faced waiter ran by and swept up the money with his big dark wrists, mumbling his thanks.

"Allow me." And now he bowed, his head receded into his shoulders, and his back became narrow and rounded. "Can we leave together? Lieutenant Bologovsky. Please do not take this for impertinence."

"You mean you can go?"

"One moment."

Now she saw that she should have left long ago. She opened and closed her compact again and took out her mirror. She was flushed from the wine and food.

He told her the story of his life, shortening the account of his marriage a little, but talking boastfully of his married daughter who lived in Bulgaria and who was always making plans to visit him but somehow never did. He told the story of his life in an hour, on the Métro and while they were drinking aniseed liqueur in a Russian bar somewhere in the fifteenth arrondissement, which was where he felt most at home. His heart was thundering, and his hands (in his haste he had forgotten to wash them) were shaking over the cigarette box, trying to introduce relative order to the table: here's her glass, here's mine; here are the cigarettes, there are the matches; here's her glove, black, warm, fragrant, and there's her hand—white, warm, fragrant. A woman was sitting before him. He couldn't quite remember how it had come about. He had had all sorts of different things to drink. His legs were sprawled out under the table, like boots, or like leggings, and he had a terrible urge to cry. It must be old age. He would not tell her how old he was—let her think forty-five; she could even think fifty, let her think what she wants.

He was looking at her breasts, at her hands, almost not looking at her face. And he was having a good time. But how could you remember all that had happened to you in your lifetime? (What was he talking about? Oh, yes, his shaky, idiotic, painful past.)

"I must confess, though, I have never spent an evening like this before. No, there's never been anything like it. Don't think I'm just trying to flatter you."

"Even if you were," said Tania, "women love flattery. You're a man, you should know that."

She was drinking too. By midnight he was talking about how hungry he was, so she ordered vodka and food as well, although only so that she would have something to eat with her three drinks. Two dark wide circles were forming around her eyes, and the vodka had made her mouth moist and deep. "What is it he's playing at?" she asked herself in a drunken reverie. "Matrimony, a one-night stand, or pimping for me? What if I asked him directly?"

The thought of that brought on a sudden fit of shrill, tearful laughter. Her head bowed, she propped her face with both hands to keep it from falling on the table.

Her sudden inability to control herself aroused his passion and tenderness. She was sobbing hard. She picked up her glass and crushed it in her slender white fingers.

"For God's sake, Tatiana Arkadievna!" he exclaimed, breaking out in a sweat. "You could cut yourself doing that."

Her hands and dress were covered with shards of glass, but he could no longer speak. Clenching his fists under the table, a roar in his head and fire in his heart, he was sitting, and watching, and drowning in a happiness of which she was the cause. He couldn't remember a thing. He was trying not to breathe, not to blink, and in the haze of his bliss everything was intoxicating, pure, happy, and sad all at once.

She was bored though. The café, with the former governor of Kaluga behind the bar, was impregnated with grease and tobacco. The wire-stemmed paper tulip— which Bologovsky kept fiddling with, not knowing where to put it, what to pair it off with—kept getting in her face. A photograph of a matador holding a guitar looked down at them from the wall. All this, and the man sitting with her, who had a tiny red insect crawling across his starched chest, seemed like such a comedown, such a terrible retribution, such a speedy path toward the end, that she wondered with anguish and horror how life could have dealt with her so brusquely and cruelly.

"If he tries to kiss me, I'll hit him hard in the face," she resolved to herself.

But he squeezed both her hands in one big rough hand, and in the taxi he embraced her and touched her, pressing his harsh lips to hers, his hard face to hers. And a minute later she was filled with pity and tenderness for herself. What was she struggling for? Why? My God, it was all so sad. She tried to look at his eyes in the gloom, more out of habit than curiosity. Totally unfamiliar eyes glittered with metallic tears, and his sparse hair (he had removed his hat) seemed equally steely.

Silently he followed her upstairs, and there in her room, where it was such a mess, where a naked bulb hung from the ceiling and a chintz blind covered the window, he pushed her rudely and greedily, hurrying and falling (she was dawdling, as if she were thinking about something). But it didn't happen as he'd planned. Exhausted, drunk with her warmth, he fell into a heavy sleep, his face in the pillow.

II

DISHEVELED, wearing a creased blue nightgown, black makeup smeared around her eyes, she lay in bed, dangling her arm almost to the floor. The silver bangle she wore was old, Russian. He was standing by the window in his coat. Outside was a courtyard three meters wide, an urban crevice, dank and dark. It was about to rain. Above him he saw other windows, but no matter how far you leaned over—no sky. Smoke was coming from somewhere above them and falling into this crevice. In his husky, singsong voice, he recited:

"Rain, rain, run along,
We are going to Arestan."

She misunderstood the last word and echoed, yawning:
"We are going to a restaurant."

He snorted, amused. Then he looked around, saw
her, and, taking a few steps, planted a kiss on her head.
Her red hair was fading and growing out; the part was
dark and streaked with gray.

"Please don't snivel," she said, lifting her hand from
the floor as if it were a dumbbell. "Well, what are you
snivelling at now?"

He wasn't crying. He was looking down at her face,
waiting for her to look up at him so that he could smile.

"You look like you're about to cry. Your eyelids are
all red, there must be something the matter with your
eyes. There's a tear running down your nose. But smile,
God damn it. Aren't you having a good time?"

Cautiously he stroked her head and kissed her part
once more.

"My teeth are too bad for me to smile," he said,
and forced a laugh.

And in truth, why did he find it so intolerably sad
to look at her? What did he regret? After all, the thing
he hadn't dared hope for the first night they met had
actually come to pass: she was with him; her body, her
warmth were with him. He had a woman of his very
own, and not one that just any man could have. She
reminded him of something he'd once perceived as real
but now saw more like a dream: sometimes (my God, if
she ever found out) her smell, or the quick touch of her

hand to his nape, reminded him of his mother. He left for work at eleven and returned at four, then went out again at six and came back at midnight. And she was always there. She saw him go; she waited for him to come back. She lay beside him in bed and warmed him, and he couldn't sleep for knowing that she was with him, that she had somehow managed to come back to him, bringing with her all he had lost.

"You know, Tania, my love, my sweetheart," he said all of a sudden, "I'm so happy I don't know what to make of it. And sad too. For some reason I keep thinking, why me? And you know, before I used to think, what am I? Why am I here? But now I've given all that up. I don't think about it anymore."

"The great philosopher."

"Some philosopher with a face like mine. But none of that matters anymore."

"Thank heaven!" She vaguely recalled the day in the restaurant when, all alone, she had philosophized too.

"I'll be going now." That was what he always said. It was as if he were working himself up to leave her. "I have to. It's time."

She stood up, threw on a short housecoat, belted it at the waist, and stood to wait for him by the door in her bare feet.

Then she lay down across the unmade bed and picked up yesterday's paper.

Before, she never so much as glanced at the paper. There were times when *he* had left her his—but she threw it out untouched. She didn't care about people she didn't know and never would. But for the past month, ever since Bologovsky moved in with her (and more and more often the conversation turned to what papers had to be filed before they could get married), ever since he had been with her, she had developed a taste for juicy crime stories reported in exquisite detail and with unusual verve, stories which always seemed to feature a blood-soaked sheet or a stiff towel stained by something suspicious, invariably foul-smelling—a lurid image that entranced Tania's imagination.

There were dramas that reminded her of a carcass being cut up in a butcher shop. And others—when a swollen body is pushed noiselessly into the water at night. Boxes are sent off to an unwitting recipient. People arm themselves with guns, kitchen knives, chisels. But the most burning and obsessive of all were the crimes inspired by a lie: the passage from arithmetic to algebra. Not just to destroy or be destroyed, but also to fool the whole world, even if you have to pay for it with your own life. Here's a woman who is jealous of her own daughter, and of her daughter's lover, whose wife she poisons. She is sentenced to life, but suspicion of a conspiracy falls on him too, something else (there's always a tiny something lurking in the background) comes into the picture, and the lover is sentenced to death. Isn't that algebra? Or another woman: she shoots herself in front of her husband but manages to whisper to the detective that it wasn't she but he who pulled the trigger, in order to get rid of her. Again there's a little something and they pack him off to hard labor. And now it doesn't matter whether she dies or pulls through. What matters is that there are things in this world that are worth paying a real price for.

It was fortunate that reading made the time and

boredom pass more easily. Tania lay there daydreaming, turning over idle thoughts of how precise and unerring she could be in doing that very thing: shooting herself. Shooting herself—because the idea of "pleasure" hadn't worked out: her roots were turning gray; Bologovsky was poor, tedious and old; and there was no one and nothing else to look forward to. She lay there on her back, her cold bare feet dangling, her arms flung back over her head, her hairless armpits exposed. But whose fault was it? Who could she blame? Ah, but wasn't it all the same? She wasn't interested in being just. Only she couldn't risk it. Maybe the detective—who would be willing to hear out her dying lie—wouldn't show up. (And it was unlikely that a priest would be around. Although it would be nice to lie once and for all in her dying confession.) No, she couldn't risk it. She would set it all up her own way. She would settle Bologovsky's fate, as a mother does for her child.

Enough for today. She got dressed (underwear that was full of holes and an old red dress which for some reason he liked) and went out to see Gulia. Again there had been a change. Now Gulia was taking a rich little girl out for her morning walk, for which Gulia received a few francs and lunch.

The kitten had grown up piebald. It scratched, walked on the table, and slept on Gulia's pillow. The whole room stank of him, an acrid, nauseating smell, rather than of Gulia's sharp perfume, which reminded Tania of methylated spirits.

Gulia's pale cheeks, her once beautiful face, which was now puffy and sickly, rested on her large open hands.

Under her low forehead were two huge bovine eyes. Her knees were spread wide, and her two fat large feet in battered slippers loomed before Tania like two inanimate, inert objects. Gulia held a cheap cigarette holder with a dead butt in her long plump fingers. Her voice was deep, almost masculine.

"Today a flunky, tomorrow kicked out. Then he can whistle for it. He'll be out of work. You've got to be tough."

"He's jealous of every dog that comes along."

"He's right in his own way. You wouldn't turn any dog down."

Tania laughed knowingly. That meant Gulia considered her a *grande amoureuse*. Once they had talked about how Nadia and Tata weren't *grandes amoureuses*. Tania liked that.

"He hasn't any money, but he can play Mr. Philosopher. Anyway, he's a little old for me, you know."

"You don't say! That good-for-nothing. And he lets himself be jealous!"

Tania lit a cigarette. "Yesterday he said to me: 'I'll marry you or I'll kill you.' "

"Why?"

"Oh, just like that. Out of hysteria."

Gulia shifted her feet.

" 'What'—he asks me—'are we all living for, you and me, everybody?' "

"But who does he think he is—Tolstoy or something? Tell him he's living so he can receive tips."

Once again Tania burst out laughing.

"But what if," she asked through her laughter, unable to tear her eyes from Gulia's legs, "what if he really does slit my throat?"

"Why would he do a thing like that?"

"Does there have to be a reason for everything? Because he's bored."

Then they started talking about other things: about how they could transform last year's hat, about Nadia, about Gulia's drunken lover, about the one really reliable form of birth control. . . . It was getting dark. It was raining. From Gulia's tiny window you could see the intersection of two bluish-purple streets. The tram stop projected a raspberry-colored star into the air, and the pavement was so wet that you couldn't tell up from down.

The days passed as if someone were dealing them out like cards, the same cards that Ella Martynovna once told Tania's fortune with and that Tania and Gulia played with now and then when there was nothing left to talk about. Tuesday, Wednesday, and another week gone by. And another. Again a Thursday. And it was already Saturday. Once more the tram stop's raspberry star receded in the distance as Tania walked out of the building. When she arrived home she felt like shouting out, "This has already happened before!" She turned on the light to wait for Bologovsky. He bored her, but she was even more bored by herself. "Tasenka mine," he said sometimes. "Mine, mine, mine. It was God who sent you to me. Tell me, my dearest, wasn't it lucky that you came into our restaurant that time? Oh, you do love to eat well! Your last money—and scraped together from embroidering at that—and you throw it away on turkey. Just wait, my precious, this month I'm definitely going to get you some caviar, some real black grain caviar."

She creased her eyes with pleasure. He kissed her and went behind the screens to undress. His stories started—who had ordered what and how much they had left behind. She listened, listened, and then fell asleep without washing. He was afraid to wake her up and so lay down cautiously beside her. The room was stuffy and full of cigarette smoke. It smelled of her, this woman, this woman. He had a woman. How wonderful it was and how terrifying. He had to write to his daughter to tell her that he was planning to get married. He hadn't told Tania that his daughter had a son, that he had a grandson, who was four. Wouldn't she be surprised! How were they doing there? Who cared though. The main thing was her. Not to wake her up.

Slowly (but his neck vertebrae cracked) he turned toward her and saw a glint in her face, the same glint that was reflected in the washbasin and the cupboard latch: it was a reflection of light, probably from the window. Her eyes were open, and she was looking past him. "Tasenka," he murmured, terrified of he didn't know what. She didn't respond, and that terrified him even more. He gripped her shoulder hard; it was warm, alive. "What's wrong?"

"In . . . som . . . nia," she muttered deliberately, her teeth set, with such hardness that it was as if someone else had said it.

He became quiet, and all his being listened. She was breathing. Wasn't she going to say something? Wasn't she going to make a move toward him?

"Have you ever thought about what my life is like?" she asked, and placed both hands on her breasts. "Have you ever thought about what all this is for?"

He felt an inner shiver, an ache between his throat and his heart, and a momentary deafness caused by his agitation. In a few seconds he would be able to hear her voice again.

". . . unbearable. Do you understand? Unbearable. That time when I bought lobster and mayonnaise, I should have bought a gun instead. You saw the dressing gown with the tassels hanging there and you didn't even ask. You just thought: her husband. It's so boring! Let me go, for the love of Christ."

He sat up on the bed, and in the darkness she saw his hands feeling his long head and then saw his narrow sloping shoulders become still again.

"I'm not holding you back. Wait, no, I am. I'm holding on to you. You're my last treasure. I already have a grandson, Volodia, Lidia's son. Where am I to . . . Tasenka? What am I supposed to do for you? What do you want? Maybe you'd like a child? You know, every woman . . ."

She raised her heavy body, and she too sat up, next to him. For a minute she couldn't get out a single word. Then she collapsed into tears and sobs and said:

"I'm talking about myself. What do you mean! I do everything to make sure there won't be one, and you ask. Good God, not to understand even that! Gulia would be laughing at me."

Her tears, the darkness and stuffiness, and the patches of light jumped like fireflies from one object to another—but the main thing was her tears, which churned up everything inside him that was still unclouded. He switched on the light.

"What's the matter with you? What? Tasenka . . ."

But her tears had made her lose her train of thought. She could no longer remember how the conversation, this weeping, had started, or why. Was this what she'd been dreaming of all those years? Someone by her side who was prepared to love her and care for her all her life, so that she could lie around all day long without it mattering, remaking old dresses, shuffling cards? But revulsion for herself and for him as well had broken her spirit. She didn't know what life was, but she had a sense that this was not it. The years were slipping away from her. Now, with those oppressive thoughts, this tedium in her heart, her aging breasts and sour face, where was she to go? Who would take her in hand and show her what to do? It was impossible that everything in the world could be this wretched, this bitter.

"I won't let you go. I love you, and I'm going to keep you. I'm holding on to you." He repeated this. The light burned in the ceiling. His shoulders sloped, and his coarse gray chest appeared through the slit in his shirt.

"Turn out the light," she said quietly. "It's time to go to sleep."

And, indeed, she soon fell asleep.

The night was long and flowed like a silent, endless river that seemed never to have had a beginning. For the first time in all these months of living with Tania, Bologovsky, downcast and filled with worry, recalled his former life, and suddenly he doubted that she could make him happy. He knew that in his memories everything fell into more or less the same order as it did for everyone else: the purity of childhood and the mistakes of youth;

the burden of his fate in connection with his motherland; the loss of home, family; his wife's death; his daughter's marriage. Ten years working as a waiter. Two, no, three women in that time: one middle-aged relative; his dead wife's girlfriend, whom they had wanted him to marry; and a Frenchwoman he met on the boulevard on New Year's Eve. Which one? '32? '34?

He was drinking then . . . it had not been a happy period in his life, though it was the same for everyone, of course. He bet on the horses and drank. His daughter sent him money for a ticket and he drank that up as well. Then it passed, and a weariness set in that sometimes kept him from falling asleep at night and broke his back and shoulders. Especially that staggering around with the plates. Nonetheless, many people envied him.

And then she had appeared. Actually, he could hardly remember that memorable evening. She was sitting at a table stirring her coffee. Then they were sitting opposite one another, and there was a paper tulip, which also reminded him of his childhood. Later she turned out to have a white spot under her left breast, a scar from a childhood abscess, and two tender but sturdy tendons under her soft strong knee. So it was that then? Was that what all those years were for? Those and the others. Everything had come full circle; everything had been restored to him, maybe even more than had been promised.

Fear, sadness. What for? She was lying next to him, she was dreaming, and he was remembering, worried and sad, remembering his life without her. And when mentally he flung a bridge across that night, which coursed like a river, a bridge from the past into the future, he could not see Tania next to him. Once again he saw only himself, utterly alone, even more alone than before. Why? Probably because he had no imagination.

Morning, again morning, yet another morning, and yesterday's was gone. Maybe it hadn't happened at all. Maybe it was all the same morning repeating itself over and over and over again. The chipped blue coffeepot shuddered on the spirit lamp, and through the open window Tania could hear the swallows twittering as if it were spring. One thought, the same thought, took Tania's breath away. One sole thought.

When Bologovsky had moved in with her and brought over his two old trunks, she had hardly so much as glanced into his things, disdaining that old rag heap, his relics and old clothes, even a greasy volume of Kuprin. But at the time she did catch a glimpse in the rags of a very useful item (even then!), and she decided to confirm that that was what it was.

"Well, I'll be going now," he said, like the tick of a pendulum. As soon as his steps died away she opened the first trunk, but there was nothing in it apart from some old and very dirty starched collars. The second was nearly full though. Tania sat down on a chair, tying a scarf over her housecoat, and plunged her head and arms under the lid.

What didn't he have there! Old suspenders and a few dozen razor blades, all rusty and black; empty cartridges; an oil lamp without its shade; pencils, rags, and a pile of brightly colored socks with holes you could put a fist through; used church tapers; a meter and a half of yellow and black ribbon for Saint George crosses; a box that held an officer's cross wrapped in tissue paper; a piece of nice thick paper with gold seals on it that was disintegrating at the folds; letters scattered in and among the socks. In the bottom corner—the object she thought she'd seen (now she remembered his telling her at the time: "It's not mine, no, but it does shoot quite well") wrapped in a piece of a Bukhara silk shawl (blue and yellow paisleys along a dark red border), a small, heavy, long-since Russified Browning, its muzzle aimed at the corner of the trunk.

She picked it up as it was, in the shawl, but the shawl was so gaudy that she wrapped it all up together in a newspaper, yesterday's, which she had already devoured. And as she slipped the packet under her sheets she thought it was already starting to resemble one of the stories she'd read the day before, the one with the picture. . . .

She had a plan. Like a military commander, like a traveler or a criminal, she had her very own plan. She had thought it up over the last few days while at home alone, and not just her brain but her whole being was consumed with it. Thinking about it made her thirsty, so she got up and walked over to the washstand and drank straight from the tap. The next thing was to take two precautionary measures: write a letter, one little letter, it didn't matter to whom—it might as well be Belova, who was thorough and was likely to hold on to it; and go and see Gulia for one last time and say: "I have this feeling, I'm scared."

No, there was a third thing as well, maybe the most

important: warn the hotel concierge, get her worrying. "Oh, Inspector, right then I thought: he's going to kill that woman, the brute. She looked at me so sweetly when she said: 'Yes, we're definitely going to see that film tomorrow evening.' (We have a cinema across the street, Inspector. We go there once a week, and so do all our lodgers.) 'We're definitely going,' that poor Russian lady said, 'if we live that long.' "

But why, what did she have to live for? What did Lila, her sister, live for, all dried up in her export office, or her father, rotting away paralyzed? Had the land where she had married, where she had lived with Alexei Ivanovich, and where she had betrayed him, ever really existed? Nothing had happened in those years that was worth regretting, or worth loving. It always seemed to her that things could have been better, that they would get better, that others had it richer, happier, and fuller—what they call happiness. And even before that, in her childhood, in another country which she had long since forgotten. Ruses that were not completely innocent, a tortuous vanity, and, since she was nine, obscene dreams. It wasn't worth thinking about. Six feet under! Six feet under! To get out of here as fast as possible, having taken her revenge out on someone, anyone, revenge for her whole life all at once, having taken her revenge out on Bologovsky because the rest were all gone, scattered, hiding, the bastards.

He didn't give her much money, not because he was mean but because he didn't have it. When he lived alone he always had money, enough for himself, and once in a while there was even a hundred or two left over, which he sent to his daughter. Now things were tight sometimes, but nevertheless, as he rode home in the close air of the Métro surrounded by a wall of strange bodies and the smell of human breathing, he thought how he had something in common with that couple hugging in the corner, drunk with joy. Dark, stuffy stations went by. Sometimes he would notice a hunchbacked, gray-haired beggar woman sitting on a bench carrying a cane and a brown bag, or an armless worker chewing on some bread, neither of them paying the slightest attention to the passing trains. Sometimes then strange thoughts would occur to Bologovsky, fear of some end, old age maybe, and the future loomed like a weight that he couldn't budge.

More and more insistently, more and more obstinately, not realizing it himself, he was waiting for love to help him. He couldn't have said precisely what it was he required from that woman. Probably if asked he would have replied that he was completely content. But without putting it into words, in his heart, he was waiting for warmth, more warmth, a kind word, an understanding move in his direction, and maybe even . . . embroidery, which was how he imagined she had got by before she'd met him. Something to alleviate all that exhausting joy, in essence so much like a constant torment, which he kept skimming like foam off his trembling bliss—with kisses, with words, with his muffled laughter.

"Maybe," he thought (these thoughts usually began as he was walking toward her hotel), "maybe she had someone after her husband. After all, it's been five or six years since then. In the old days I wouldn't have dared think such a thing, but now everything's changed so much. She was living alone, and it was hard on her. Oh, so what! What do I care? But what if she's deceiving me now? No, that's ridiculous."

He himself was neither jealous nor suspicious, but he needed his daily ration of torment or reassurance, and it was precisely that which was missing. Every time he reached the front door, on the very threshold, the worry that there, inside, things had changed pressed on his heart; he was afraid to think that everything had gone cold up there, that there was nothing up there at all. Then as the door slammed shut he would run up the stairs on his thin legs, three steps at a time, simply to convince himself that Tania still existed.

She was sitting on a chair in the middle of the room completely undressed, waiting for the ten red nails on her hands and the ten on her feet to dry. She was very white, and her large round stomach and belly changed shape depending on how she sat. There was practically no hair on her body—her lack of eyebrows gave a hint of that. She had her legs stretched out in front of her and her arms hanging by her sides, and she was waiting. Her face wore the expression, resigned and obtuse, that she herself never saw but others did.

"Someone's been here," he said, sensing a presence in the air. The ashtray was full of butts.

"Gulia," she responded, not stirring.

"What's wrong with her?"

"She got worried so she dropped in."

He started to undress.

"What was she worried about?"

"Me. How you and I are getting along."

He took off his coat, hat, and jacket and tugged his feet, stiff with exhaustion, out of his shoes. He sat down at the table and started looking at her, naked and still, at her heavy breasts, at her twenty nails as red as radishes.

"So it's you? The same old you?" he asked himself cautiously. "Lord, but who are you? Why are you so naked? Cover yourself, for God's sake. I beg you!" He said this to himself, and at the same time he felt that he was losing the gift of speech, as if his voice and tongue were being taken away from him. "Keep quiet. Better keep quiet." Suddenly he made a strange face as if his mouth had been slit with a razor and then pressed together. Bologovsky stretched his hairy arms across the table and waited for this woman to get up and cover her nakedness.

Finally she got up, found her slippers, and started dressing two steps from him. It was strange for him to have her so close, so accessible, and to have no desire even to watch her.

"Gulia's worried about me and so is Belova. Even the concierge downstairs says '*Dieu merci*' every time she sees me. I can tell by their faces that if I croaked after eating mushrooms or rotten fish they'd suspect you of poisoning me." She chuckled, tugging at her soiled, purplish-pink girdle. "Well, why don't you say something? Just you wait. I'll die and then you'll find out. Talk! Oh, I'm so fed up with it all, fed up. Everything's old and worn out." She hitched her brassiere with a safety pin. "My hair's a mess, and my powder's almost run out. Say something!" And she froze, in one stocking, looking at

Bologovsky with hatred. "If you're going to live with me, then talk! Why do you go on living? Why do you go on living at all? Do you hear what I'm asking you or not?" she yelled, sobbing.

He moved his fingers but said nothing, a shiver passed across his face, and his eyes grew even more metallic.

"And I thought I could live with a man like that somehow . . . somehow," she muttered, grabbing her hair with both hands in anguish. "Do you understand that I feel nothing for you but hatred? Nothing! Why have you been feeding me for three months? Why have you been sleeping with me? Watch, I'll shoot myself right now, and the police will arrest you. And just before I do I'll ring the bell. I'll scream. . . ."

She jumped up, but he jumped up too and barred the way.

Where was she running to? Not to him. Not to the bell, which was at the head of the bed. To the cupboard. He was still unable to overcome his muteness, and couldn't utter a word. What kind of words did he have anyway? Tenderness? Anger? She had stopped by the cupboard doors, half-dressed and holding a stocking in her hand. While he quickly slipped his feet into the shoes tossed under the table, while he pulled on his jacket and coat—still mute—she remained by the cupboard, apparently lacking the nerve to go through with what she had intended. Her face was frightening now; another four, three . . . two seconds . . . no, she couldn't do what had seemed so simple and easy before. One second. Not even unwrapping the Bukhara shawl, if she could only reach the bell; through the shawl into my stomach, into my soft warm stomach, sending the shot and my scream all through the building. (By that time he was running down the stairs.) "What happened?" "She's shot herself," he tells the people running toward him. "See, she's still holding the gun." "Not on your life, you're under arrest," they reply. "If she'd shot herself she wouldn't have rung the bell. She wouldn't have called out for help. She wouldn't have made every other person all this past week think she was afraid of you. You killed her." "But I ran out onto the stairs *before* the shot. Ask the neighbors." And then someone will say (under oath) that first there came the shot and then the steps on the landing, and another someone (also under oath) that first there came the steps and then the shot.

He was already far away, out on the street, and she was still standing next to the cupboard, stock-still. Instead of thinking about what in fact had kept her from carrying out what she had intended, she thought about trivial things: "What time could it be? Look at that cobweb hanging from the ceiling. What was that over there? What is this kind of mental illness called? Mania. Some kind of mania. Lympho . . . lymphomania. No, what am I saying! Mythomania. From the word 'myth.' I dreamed up a story which you could get money for from one of those newspapers if you wrote it down. I dreamed up . . . My God, where is he? My God, he's run out on me!"

Six o'clock. A green-shaded lamp is lit near the cashier's dish. Seven men in identical white jackets are soundlessly setting the tables. The trolley, with a rustling noise, brings hors d'oeuvres and the *tarte maison* topped with cream up from the refrigerator. Someone wipes glasses and carries them stem up. Bologovsky moves back and forth in the aquarium light, sorting silver forks. At seven-fifteen the front door starts swinging: the first customers walk in; others follow. First places are taken in the four corners of the room; then in the middle. The light burns. Voices. Hot bowls sail past, an ice bucket for one table, *shashlik* brought in on long skewers. The room fills up. Eight o'clock. There isn't a single free table. Fortissimo sounds from the invisible orchestra and then a gradual quieting of voices and movements, an ebb of people, plates, and glasses (stem down); the gathering of napkins, the stacking of chairs; one lamp goes out, another, a third. The clock says ten, ten on the dot. Outside is a spring night, a May night. Paris hasn't changed. It is hard to believe somehow.

He walked along, thinking, but his thoughts did not come easily. All he felt was disgust at her nakedness and her tears. As he went over in his mind the three months he had lived with her, everything, or nearly everything, took on that aspect—cynical, insulting, false. There was nothing you could grab hold of; it was all so slippery, so vile. And hardest of all to bear was the awareness of his own vain self-deception. In that respect she was not herself, nor was he himself.

He walked the streets through the gloom and damp of the evening, taking no notice of passersby. At the lights he stopped in for a drink, and the alcohol helped his soul—yes, here was proof of its existence—stretch its dusty wings. To let change jangle on zinc one last time, to take a swig and feel the warmth run down his shoulders and ribs, the very warmth he had had so little of. Here was another corner, a streetlamp, a chemist. There was a big muddy ice wagon; there was a horse. Don't get confused please. What does artillery have to do with it? The Nikolaevsky Cavalry, a great institution . . .

"Oh, go on with you," he says, pushing his hat back on his head and putting his arms around the docile, big-eyed light chestnut's muzzle. "Oh, go on with you."

He strokes it, tousles its mane, kisses it on the lips, and sniffs the air blowing in his face from its obliging nostrils. And it sniffs him back so that they're both sniffing each other.

"Oh, go on with you, you recognized me. You remembered," Bologovsky says. "You haven't forgotten." He rubs his cheek, his cheek and his whole face, against the horse and strokes it with both hands.

The iceman comes back from delivering a block of ice to the café, silently crawls into his box, silently lifts his whip. And the horse walks away, indifferent, submissive, leaving Bologovsky alone.

When he flung the door open and entered, Tania was standing in the dark pressed up against the wall, kneading her hands and clutching an end of the Bukhara shawl to her breast. (Where had he seen that shawl, and when?)

"Tasenka, what's the matter with you? Anyone would think you were trying to scare me," he said and smiled.

She moved away from him, mistrustful.

"Where have you been?"

"What do you mean, where have I been? I've been working. I'm a waiter, remember?"

He reeked of wine, and his hat was crushed to one side.

"Tasenka, tell me . . ."

She clutched the bit of shawl tightly to her breast. He came toward her, and a depth she didn't know opened up in his eyes.

"So tell me, you don't love me? 'In a sort of way,' you say. I don't think it's a 'sort of way,' but in a very particular way, so particular that it's frightening to say out loud."

He stood close to her, put his hands on her shoulders, and pressed his chest against hers.

"So there wasn't any point to it after all, eh? Come on, sweetheart, how many were there before me?"

She didn't respond. The gun was poking into her chest and his too, but he hadn't noticed it.

"Tell me how many there were and I'll let you go. You'll be free, the way you were before. Damn you, little idiot! It didn't work out. Forget it!"

"You're running out on me?" she whispered, frightened, and tried to reach the trigger under the silk. Suddenly he moved back and grabbed the muzzle with his right hand.

"What the hell is this?" he asked, sobering up a little. She began to fall back slowly. "No, don't you faint. You're a good actress, I should know. I know how well. . . . So what on earth is this?" She stopped her fall and leaned against the wall, breathing heavily. Her face was frozen, white, wet. He gripped her wrist with one hand and twirled the Browning in the other, holding it by the muzzle, and the shawl fluttered like a flag. "What on earth is this? What is it?" he spluttered. Letting the gun drop to the floor with a thud, he grabbed her arms with both hands now and, digging his fingers into their fleshiness, panting, forced her to bend and jerked her away from the door.

"I'll scream," she cried, bumping her head on the headboard and watching to see he didn't pick the weapon up again.

"Kill? Me? She wanted to kill me!" he whispered, making her bend over even farther, dragging her, pulling her, shaking her so hard that she finally gasped and fell between the bed and the table.

"Let me go," she wailed. She struggled, like a big fish, squirming to get out from under him, feeling his familiar heavy body on top of her. He crushed her with his knees and chest, pressing, breaking her arms: "Why did you do it, you viper? Why?" he muttered. His whole face—so close to hers—was covered with a grid of swollen veins.

"I was joking, joking, jo-king," she repeated senselessly, still trying to throw him off, knocking her head on something hard in the process. He turned her face toward him with his elbow, crushed her arms even tighter with his chest and left arm, and with his right grabbed her by her velvety white throat, which felt so much like the place behind her knee that he touched sometimes, above the calf: two firm tendons and that soft skin, strength and weakness.

"A-a-ah," she wailed, and her two terrified and dulled blue eyes bulged. "A-a-ah!" But the second time it came out as a rasp, not a wail.

Yes, those same two firm, sturdy tendons, he realized

soberly, something round in the middle and all wrapped in quivering lard, into which he dug his hairy fingers. He squeezed it for a long time until it stopped throbbing. Was she really dead? What if she was still alive? He grabbed a pillow from the bed and threw it on her face, threw another on her chest, and lay down again, crushing her, unable to believe she wouldn't revive.

There was a loud crash against the door. Wait . . . He'd better make sure there aren't any gaps. Otherwise— it would be too frightening if she turned out to be alive, with those nails, those moans and those spasms, that past he didn't know, that future. . . . But, thank God, there was no future.

Astashev in Paris

I

MAMA LIVED ON THE SEVENTH FLOOR of a very large old building. The entire floor was rented out by the room; people ate, slept, and cooked in each room, and in the evening they took their rubbish bins out to a common hallway. The old-fashioned hydraulic elevator broke down every other day. The stairwell, which had no windows, was not always lit, and the cast-iron door to the street was too heavy, and that was why Mama almost never went out. A neighbor ran to the shop for her, and Mama only visited either on her own floor or one flight down—the building had been taken over by Russians. She only went downstairs to go to church, and then only for the main holy days. Afterward, getting back up, using her umbrella like a cane, took so long and made her so short of breath that she was nearly reduced to tears. When she met friends at the candle box and they said, "You must drop in for a cup of tea sometime, Klavdia Ivanovna," all she could think of was that elevator, the elevator, the unlit landings, and the steep, hollowed-out steps. "You've got a home. Stay put." That was how she saw it. "Otherwise you'll go out one day and won't come back. You'll get stranded between floors or choke to death on the pavement."

Indeed, Alyosha found his mother's apartment quite agreeably situated, as the higher up you were the fresher the air. When he came to visit he made sure the window was wide open. It looked onto a round windowless building that resembled a globe: the gas plant. Behind it you could see an endless murk of buildings, roofs, windows, and a tower that came in and out of view, sometimes with a flag, sometimes not, sometimes with its top cut off, sometimes with the statue of an angel on it.

"How lucky you are, Mama," Alyosha used to say. "Such tranquillity, such peace of mind." Then he sat down to drink tea and eat some pie, a pretzel, jam, to read the papers he had brought along with him. Or sometimes his eyes fixed absentmindedly on her trembling head, her sparse hair, her dry hands and bent fingers. "I've made it possible for you to live exactly as you please," he used to say, "and I live exactly as I please, too. You and I have already been through more than enough. *Assez*, now, *assez, assez*. You have electricity, a heated bathroom, sun—and curtains if you feel like shutting it out. Your central heating works, and your papers are in perfect order. All that is what's known as comfort, Mama. Yes! And we both have it now because I . . . well, thank God."

She sat at the table and nodded in agreement, smiling. She was knitting—without looking down—a thick white sweater for him. In front of her on the table lay a picture from a fashion magazine showing a young man with a long tanned face wearing a thick white sweater and sticking his chest out. She looked at it as she knitted, counting to herself, and it was in fact coming out very much like the picture. The ball of white wool bobbed up and down on her knees. Alexei Georgievich kept opening and closing the windows, making sure that the bolts were working. He turned the light off and on, jumped to see whether the parquet creaked, and pulled at the curtains to make sure they were up securely.

"That elevator of ours broke down again yesterday," she said sadly. "They were fixing something. They say something's broken in the basement. They never did fix it, though. Just gave up."

But he didn't pay much attention to what she said. Either he talked or he read. When he was talking to her he never said a word about his business, about the people at the office. Instead he reminisced about things that had happened long ago, as you would with an old ally with whom you have no present in common but with whom you share a past—and what a past! It had been a long battle they would both remember and respect forever: she because her Alyosha was its hero, and he—for the same reason. Or else he told her about something unusual he had seen on the street. But the past, their common forty-year past, was much more real than their shabby and soulless present.

"Mama, do you remember when we lived on Siverskaya? Remember I had a little navy-blue suit that summer Papa went away and the silver was stolen? Remember what a plump, energetic little boy I was then? And my dream was to train porcupines and join the circus?"

She remembered of course.

"Today I was walking along, and what did I see? Children sailing toy boats on the pond in the square. Mama, technology has even reached silly games like that. I felt upset. Why was it ordained from birth that I should have to make do with flat-bottom boats made of tree bark?"

His big blue eyes looked straight ahead as he recalled a Russian pond, willows, his fat knees, and his trousers rolled up. When did that end?

"Childhood stopped in a very abrupt way, Mama. Was it after college? I always seemed to be marching off with a black knapsack slung over my shoulders. March, march, march! It's just as if I'd kept on marching right up till today. I'm still young. You used to give me thirty kopecks for lunch, and I spent twelve and saved eighteen. Then, when you sent me to Moscow—remember?—I saved masses of money on my hotel. Let me have a pencil."

She nodded, crossed herself, and flicked away a tear from her old eyes.

"And now, Alyoshenka, and now!"

"It's even funny if you think of the money I saved. Yes, a lot has happened. But the main thing was having to start all over again from scratch here. You can't get away with just any old thing here, like you could back home. Here it takes something completely different. But I was born a European. It would have been simply ridiculous for me to live in Russia."

"And yet . . . if I could take just one look at it!"

"People often say to me: 'Astashev, are you really Russian? You're just like one of us.' "

Later she hugged his pudgy, flabby body and his clean hands with their pink palms and delicate triangular fingernails, stroked his dark blue jacket and fair hair, and gazed into his round, youthful, baby-smooth face.

"My clever boy," she said. "My consolation."

He kissed her, looked at his watch again, and since it was after eight, he left.

"Where are you going now?" she asked. "Have you got yourself a sweetheart?"

He replied, while fastidiously buttoning his well-made coat:

"Mama, I have no business having a sweetheart. Siring beggars is not my sort of thing. Sometimes I make an exception for the sake of my health, but I have to wait a minimum of three years to marry."

"Well, may the Lord protect you," she whispered.

She never did find out where he went. In all these years she never had the least idea.

Half an hour later he was ringing the bell at a broad polished door where the stairs were carpeted and palms flanked the downstairs mirror.

"That must be Alexei," said a woman's voice in the next room as the servant was helping him off with his coat.

"Yes, it's me, Mamenka," he replied. "Hello."

"Hello there, vulture. Whose bones did you pick clean today?"

He walked over to where she was sitting, clicked his heels, and kissed her hand. Usually there was someone else there, and Xenia Andreevna's behavior with him was playfully haughty.

"Did you hear? *'Mamenka!'* " she exclaimed. But her dyed red hair, sagging bust, and the thick layer of powder on her neck betrayed her age ruthlessly. "You make me feel old, you gangster!"

This was Alyosha's father's second wife, his step-mother, who once won a great victory over Klavdia Ivanovna.

He bloomed there like a rare and special flower. He made himself comfortable in an armchair, made endless witty remarks, laughed loudly and gazed unctuously at Xenia Andreevna and at her guests—officials, well-off, whom Mamenka was encouraging. Despite the difference in ages, Alyosha could keep up with their idiosyncratic conversation: stories of deputies, chairmen, and vice-chairmen, of elections for some committee, or committee council, or council executive. Evgraf Evgrafovich hinted at the possible candidacy of Yuli Fyodorovich to the audit commission. One guest gave a significant look; another guest felt that a recount was inevitable; and Mamenka intrigued venomously and opportunistically on behalf of Admiral Vyazminitinov, who had made someone a charitable donation.

Alexei Georgievich suddenly asked for champagne, told a funny story, kissed Xenia Andreevna's hands, and behaved like a spoiled child who can get away with anything. Then he became respectful and kind, produced a free theater ticket from his pocket and offered it to all and sundry present, and took his leave.

Alexei Georgievich had lived with his father for one-half of his life, and the other half with his mother; a month here, a week there; a winter here, a summer there. He was ten when his father had walked out on the family, moved in with a woman who called herself an actress, and continued to support his wife and the two children, he and his sister Nyuta, haphazardly and meagerly. Nyuta died a year later of meningitis. He went to one of the modern high schools. They lived on Pesk, in a dingy apartment with one entrance that was furnished with their bulky and nondescript furniture. There were small windows between the rooms to let in more light, and fat spiders spun their webs up by the ceilings. His mother and nurse, who were preoccupied with cleaning the painted floors and starching the curtains, never knocked them down. Sometimes in the evenings, engulfed in their own brocade and protected by female superstition, the spiders ran out to the middle of the ceiling, fell on one another, and sucked each other dry, whereupon they shriveled up and fell to the floor.

When he came home from school, Alexei went straight to his desk in a room full of trunks and cupboards, where the window vent stayed closed for weeks on end. He sat like that until nightfall, writing compositions, solving problems, looking a chapter ahead in history and Russian to get an idea about the next day's lesson. There was a walnut shelf over his desk where he kept his Latin texts, mimeographed solutions to theorems, *Sample Compositions for the Sixth, Seventh and Eighth Classes; Teach Yourself Physics*; and *Geography Exam Questions with Their Answers*. He only had to have one textbook per subject, but he had several: Sipovsky, Savodnik, Nezelenov, Smirnovsky, Kraievich, and Zinger, Lebedev, Smirnov, and Yanchev,

Kiselev, and Davydov, and for history Illovaisky, Platonov, Vinogradov, Belyarminov, Elpatievsky, and someone else whose name he didn't know because the title page had been torn out. Alexei Georgievich had acquired all these textbooks through exchange: he took his mother's books—Pushkin, Lermontov, Mamin-Sibiryak, Sheller-Mikhailov, and sometimes Zola's novels in translation—out of their narrow, glass-doored, silk-curtained bookcase and swapped them at school (they all knew him there) for textbooks, which students in all grades passed on to him—not just theirs but their older brothers' and sisters' as well.

He was at the top of his class. He sat right under the teacher's nose in the first row. For a very long time he was shorter than everyone else, and since his last name began with an *A*, he was all the more visible. Everything started with him: the two-by-two procession, examinations, question-and-answer periods. He always recited whatever greeting was called for, and it was he who always answered the inspector's questions as well. Cleaning the blackboard was his job, and so was the chalk, for some reason. And despite all this no one ever took it into his head to be jealous of him.

On Saturdays Alyosha didn't go home after school. Instead he took the number 14 tram to Sennaya Street. A year before his father had been disbarred for some rather less than honest dealings, and now he was "in business." The apartment was quite pleasant, with a gilded frieze in the foyer and velvet and leather and even a servant—a grubby, pimply boy with greasy hair and a drinker's nose. Alyosha had the utmost respect for his father and his father's servant, apartment, and new wife.

Here was a real woman, the first woman he'd had a chance to study at close hand—dressed, half-dressed, undressed, in sickness and in health. Here was a real woman, who bore some inexplicable relationship to his father's wallet. In her vicinity Alyosha always felt a little anxious, giddy, and not altogether comfortable.

He stayed there until Monday morning. His life for those two days bore no resemblance to life with Klavdia Ivanovna. Saturday was Mamenka's *jour fixe*: guests sat in the drawing room drinking tea, making witty remarks, and gossiping. And he would put his homework off until later, until that night, and sit in an armchair, his eyes bulging, unable to tear himself away, mentally unbuttoning the women's gathered silk dresses, mentally crawling into the men's shoes and swallowing whole the éclairs, napoleons, cream puffs, and bouchées, and all their words and puns, which showered down like peas, like shot, like pearls.

They were three at the evening meal: Papa, bald, with thick eyebrows and a handlebar mustache, looking like something off the cover of a gypsy romance; Mamenka, Xenia Andreevna, wearing a transparent robe with flowing sleeves; and Alexei. Sometimes after supper his father and stepmother drove to the theater, and he lounged about the apartment for a long time examining the contents of drawers—both locked and unlocked—and then sat down to his homework. Sometimes they took him with them to the theater—operetta, farce, Suvorin. Once, one Sunday afternoon, they took him to see *The Inspector General* because he had studied Gogol recently at school.

Usually on Sunday, though, he got up late and read

the newspapers from cover to cover over tea, like a novel, from the front-page obituaries to the personal columns at the back. After breakfast Xenia Andreevna took him for a walk. They walked down Nevsky and Sadovaya to the Summer Garden, where they ran into people they knew.

"Oh, my God! Whose young man is this?"

"This is my son," she would say. "Isn't it odd that I should have such a grown-up son?"

The bewildered listener would smile in silence.

"Doesn't he look like me?"

And when the whole thing was cleared up there would be lots of laughter, lots of teasing on her part, and lots of feeble jokes on the other's.

Drifting off to sleep at night, Alexei Georgievich used to hear his father quarreling with Xenia Andreevna, things breaking—a pitcher, a perfume bottle—a chair falling, their whispers and shouts becoming less and less constrained, less and less self-conscious. In the morning he never saw anyone. The servant brought him his glass of tea, and he ate a roll and walked his quick, rolling walk to the tram stop. During the winter the streetlamps were still burning through the snow and fog. Cutting through the gloom, the tram car rolled along, jingling its bell, and Alyosha sat and looked at the old ladies, at the women, at the fine ladies swathed in fox and sable, and found that there was something which attracted him in nearly all of them.

On Monday he went back home after school. Klavdia Ivanovna latched on to his overcoat, his nurse came out of the kitchen, and they both set about tormenting him.

What did he have to eat? Didn't he starve? Didn't he
catch a chill? Didn't anyone insult him? He fended them
off, saying as he walked away: "It's always the same,
tiresome really. Xenia Andreevna ordered herself a new
fur coat with foxtails. I think Papa is going to get himself
horses."

Having driven this nail into the maternal heart, he
went to do his math, nestling his round chin (on which
nothing would grow for a long time) in the soft bed of
his hand. This studying, this effort, this sweat, went on
all week until the weekend came around once more, like
an unexpected and illicit flourish on a plain government
building.

He was blue-eyed, quiet, and combined when necessary both speed (serving and fetching) and dependa-
bility. His face was pale and serious, and his disposition
excellent. He never got particularly close to anyone, never
played darts or cards, and never lent money. He was
growing up, and it was gradually becoming clear that he
hadn't read anything apart from his textbooks. On the
other hand, he knew what he needed to know by heart.
When he turned sixteen he heard a conversation about
women. The conversation was eminently pragmatic and
dry, more as if it were a matter of choosing a subject to
study at the university or an obligatory Lenten fast. It
was one of those Saturdays. In the evening he was at his
father's, having mapped out his plan of action. Late that
night, when everyone was asleep, he pulled his trousers
on and went barefoot to the cook, a young, still attractive,
furtive woman, and within half an hour he was back in
his room. In that half hour he had not opened his mouth

or uttered a word, so that finally the cook had said to him: "But why, Alyoshenka? Why don't you say something? You're so quiet for such a young man."

At twenty he lost his father. At the time Xenia Andreevna was in Kislovodsk, where she hobnobbed with White generals, with second lieutenants, wore white lace shirts, and composed and published a patriotic novel. Alyosha stayed in Petersburg with Klavdia Ivanovna, working in a Soviet institution, going hungry. In his humiliated thoughts he cherished proud Bonapartist plans without even being able to give them a name. It was during those years that his savage hatred for authority, for the people, for his country, was born. No prince of the blood or old-line nobleman could have contemplated the goings-on in Russia with the same rage and shiver as Alyosha.

He hated all of it: the vast expanses, which themselves could lead to ruin due to the impossibility of keeping a people who cracked sunflower seeds in their teeth and blew their noses into their hand under police control all the way to the trackless frontiers; the disorder of history, right up to the succession after Peter the First, which he perceived as an unforgivable blunder, from which he was now forced to extricate himself. He hated the entire nineteenth century, which seemed like an apocalyptic sign, each decade speaking of the future in the accursed tongue of prophecy. He liked to recall the last four lost wars and the tattered, unkempt "vanguard," which had been half infiltrated with police agents, who joined them in tossing bombs.

When the borders opened up in 1925 and he found

himself in Paris he used to refer to Russia as the Soviet Republic, the Bolsheviks as the comrades, and Lenin as the German spy. He believed that he had miraculously escaped execution and used to say that they were raising fourteen-year-olds of unknown patrimony at the state's expense and that the peasants were eating human flesh. Then that passed and he forgot all about Russia. A new life began in a new place. And at first he had such a life-and-death struggle with it that he nearly gave up.

The two of them were living in the suburbs in an unheated room. Klavdia Ivanovna went out to iron during the day. He watched this relatively young, strong woman being transformed into an old woman who suffered from a hernia and had bleeding calluses on her overworked fingers. He ran all over town. What did he know how to do? What could he do? Work in an office, wash dishes in a restaurant, be a delivery boy in a Russian pastry shop, sell vacuum cleaners door-to-door? He did all those things until he finally grew numb from it all and got fed up with it, fed up with trembling over every penny he made. Had he been able to steal without getting caught he would have stolen, but he didn't have any idea of where or how business of that kind was carried out.

Even in that restless indigence, from one niggardly day to the next, he was being drawn in a specific direction and had made a definite choice, adamantly preferring selling for a commission—long hours and fruitless running from house to house and up and down stairs—to sitting in an office. They told him to find someone who would like to acquire a piano (or a sewing machine, or a radio, to say nothing of a bicycle, encyclopedia, or the latest model carpet sweeper), and he looked—but he never found anyone. He felt the stony damp cold of the pavement through his soles and the hundreds of steps in his heart, but he did not give up his vague hope that on that very pavement, on those very stairs, he would catch a glimpse of his prosperity.

Toward the end of the third winter, when Klavdia Ivanovna was taken to the hospital for an operation, he took advantage of the fact that she wouldn't be seeing the papers and placed an advertisement: "Xenia Andreevna Astasheva—Please contact your son." A letter arrived at the office of the newspaper. Xenia Andreevna gave him her address, asked him to come to see her right away, and expressed her amazement that neither Nadezhda Petrovna, Vassily Vassilievich, Zhenya Sokolova, nor the Sipatievs had told him that she was in Paris. He had never known these people.

She understood everything the moment he walked in, and although she was considerably changed (she had been forty, now she was fifty), he had changed even more. A kind of dark puffiness, a crushed look, had appeared in his face, and his voice was louder. It was as if Alyosha were in a state of constant indignation over something. His eyes had become furtive and lackluster, and his mouth, pale and wet, had spread out across his face. He still didn't know whether he could—or should—tell her. He hitched his thumb in the armhole of his vest and smoked the cigarette she offered him. He didn't know whether to launch into his story snorting and foaming. It was certainly a story beyond her wildest dreams.

"Well, my handsome blond," she said in her deep

voice, toying with the chain at her neck that he had known since childhood, "tell me about it, don't be a fool."

The room was not hers. She had rented it furnished, but it was an expensive room with red silk curtains and a grand piano. (She didn't need a vacuum cleaner, did she? No, probably not.) There were three bottles on the table—refreshments she planned to treat him to, although he felt like a veal chop, baked ham, beef, roasted or stewed beef.

"I'm lost here," he said. He placed his unlit cigarette back on the table and looked down at his hands, at his bitten fingernails. "Can't you think up something, Mamenka?"

She had him drink a small glass of Benedictine, which made him feel warm, and his thoughts became sweet and misty. Crossing one large elegant leg over the other, revealing a silken knee under her short slim skirt, she sat before him—not young and not old, her hair dyed, her veins prominent, self-assured—and smoked. She didn't smile. There was nothing to smile at.

"I'll give you a chance," she said in her bass voice, giving him a penetrating look. "Listen closely, my number-one student. Just a moment and I'll get you something to eat. There's something left from lunch."

She went out. Her perfume lingered in the air, strong heavy perfume. He looked around. Who was she? What was she? In the morning, for example, when she gets up, what does she do? Where does she go? Who pays for all of this?

She came back. Roast beef with mustard and bread.

He ate it all. He drank another liqueur. Mustard and Benedictine. He liked it. He would have to do it again sometime, when he could afford it.

"Listen. First of all, about me. I have a Frenchman. God save the soul of Georgy Ivanovich"—she crossed herself deliberately—"there'll never be anyone like him: talent, spirit, the old guard. But I don't have to tell you—you're his son. Remember one thing: he was an extraordinary man. But this Frenchman cropped up on a train, and it's been a fairy tale, a novel! He got hooked, like a trout on a line. He's been keeping me for over three years. Fantastically intelligent, magnificent blood, a musician. He was an expert adviser in affairs of state, but now he's retired. There's one drawback though: he's over seventy."

"Oh, my God!" he sighed sympathetically.

"What are you gasping for? Think! That's not so much for a well-preserved man. After all, I'm not sixteen anymore. But there is still a danger. He nearly died of a heart attack this autumn. And there's a family, a wife, children. There's another mistress he's had for thirty years. And there's yet another actress, a horrible bitch, she sleeps with ministers. He needs her for business purposes, he meets useful people at her place. In short, I'm giving you a chance. Instead of going around trying to talk people into providing themselves with things they don't need—insure him, making me the beneficiary."

"What did you say?" He didn't understand, but by her face he could tell she had come to the crucial point.

"Are you drunk? On one glass? I said: Go and make yourself an insurance agent. You'll meet him here and

get friendly. Only no 'Mamenka' when he's around. Use
something vague, '*ma cousine*,' for example, for that matter,
on my husband's side, a distant relative . . . twice removed.
He'll ask you: 'And what do you do, young man?' You'll
see, he's a true gentleman, he talks like a professor. You
tell him about some real-life cases. Make him understand
what it means to leave your loved ones beggars. Don't
scare him off with death, no one likes that. But allude
to the fifth act, to the last curtain that falls without
warning."

He laughed knowingly, by now completely drunk.
He wasn't used to drinking.

"Oh, Mamenka, you're amazing! You're so good, so
sweet, so clever! I'm going to kiss you. I'm definitely
going to kiss you! You always seemed like perfection itself
to me. At one time your peignoirs got me quite excited.
At least give me your hand, if that's the way you want
it, like mother and son."

"You idiot," she said, flattered nonetheless.

All of a sudden he sobered up, pulled himself together, and coughed.

"But what if it doesn't work out? I mean, what I
meant to say was, what if it does work out?"

"You'll get a percentage. If you get him up to half
a million, that will mean a pretty penny."

"But that's likely to cost him a small fortune, especially if he's getting old."

"It will cost him a lot of money, but he's rich."

Alyosha thought it over. He touched the glass and
licked his sticky finger.

"But what then?"

"To start out all you need is the first fifty thousand francs," she said simply. She drained her glass, her eyes half-closed.

He watched her and suddenly began to laugh again, but differently now—a moist, pensive laugh.

"It really would be nice, my dear Mamenka," he mumbled, and something joyful shone in his face. "Oh, it really would be nice! Is it possible? And in such an honest, such a good way? You know, Mamenka, I do like honesty. I'm not a rascal. I could never kill anyone, for instance. I couldn't even rob. I've never tried to seduce a married woman, I swear. I've always preferred unattached ones. I can't think of a single sin I've ever committed. So why should I suffer like this?" He fell silent, waiting for the tears under his eyelids to go away. "My God, why? I don't have a bad disposition, I'm clean, polite, and if I don't recite poetry or go to concerts, that's no crime, after all."

She listened to him ramble. The light was failing in the room. The long noses of the silk dolls on the sofa were drooping into the festoons of their colorful dresses. Then she stood up, switched on the light, powdered her face, put on a striking tall hat, and took him out to shop. She enjoyed the fact that he was young and decent-looking, that they were as close as ever, and that together they would follow through on an idea that had been obsessing her for over a year.

When he recalled now—which he did very rarely— that old man, who turned out to be sixty-nine (he found out his exact age when, in accordance with all the rules of the insurance game, he brought the doctor to examine him before the policy signing and first payment), when he now recalled that enchanting, silver-haired, frail old man, who when it was all over gave him a little notebook with a place for a pencil on the side and who proceeded, very shortly thereafter, to die, it seemed as if it had all happened long long ago, on the threshold between child-hood and adulthood. And what a wretch he had been when he was so down and out that he was driven to placing that announcement in the paper and then brought Klavdia Ivanovna home from the hospital, back to their unheated room, so that she could start doing daywork again! But he didn't think about that very much, and gradually all of it—the meeting with Xenia Andreevna, the new shirts, "*ma cousine*," evening chess games with Monsieur Robert, turning pages for him when he did his relaxed, tender rendition of Schumann—all of it had grown so bent and twisted that now he found it offensive and ridiculous to dredge it up from his memory, where it slumbered. His life had changed so drastically. Things were moving along with such energy and smoothness, he was living so independently, with such confidence, that he even permitted himself little affairs now and then. He felt so on top of everything that once in a while he would whistle a popular fox-trot around his neatly kept, com-fortable, bachelor apartment.

II

THE MORNING WAS FRESH and sparkling. The sun had already managed to break through twice, and twice it had poured with rain, lacquering the pavement. The sky was azure and black, and the wind made Alexei Georgievich's nostrils twitch like an animal's when he emerged wearing a bowler and carrying an umbrella and briefcase, set out down the street, and turned toward the bus stop. His face, which he had just washed, glowed, and there was a clarity and a blueness in his eyes. In fact, there was something about his entire appearance that corresponded to that morning, that hour, the air, the weather, something healthy, vigorous, intense, and restless.

Astashev had still not altogether adjusted to his new apartment, which he had moved into a month before. He changed his place of residence rather frequently and left without leaving a forwarding address. Usually his departures coincided with the end of an affair. "A clean break," "not striking the last chord"—as he referred to the liquidation of his relationships with women. Recently he found himself thinking more in French than Russian, and he already knew all kinds of appropriate expressions for this in French. At the same time they were much more in keeping with the actual essence of his affairs, since the objects of his affection tended more and more to be French—he did not care for Russian women.

His breath was a blend of strong coffee and Swiss mouthwash. He never smoked. In his head he had the address of a prominent businessman—his home address. Astashev tried not to go to offices. He hurried, as he was anxious to catch his client at home. His thoughts took their usual course. Early in the morning he was all attention. A working day stretched out ahead of him.

He bought a paper at the kiosk. He preferred French to Russian and right wing to left. On the bus there was a pretty girl, and he looked at her for a long time. He was curious about women and liked to observe ones he didn't know: how they powdered themselves, what they talked about, how they fixed their hair, how they crossed their legs. He got off at a broad, deserted street where at that hour only the dogs were out, and the maids walking the dogs chatted to each other. A dark blue-gray poodle covered with curls except for a shaved back stepped out of his way.

He walked past gardens. The wind rustled among the fallen leaves. Damn it, what a garden, what a house! White house, black door—and you don't hear a thing because you're stepping across something sandlike, so thick and deep it's like leaving tracks in velvety dust.

One tall mirror was reflected in another, and there, in that other one, he saw the edge of a laden table, a wisp of steam over a cup, and someone's elbow, and another door, and you couldn't tell which way to go: through that one, through the mirror, or through that closer one, where the hand of an elderly clean-shaven man wearing a butler's coat and a pince-nez on a black cord was beckoning to him.

"Tell him Mr. Astashev is here," said Alexei Georgievich without changing the expression on his ruddy face. He had a name, and he never attempted to explain in the foyer what it meant, why he had come.

The study was white, like a hospital ward, with white leather furniture so deep that the couch and armchair were just waiting to swallow up anyone who sat in them. Into the white of the rug, the armchair, the telephone, and the glass desk, and through the white door walked a big, powerfully built man with an expression of absolute boredom on his face. He looked at Alexei Georgievich, shook his head, and leaned his two fists on the desk, preparing to listen.

"I'll only keep you five minutes, not a second longer," said Astashev ponderously, gravely, as if he wanted to impress him at the very outset with his youth and reliability. His blue eyes spoke with purity and lucidity of his integrity, his straightforwardness, his Orthodox christening, of the fact that had it gone a little further nature would have transformed them into the eyes of a young woman, a nun who had selflessly yielded to fate. "Allow me to inform you of some important news."

"How much is it going to cost me?" the businessman asked in a hoarse and careless voice, not yet aware of who it was before him. His heavy torso balanced on top of spread legs.

"Not a penny, if you decide not to take advantage of it. I came to tell you something that will seem like an awful truism to you: *We are all mortal.* Fyodor Grigorievich sent me to you."

"I don't know any Fyodor Grigorievich," said the businessman, with an impenetrable look.

"Here is my watch: I promised not to keep you long. It tells me the time. One day it will tell *us* the time. Yes, yes, let us not shut our eyes to it: the bell will toll for each and every one of us."

The businessman dropped his fists, nudged the arm-chair with his foot, and sank into it.

"What do you want from me?"

"I came here to remind you"—and Alexei Geor-gievich also lowered himself, but with caution, so as not to drown—"we all persist in unforgivable thoughtless-ness. After all, sooner or later *it* will come for you. Then I'm going to come and see your wife, then your children. I'm going to come and take a look at you. Have you thought about that?"

He rested his chin on his half-empty, soft briefcase and looked dreamily into the distance.

"We are giving you the opportunity to provide for your family—there'll be nothing to worry about. You'll have plenty to think over at the last moment as it is— your soul, for instance. I'm not a believer myself, but many are. In any event, it is frightening, and it happens to everyone no matter what. We are giving your nearest and dearest the opportunity to abandon themselves one hundred percent to their grief without having to worry about their daily bread during those first few days. Oh, those first few days! We pay reliably, promptly, gladly. We pay faster than the Banque de France, while you're laid out, while the deceased is still laid out on the table. You can make direct payment to insure yourself in the event of death, which will come one way or another."

"Ah, so that's who you are." The businessman stretched out his well-manicured white hand and wiped it across his dark tough face.

Alexei Georgievich went on, a little more calmly now.

"You'll pay every first of the month. I advise you to insure yourself for a million. The usual amount. Every man has moments when he thinks about his own end. Forgive me for speaking so candidly, so frankly about it, but we are alone after all. Those moments are terrible because whatever it is that awaits us is inescapable. Do you understand? Inescapable. As inescapable as the fact that today, whatever the weather, night will come. You can make phone calls, buy, sell, rush about, or go to sleep right now on this sofa. It makes no difference. Night will still come. And *it* will come too. That's it." Astashev pinched the tender white flesh on his hand. "All this will come to an end. And then what?"

A pause—two seconds. Then the blue poodle he'd seen in the street pushed the door open with its solid frame and walked in, leapt slowly and confidently onto the sofa, walking across and leaving tracks on the morocco leather, the rug, the morocco pillow. The businessman neither saw it nor stirred.

"What a marvelous animal. May I ask your age?"

"What's it to you? And anyway, why . . . ?"

"You mean you can't guess? The closer to the end, the larger the payments: the greater the odds. At fifty there are certain odds and at sixty others. At seventy . . . But you're not seventy. You can't fool me! Just your signature will take care of everything."

"Greater chances of what?" He was slowly turning pale, as if he were growing tired right then and there and didn't have the strength to chase away, to cut off this visitor.

"Of turning into a heavy, burdensome, and rapidly decaying object. You're probably sitting there thinking, why should I take out insurance when I have property, capital, bonds . . . ? Let me tell you a story, a true story. I went to see a very important scholar—I won't say 'great' because I never call anyone that on principle. The scholar said, 'Forgive me, but why should I take out insurance? I have ten volumes of scholarly work, each one a thousand pages long. That's enough for my children and grand-children as well.' What do you think happened? Less than two years passed, he died, and some young upstart came along with a pamphlet he had thrown together exposing the old man, and now those ten volumes"—Alyosha sud-denly gave a sharp whistle—"and the widow is going hungry, actually going hungry."

The businessman sat up with a start, looked at the dog's paw prints, and imperceptibly let out a slow deep breath.

"Thank you. I'll think it over," he said. And he did indeed make it seem as if he were planning to give serious thought to what he had just heard. "Good-day."

"Just one more thing," Astashev exclaimed, as the businessman was already preparing to scramble out of the armchair on his sturdy legs. "Of all things, do not think, or think about it as little as possible. Your signature is all." He shook a piece of light-blue patterned cardboard out of his briefcase. "Right here in the corner. I remember

a singer (a famous baritone, I can't tell you his name—
professional confidence) who thought and thought and
then he died. Can we ever know what's going to happen
to us?"

"Go. Enough," said the businessman staring straight
ahead. The yellowed whites of his swollen eyes looked
like a child's cheap plastic toy. "You've left your mark,
Teacher, so get out. Out! General, take Teacher out."

The butler with the pince-nez on the cord came in
and took the poodle out. The businessman stirred heavily
and started to climb out of his chair. Alexei Georgievich
shot out of his like a coiled spring.

"Be sensible," he said, again clearly, honestly, and
loyally. "If we don't know what's going to happen to us
there, at least we can put our affairs in good order *here*."

"Leave me," pronounced the businessman very quietly, as if he were addressing some third party standing
between them and Astashev, or even the armchair that
wouldn't let him go.

Finally he got up. The deadly boredom on his face
had become even gloomier, and there was something
frightening about the cast of his expression.

"I'll leave you my card," said Astashev. Once again
his pink fingers went into action, scooping up something
that had slipped out of his briefcase.

"No need. I'm very busy. General, show the insurance agent out."

Alexei Georgievich roused himself and walked to
the door, and other doors, lacquered doors, glass doors.
He was all attention. He already had a new address in
his head. The trees stormed in the gardens he was passing.

He was swinging his umbrella. There were no more dogs, or maids either for that matter. Chauffeurs were standing at attention by their automobiles, waiting for their employers, and two Chinese cooks were walking to market, debating something in their ringing language.

Passing. Passing pleasant, tantalizing thoughts of what the cooks would bring back from market: lobster, partridges, pineapple. He thought: "Does the businessman have a wife? Probably a silly, capricious woman who loses at the casino in summer and eats too many pastries with whipped cream. Does the businessman have a daughter? Doubtless an easily bored, amorous creature with her sights set on a foreigner (the right approach!)." How could he find them? Or talk to them? Maybe he has a son? Yes, of course, he does have a son, and his address is even entered in Astashev's little book. A film production business, a star-studded office twinkling away under that very sky, on the Champs-Élysées. Go there tomorrow, cajole him, apply some pressure, reel in some contacts, and leave a mark there as well. But that was for tomorrow. He had three more appointments for today.

The city, the streets, this race to meet life head-on. He swam along in it freely and easily, he was comfortable in it—citizen, taxpayer . . . but not a soldier! Naturally, he had not changed his nationality. "A Frenchman in spirit," he often said, but he carried the same useless international passport, which had in fact been no hindrance to him at all. He had no wish to link his fate, his warm, precious, secure, unique life with an entire country, with a state that was not always peaceful and that, at times, went through upheaval. He kept his money in an

American bank in case times got rough. He could hop on a train, or a boat, or a plane and keep his happy, industrious, and yet vulnerable existence going at full tilt.

"From Ivan Stepanovich Besser," he uttered with a bow as he entered the stale but spacious drawing room cluttered with cheap antiques, deriving a certain satisfaction from shaking the soft hand of its owner, which felt as if it had just been washed. "Excuse me if I'm interrupting, but Ivan Stepanovich urgently requested that I stop by to see you."

"Sit down, sit down, dear man." A short, tubby, rusty-haired man, with large intelligent eyes, led him to a small table where flowers trembled precariously in a vase.

"I'll take up a minimum of your time and will inform you—alas!—what I am obliged by my profession to say: sooner or later the curtain will fall."

His host gasped and wrung his hands.

"Oh, I know what you mean. Don't remind me. It's dreadful! Haven't they invented something for that yet? You know there was an article in America about some kind of pill. . . . And they call this progress!"

Alexei Georgievich smiled.

"What pills? Come now, everything on earth, from the tiniest insect to the greatest genius, has its end. Can pills really do anything about that?"

"Then they should say what's *there*! What use are all their academies and universities and laboratories? No, no, I refuse to talk about that. I don't want to. Let's change the subject. I know, Ivan Stepanovich insured himself for a hundred thousand. I've decided to insure myself for a hundred thousand, too. I'm even going to insure my wife for a hundred thousand (will you give me a discount for two?). But we're going to handle the whole thing discreetly. We're not going to think about the meaning of what we're doing. I'm not going to be able to sleep tonight. I'm too scared."

Astashev smiled once more and nodded slightly in assent.

"Then let's not. I've already forgotten what we were talking about. If struggle is impossible we must take measures to see that it all goes smoothly, as discreetly as possible, that the payment is made—"

"Ah, by the way, I'm told you're not always prompt about paying."

"Prompter than the Bank of England."

"But you sometimes get taken to court?"

"Just by cranks. I beg you not to say such a thing, even in jest."

"Ah, how interesting. You mean there are cranks? And do you pay for suicides?"

"What on earth for?" Astashev made an ugly face. "With one foolhardy act a man cancels out his entire life. Why reward him? That just makes him someone who never existed, a chimera. We pay for a normal end. And therefore we can only pay for people who were, who existed, not suicides."

"Most interesting. Go on, please. I'll get my wife."

He stood up, opened the door to the adjoining room, and said lovingly:

"Darling, come on in. . . . That's all right. Our guest doesn't mind."

A woman came in. Her hair was uncombed and she wore a housecoat. She had a broad Russian face and a full ungirdled figure.

"I beg of you, go on."

Alexei Georgievich, taking up the woman's point of view, quickly sketched out the business that had brought him.

"Well, that's clear," said the hostess, combing her fingers through her hair. "Everyone in America took out insurance a long time ago. We're the ones who are behind the times."

Documents with seals, documents with writing, documents with blanks that needed filling in, slipped out of the briefcase and into Astashev's hands. He quickly located the right amount on the chart and made some calculations.

"Isn't that interesting, darling," said the host, signing first here, then there. "One of us will collect on the other."

"Well, naturally. It works out very nicely."

Alexei Georgievich blotted the signatures first here, then there, with a square of pink blotting paper.

"When does it go into effect?"

"This very minute."

"Do you hear that, darling? Isn't that interesting. We're already insured."

She signed where she had to as well, and they immediately wrote Astashev a check, despite his protests. He put everything back in his briefcase, clipped his pen to his pocket, and started saying good-bye. They thanked him for what seemed like forever, tried to talk him into staying for lunch, and gave him the address of a family acquaintance ("Zhenya Sokolova's uncle. You probably know him") who had wanted to for a long time. . . .

When they reached the door Astashev asked when he could send the doctor by.

"Oh, don't bother, don't bother," exclaimed the host with tears in his voice. "He'll just find all sorts of diseases. That's right, darling, isn't it? He shouldn't bother."

But Astashev said he couldn't go ahead without it, so they agreed. Then they thanked him again and asked him to thank Ivan Stepanovich for his unfailing concern for them.

It was lunchtime. Every day he had lunch in a clean, inexpensive, rather institutional-looking restaurant where they knew him well and where the same people always sat on his right, people from the South who ate an extraordinary amount of very good food, and a thin woman with a big nose and a brightly painted mouth sat on his left. He made no exceptions, even on Sundays. He ate slowly, read the newspaper, did some calculations in its margins, made notes in his little book, worked things out in his head, occasionally asked to see the phone directory, and carefully turned its pages between the plates. He never drank wine; he was served a bottle of mineral water. A few words about the weather to the *garçon*, a nod in the direction of the big-nosed woman (hadn't she grown prettier since yesterday?), a half bow to his neighbors. Poached fish and roast meat, or roast meat and dessert, coffee, cake. Three lumps of sugar in a small white cup with a crack. After lunch he went to wash his hands, clean his nails, tidy his hair with the comb and thick brush he carried with him, and brush the dandruff and crumbs off his shoulders. Then he left—with his umbrella and briefcase in his hands and a new route, a new address, in his head. He moved along this urban conveyor belt that knew no beginning, no end, and no pause. He was conveyed, moved along, like a spoke or a screw, and to do so came to him as naturally as it does to a tree to grow in the same place.

"*Permettez.*"

But they wouldn't let him in. The door opened a crack, an eye glittered, and a man's voice said:

"Yes, it's me. Who are you?"

"I already came once, but I missed you. I—"

"Are you selling brushes? Sewing machines?"

Alexei Georgievich tried to edge in with one shoulder.

"I make the hardest thing of all a little easier. I sell life insurance."

The door gave way but immediately closed shut on him, catching him so that the umbrella was inside but the briefcase was stuck on the outside.

"Go away!" And the person standing in the foyer jangled something metal in his hand. It was a set of keys. "Are you insuring *against* life?"

"What do you mean, against life?" That caught Astashev off his guard. And the thought flashed briefly: Could something like that really be done?

"Go to hell!" shouted the man, squeezing him in the door harder and harder. "I'd rather be done with it. You can't frighten me! What I want is someone to insure me against life, this damned life."

"If you don't mind, I don't deserve . . . I have something very important to tell you."

"That no one lives forever? Well, all the better. That's just what I'm waiting for."

"But your wife, your children," prattled Alexei Georgievich as he tried to free himself from the crack. "To leave them unprovided for—"

"Wife? Children?" the voice exclaimed hysterically. "Leave money to that old idiot for her lover? To those little bastards to bet on the horses? Get out. You're not needed here."

"No one has ever spoken to me like—"

"Out! Out!" And Astashev felt something pressing on his chest and shoving him. He summoned all his strength and darted sideways out of the door. It slammed in his pink face so hard that it shook the house. "They've been hanging around here since the morning," moaned the voice behind the door. "Vacuums! Typewriters!"

Astashev spit coarsely, landing just above the keyhole. "Barbarians," he said loudly. "Mongols." He descended the steps slowly, opened his umbrella because it was drizzling, and walked off, calming himself, letting his blood cool. And suddenly he remembered he still had one more place to go, one more name. A rendezvous set for today. The most intriguing thing he had to do.

But before making that rendezvous—a visit to the sculptor Engel, whom he had already been to see twice without managing to come to terms with him on either occasion—he decided to stop off at the insurance company he represented. He usually passed by most days, usually in the late afternoon.

Nearly two hundred employees and at least a hundred clients crowded into a big hall that was divided up by grilles. In the grilles were small openings, and above each opening there was a number and a sign. Astashev shook several hands, slapped someone lightly on the back, and having received a gentle slap on the shoulder in return, went over to window 53, above which was written DEATHS. Now that his French was perfect, though, he knew that the word "death" never crossed the lips of the mustached, middle-aged, high-collared employee who sat at that window. What he heard was the word "decease," which sounded so much more agreeable to the client's ear.

He took care of everything for the two policies signed that day, set up a doctor's visit, obtained the necessary blanks (supplementary to the blue patterned papers), and graciously acknowledged the comments about how he was one of the most successful agents in the company's entire hundred-year existence. Only then did he find out that the day before they had got word of the death of a client whom he had insured eight years ago. He promised to stop by to pay a call tomorrow, told the young lady sitting at the back of the DEATHS section to find the file for that case, and while she was taking one of the first policies marked by his hand out of a thick file, turned to chat at the next window, under the sign PERSONAL ACCIDENTS.

At five o'clock he was already at Engel's.

Blocks of clay wound in wet rags, a piece of stone torso with spread legs, the square beaten-up face of a famous boxer just cast in bronze with the crown of the head lopped off, and an overgrown bronze cauliflower ear were stacked up in the chilly, high-ceilinged studio where he was ushered in by Engel himself, a dry, small man with no beard and no eyebrows, who looked Japanese and wore a long white smock.

"I've been expecting you. Eagerly," he said, spreading his thin greenish lips to show a mouth full of heavy, close-set teeth that made his whole weak, fragile face jut forward. "You did such an astounding job last time explaining about why you'd come. I've been hoping I'd get to listen to you some more. It was so odd, what you were saying. As if you'd been sent from the next world as a reminder. (You don't talk with everyone like that, now, do you?) But I couldn't then. I had a model sitting here, there, that one." He poked a childish hand at a stone torso, and it seemed incredible that such a giant had visited him and not crushed him. "I've thought a lot about all that since then. It was the first time I'd ever had to think about it. And I realized that my conviction that there isn't anything *there* makes living impossible. Do you smoke?"

"I don't smoke and I don't philosophize," said Astashev, moving from the shaky stool he had sat down on for some reason to the soft upholstered sofa in the corner of the studio. "Last time you and I were talking about two hundred thousand. Given your relative youth, it's really worth it."

"Fine," Engel replied, wiping his low sallow forehead pensively and deliberately with two fingers. "But that's not the most important thing. You came to see me with your talk about the fifth act, the final curtain, the finale, saying that everything has an end. All those metaphors which were hardly in the best taste. That's what's important—terribly important for me. You've become indispensable to me. I thought you might make it possible for me to think this whole horror show through to the end."

"I'm flattered."

"There's something offensive about you. . . . But we can talk about you later. First let's talk about me, because I haven't slept for ages, and I haven't been able to work at all for almost two weeks now. I've started to doubt everything. I've started to think that if there's a *here*, then there has to be a *there*. That is, it's impossible that there's nothing *there* if there's something *here*. I've lost some of my conviction, and that's made things a little easier for me."

"If you please," exclaimed Astashev, and he smiled the most simplehearted of his smiles, "what kind of *there* can there be? You're not sixteen anymore. You're experienced, you've lived. You're probably even—don't be offended—a bit of a libertine. What kind of doubts can there be that there isn't anything *there* at all? What have you come across *here* that could have made you so wrong about *there*? Good food, young women, the beauty of nature, comfort, security?"

"No, there's got to be more to it," said Engel adamantly, and he looked closely at Astashev.

"God help me then, because I don't see it. And believe me, when I say 'good food' I'm talking about the rarest of delicacies, not about stuffing yourself stupid every day. And as for women: there was a time when people blushed, perspired, sighed (perhaps not me personally), but by now everyone realizes perfectly well what love consists of. Even the women. And if they don't— so much the worse for them."

"No, that's not it at all. I don't know myself, but there's more to it than that. There's no other way."

"Art? Literature? There used to be that. People read until daybreak, got swept up in politics (though I never have). But by now they know better. They've learned. What's left?"

Engel walked away to the window and looked out at the September twilight.

"But if you think that, then how can you live? How can you die?"

"How can you live? Listen to this: I was on my way to see a client today. A male dog was having it off with a bitch on the pavement. And do you know what I said to myself? How simple happiness is!" He laughed.

Engel went back to the sofa, stubbed his cigarette out in a saucer, and said slowly:

"But what's someone supposed to do who can't be like that?"

"Try to make things as logical as possible. Watch his health, work, live like everyone else does. Take out insurance. The state rests on people like you and me, not on dreamers and failures. It is the collective guarantee of sober people to facilitate their own life and death."

"No, that won't do."

Astashev peeked at his watch under his cuff, fumbled with the booklet in his hands, and then put it back down beside him.

"My objective is modest," he said, as if excusing himself. "To remind people that the inevitable will come and that they should prepare for it well in advance and in the most advantageous and convenient way possible."

Engel's slanted eyes fixed once more with a kind of melancholy hope on Alexei Georgievich's smooth round face. Neither said anything.

"I can imagine," Engel now spoke more dispassionately, "the kind of experiences you've had with people. I bet your presence makes a lot of them very uneasy. Perhaps you should write your memoirs? But maybe you're writing them now?"

Astashev drew himself up.

"I place very high demands on literature," he said with dignity. "If I were a writer I would delve deep into the human spirit and write somewhere between Tolstoy and Dostoyevsky, but in French."

Again neither said anything. Finally Astashev, who had been casting around in his thoughts for the broken thread, found the words he'd been looking for:

"And so, allow me to be perfectly frank. You're frightened, you're confused. But you can't stop thinking about the practical aspect of the matter. Today I've brought along all the necessary papers. Since you're under forty it can all be taken care of without a medical examination. We just need one test, and if there's no sugar—"

"Listen," said Engel with childlike amazement. "Why should I insure myself? I'm completely alone. I don't have a wife, or children, or nephews. I live, work, and sell. I give money to whoever needs it and asks me for it. A suit lasts me for four years and I eat nothing but vegetables. I'm not going to take out insurance."

Astashev stood up sharply.

"Excuse me," he said loudly and bad-temperedly. "This is the third time I've come to see you and sat here and explained. My time is valuable. Why do you keep inviting me here? If you haven't got anyone to insure yourself for, you should have told me that before. You're committing a grave error: you're young, you're healthy, you could insure yourself for your retirement."

"Don't get angry, please," said Engel. He turned his back to Astashev. "I asked you to come because it seemed to me you knew something. You probably don't notice yourself what it is you're dodging. Just tell me one thing: How do you think it will come?"

Astashev was already putting on his coat in the entryway.

"It will come as it does for a hare in a hunt or a fly in a glass," he said angrily. "I'm a self-made man, and those trivialities don't concern me."

He picked up his umbrella and briefcase, raised his hat, and without saying another word, left. Engel wiped his perspiring palms with a handkerchief and went to the window to watch him go. The window of the studio looked out on the square and he saw Astashev emerge, walk away, hail a taxi, get in it, and drive away.

The day was drawing to a close. As usual the elevator wasn't working at Klavdia Ivanovna's. He drank tea and she knit. Today they talked politics, and Alyosha tried to explain to his mother that the proletariat were the people who smelled. Then he left, and by the time he got to Xenia Andreevna's he was completely unwound and happy.

"Mamenka," he said, taking a bite of cold veal and choosing a moment when the admiral and governor weren't listening, "yesterday I went from here to the Tabarain . . . with two cancan dancers. We were out very late, and I gave them caviar and champagne. Give me the address of Doctor Markelov just in case. We parted on good terms."

She nodded her head with unconcealed satisfaction and replied in her low whisper:

"Sit back a little, gravedigger. I can smell the corpses on you."

III

H E H A D M E T H E R two years before. She was living with her two old aunts in the same building as Xenia Andreevna, but downstairs, and once she stopped in to say that if Vyazminitinov came he should come down because someone had been to see them that day who had seen his son recently in Moscow. In short, she had come to deliver a message. Mamenka didn't even look at her: "Fine, I'll tell him." But when Vyazminitinov came she forgot all about Zhenya, and the next day Zhenya had to come again. She begged her pardon for the inconvenience and left Vyazminitinov a note. Astashev was there again. He got up, said hello, asked whether Zhenya had been to see the popular play that featured the actress with the magnificent bosom. Zhenya blushed. Her eyes glittered, and she said she didn't go to theaters at all because she was busy every evening.

"And the cinema?" he asked, appraising her more attentively.

"Oh, every day," she replied. "I sell the tickets."

She was wearing a dark blue woolen dress with buttons that ran down her flat chest from collar to waist.

"What exceedingly original buttons," said Astashev. He wanted to touch one of them. She recoiled, and her eyes darkened (they were light brown). Quickly gathering up her fair, gold-flecked hair and coiling it at her nape, she turned to go. And suddenly he noticed that she was slim and graceful, on the tall side, with a high waist and long straight legs.

"Her mother has remarried. To Count Loder," said Xenia Andreevna. "Her aunts are half-wits who keep her under lock and key. And she's innocent. I'd lay odds on it. A virgin. It's phenomenal, but it's a fact."

A week later he ran into her at the main entrance.

He was on his way out, and she was coming in from work.

"Right here." He pointed to her black purse. "This is where you carry the cash box."

"No," she replied, "I turn the money over to the owner. He comes by for it."

"Oh well, too bad. Otherwise I could have robbed you in some alley."

She smiled, confused.

"For some reason there's a gun at the ticket office,"

she said trustingly. "I haven't the faintest idea why it's there though. I don't know how to shoot."

"Are there really ever such large amounts of money there?"

"That's just it. There aren't. I think someone just forgot it, or dropped it. I've had five gloves lying there for, oh, a year—all for the right hand. Also two sets of keys, a compact, a lighter, and a stickpin with a fake stone. They're just there."

"Would you like to take a little walk? It's early still, and it's a fine evening."

"No," she said. "They're expecting me at home."

And as if she hadn't quite finished saying something, she gave him her thin hand in its suede glove.

"You never flirt, and you always go home on time?"

"I never flirt and never have," she replied, and left.

"But she's gorgeous, just gorgeous! Sweet, innocent, delicate, young. She has such a happy look and sad voice. Odd she hasn't married before. She's probably almost thirty," he thought en route. But by the next day he was no longer thinking of her, and when he ran into her again on the stairs a month later he didn't recognize her.

He turned around, and she turned around at the same time, and in the darkness both of them stopped.

"You're back from work? So late?"

"Always at the same time, a quarter to eleven."

"And tomorrow, too? Every day?"

She suddenly collected herself and didn't answer, sneaking a look but not looking.

"You're prettier than when I saw you last," he said. "How are the buttons doing? Still there? And still no flirting?"

She slowly opened her long rouged lips, showing her white, even, narrow teeth, and said gravely:

"Not counting you."

And she left the darkness of the lower landing. When he switched on the light her steps died and a door slammed shut somewhere.

Every evening he met her, but on the street, not on the stairs. They talked for a few minutes, and they always found something to talk about. He walked with her to her building, listening to her stories about work, about her aunts, about her mother, about her girlfriends.

"Are they pretty?" he asked.

And she answered, "Not very. Like me."

"From the fact that you come to see Xenia Andreevna every evening I've come to the conclusion that you don't have anyone to flirt with now either," she once said, smiling with embarrassment. "Not counting me."

But he answered with unexpected frankness.

"No flirting, but there is a lady I know. She has a corset shop. She's French, of course. One can go and see her as late as twelve at night. Before that there's not much to do there. But I have a feeling she's going to start boring me pretty soon. You don't know men. We're awful swine. Of course, that's just what women love us for."

She walked to the door with a firm tread and, saying good-bye, pale, announced that her holiday began the next day.

"What, in the middle of winter? Where are you going to go?"

"Nowhere. Is it really absolutely obligatory to go somewhere?"

Then her aunts moved to another apartment. He

never asked after Zhenya, but sometimes he remembered her as a very frail, slender, flexible plant, almost translucent, and a little poisonous. Then he forgot about her.

The aunt who had the money died, and Zhenya and the other aunt could not touch the inheritance. Months passed, and life got hard. It was being challenged, the trial date was approaching, but the will was never found. Life changed completely—restricted now in every aspect and very quiet. Zhenya had worked all her life; she had always supported herself. But now there were two living on her salary. Moreover, the aunt who was alive was weak and constantly ill, and there was no one to turn to for help because she was the sister of Zhenya's father, and Zhenya's mother had not been on speaking terms with her for a long time.

Day and night Zhenya sat in the ticket window of the small, elegant cinema, so that the customers saw only her hands, her delicate fingers and their long, dark red, lacquered nails, and the agate ring set in platinum. Sometimes someone buying a ticket tried to bend over, breathe into the opening in the glass, and take a look at her face, but she just jotted something down in pencil without raising her head, tore off a green ticket, and handed out silver and copper change from the cash box. Her hands kept taking in those ticket booklets, dozens of them, which she carefully hid in the box, the same box that held the five lost gloves, compact, and lighter. And every so often the hope crept up on her, as furtively as a cat, that Astashev would all of a sudden show up—not for her, not to see her, but at the cinema, as a viewer. That he would buy a ticket from her and she would shake his hand through the low-cut glass.

She was living far away now, on the opposite bank of the Seine, and no longer had any chance of running into him at night. She thought of those past encounters when—or so it seemed to her—he had been waiting for her, with something like madness. She thought about how here she'd been living her life for such a long time and she knew nothing about him. Did he still go to see Xenia Andreevna? Was he still seeing the corset shop owner? Did he still smile broadly and gaily, did he still dress fastidiously, was he still a little overweight as before?

She felt such sadness some mornings when, sleepy, still in her dressing gown, blue smudged under her eyes, she stood over the bubbling percolator and thought about writing him a letter. In fact, she had already composed the first sentence:

"Evgenia, you should call me Evgenia, dear Alexei Georgievich, because I am writing you this letter, exactly like Tatiana in the opera. . . ."

On those mornings she realized she would never write to him, never seek his affection, or his name.

"But what shall I do? What can I do?" she asked her large, drab window, which let the cold in during the winter and in the summer a warm rustle of fragrant bushes from the neighbor's garden far below, as if it were the bottom of a well.

Days were either dreamy and melancholy or else so busily tedious that his voice, his manner, his whole being flickered in her memory, and when she was finally left to herself, weary, it reappeared and seemed fainter and somehow more touching.

She did not have her own room. She slept in the dining room, and her aunt slept in the next room. That was now the sum total of their living quarters. Zhenya never went visiting and never invited anyone as she was too busy for chitchat and anyway was incapable of making conversation. Gradually she even stopped seeing her mother because she felt as if she were an embarrassment to her—and little by little she drew apart from her girl-friends as well. There was no doubt about it: she was poor, and she was lonely. She had been condemned by fate to a lackluster life bereft of happiness, bereft of rapture, so that her innate elegance, her long eyes, her sleek, smooth, golden hair, and her long legs, which she liked to put into rough shoes and thin stockings so that the hairs poked through and the birthmark on her ankle was clearly visible, seemed almost incongruous.

The obese old lady got around with great difficulty. Insulted by the litigation over the inheritance and ac-customed to an idle and well-provided life, she sometimes did not say a word for days on end. Zhenya wrote the letters to the lawyers for her, fed her her meals in bed or in her easy chair, and then left for work. She watched before her the changing line of people come to be en-tertained as if in a dream. Thus her day passed, and she thought about how that was life and how sometimes there was misery on top of that as well.

Almost without having thought about it—later, she couldn't work out how it had happened—one day, in the autumn, after more than a year and a half had passed since she had seen Astashev, she had the idea of paying Xenia Andreevna a call. They found someone to fill in for her at the cinema that night, and she went out wearing the same dark blue woolen dress—not knowing herself what she intended to accomplish and unable to explain this action to herself—and returned to the street where she had once lived.

The building seemed utterly foreign and gloomy to her. The entrance stirred up memories. But nothing had really happened. He hadn't told her anything definite, and she didn't care what he said anyway. But she still couldn't manage to come up with an excuse to explain why she had come.

But an excuse turned out to be utterly unnecessary. Xenia Andreevna was in an excited, keyed-up state, and she included Zhenya in her powerful, suffocating embraces. Besides Astashev there were two other guests, neither of whom Zhenya knew.

"Zhenechka Sokolova," said Astashev. "Can I offer you a liqueur with mustard?"

And suddenly he felt an animal joy from her presence.

She drank in tiny sips and smiled. And she was amazed at the air, which made you breathe in a completely different way from anywhere else on earth. There was something heady about this silk-draped, still straight-backed, painted, older woman and in the two men, who were obviously infected by this headiness and who were courting her in a crude and passionate way. And finally there was something special about Astashev, Alyosha Astashev, as she called him to herself, something suddenly strange, near, and momentous that changed her forever.

"Well, if you'd really like to, then that's that. Go ahead," he said, forgetting that he himself had only just now asked her to tell how she had been occupying herself all that time. But she was silent, her pale face shining as she looked into his round blue eyes.

"You have such blue eyes. Only children and very old men have eyes like that," she said with great love.

"I've been told that a million times." He flashed his teeth, and she noticed a new gold tooth on one side of his mouth. "Listen, my sweetheart, have you ever kissed a man?"

"No," she replied, and shook her golden hair.

"What a little fool you must be then!"

They both laughed. And suddenly she felt like confessing. She sat for another five minutes without moving or speaking while he told her an "absolutely true story" from his own life, and although it had something to do with a woman, Zhenya was too preoccupied with what was going on inside her to make sense of what he was telling her.

"I don't know him at all. Why should I love him? For his beauty? But he probably doesn't seem wonderful to anybody but me, and can I really love somebody just for being handsome? Look how coarsely he eats, and anyway, if he were really that handsome he would have been married a long time ago. There's no such thing as a handsome bachelor. Maybe I love him because of the attention he pays me? But where's the attention? Once he asked me about the buttons on this dress, but that doesn't prove he was thinking about me. I love him for all of it, for his crudeness, for his obvious meanness, for his bandit's laugh, for the boorish way he moves."

"I must confess, Zhenechka, I've never kissed anyone either." He made a guilty face. "There was never time.

Other things—well, I'm not saying, but as for kisses—I just never had time. Generally speaking I've always been in a dreadful rush. And, you know, when I was sixteen there was an alarm clock in the cook's room that made a terrible noise, a real din. Why, I never even took the time to find out whether it was on a chest of drawers, or a windowsill, or even on a shelf of some kind. Good Lord! Life is too short, and there's too much to do."

"What if this was the limit of possible happiness," the thought occurred to her, "and there could never be better moments than this, ever?"

"You know what would be the most interesting thing right now?" said Alexei Georgievich. "Let's go somewhere. We might even go to your cinema. We can take the best seats in the house."

"No. Why go to the cinema? It's too late anyway. And today the film isn't particularly good."

"Well then, let's go to the fair. I still haven't been to the fair. Have you?"

"I went with my aunt, but I hardly saw anything."

"With your aunt. Well, today you can go with your uncle. Only you won't see anything this time either."

It was the autumn, and the year of the World's Fair, the one that disfigured Paris for a few months and then vanished into thin air leaving no mark or monument behind it, nothing except the memory of a chaotic profusion of lights, objects, and crowds.

When they walked onto the bridge they were in the middle of a dense crowd that pressed in on all sides (Astashev led Zhenya by the arm to make sure he didn't lose her), and overhead, in the moonlit September sky, a prolonged salvo of fireworks was blazing away. It was already night, and this gaiety, which amazed rather than infected the visitors, was already on the wane. Under the bridge, in the sluggish Seine made violet by the reflected fountains, lights trembled, flickered, flared, and danced. Rockets shot straight up from its banks and exploded, and children's balloons fell to earth through the deep black heights. Thousands of balloons flowed across the sky like the Milky Way and were lost, the last of them resembling in color and size the moon which sailed close by. From the Eiffel Tower wailed metallic music, a chorus of voices, and an organ whose grindings brought tears to the eyes. A siren screamed in the distance, and once again the gold of Roman candles spilled into the sky, falling into the blackness of a straying sailing cloud.

Everything was rocking—the water under the bridge, the crowd on the shore, the air shot with light. A lost child pressed to the rails of the bridge was crying. A policeman was trying to make his way to him through the density of swaying bodies. And breathing in the rocket smoke and that wailing music, it seemed to Zhenya that all this, this madness of a holiday, had been hurled down onto this city, into this evening, turning it into a place where there was no sorrow or sighs, no human wickedness, no deceit, no separations, no shabby dance-hall decorations. But all Zhenya could really hear was the chorus of her own heart, like a motorboat tearing across a lake of happy tears.

They sat on the bridge of a yacht until everything was over. He told her that she should go home with him, that generally Russian women were dreadful teasers.

Whenever a woman walked by he started following her with his eyes and made a comment.

"I have very specific tastes," he said, sucking through a straw, his hat pushed to the back of his head. "I like brunettes more than blonds. About five years ago I had this blond. My God, how she messed me about. We men are awful swine. You've got a lot to learn, Zhenechka. I suggest you start taking instruction from me."

Now it was no longer an impression. She knew for certain, clearly, that there would never be another evening like this. It was going to be the only one. And she had to do something to make it last, because the night and the morning were going to rip everything apart, throw everything into confusion, wreck her life. She wasn't thinking about why she loved him anymore. Everything, from his name to his Russianness, which no number of French expressions could overcome, charmed her, oppressed her. Why did she think she had to explain or vindicate herself to anyone? She had never sat like this with a man before at night on the bridge of a moored yacht (which could have set off on a round-the-world cruise of fairy-tale lands, but which wouldn't leave, a yacht with its lights out). It seemed to her that together he and she could live a life unafraid, like lovebirds, or half a life, or at least a quarter of a life. She had never felt like spending so much as twenty-four hours with anyone before. She thought about how she could stand by and help him do something, unnoticed and brave. And maybe something that he couldn't have done alone and she couldn't have done alone they could do together.

In total darkness the crowd flocked to the exits.

Both of them walked quickly, with the rest, to the Métro stop. She was going one way; he the other.

"Come and tuck me in for the night," he said, holding her hand in his. "No one will ever find out. Don't be provincial."

She tore her hand away, ran down the stairs, stopped, and looked back, remembering that he hadn't told her where or when they would see each other again. But he was already gone, and a crowd of tired, crumpled, dusty, sweaty people was piling on top of her. They bore her to the train and down the street right up to her doorstep, and someone even came in with her and followed her upstairs—but went up another floor. Then, when she was alone on her sofa in the dining room, where it always smelled of meals, tears suddenly poured down on her hands. She didn't know what to do about them, how to catch them, how to stop them. It had been too cruel, this approach by an utter stranger, a person like a million others, whom she hadn't known before, whom something had marked out for her, who had cast a long shadow over her world. In this approach she sensed destiny, the threshold of life, and clutching her breasts in both hands, she whispered his name.

The rain was coming down in sheets, the wind was howling, the cold, wet, and tedium were truly autumnlike when, after what were for Zhenya four very long, hard days, he came to see her at the cinema. It was about half past ten. She was handing over the cash box to the owner, the last show was in progress, and Astashev, seeing the owner, said to her calmly, "*Bonsoir, chérie*," and shook out his umbrella. She lost her voice from sheer happiness and shame, finished counting up the money and tickets, and as she tidied things away, and locked up, and switched off the overhead light, looked at him several times and smiled. He was examining the posters on the walls with his back to her.

When they came out a taxi was already waiting.

"Where are we going?" she asked. "It's already so late."

Without speaking, he pushed her forward, and when they got into the taxi, not looking her in the face, said quickly and dryly:

"I'm not the kind of man who embraces in cars. Don't be afraid. In the first place, it's clumsy and un-comfortable. In the second . . . How are you feeling today?"

"Where are we going?" she asked again and saw a bottle of champagne sticking out of his pocket.

"Zhenechka, Zhenechka," he said with annoyance. "You ask an awful lot of questions."

"All my life has been a pledge," she said softly and dropped her face in her hand. "That's from *Onegin*."

"A fine opera," he responded and harrumphed.

"Do you like music?" And her face lit up with such joy that even he was surprised.

"I do. But I don't get much chance to listen to it. Well, here we are. This is it."

They got out. Because of the rain, she ran straight inside. He paid the fare, opened his coat and stuffed the change in a side pocket, and walked right up to her, put his arms around her, pressed her against the door, kissed her, grabbed her by the elbows, and without giving her a chance to catch her breath, silently holding her, dragged her over to the stairs.

"Let me go, dear Alexei Georgievich. Let me go," she whispered. "I have something to say to you. I'm frightened. I'll come some other time. I'm not going to make a scene. I'll be quiet. Let me go."

He twisted her arms painfully behind her with surprising skill, and greedily kissed her lips twice, touching her breasts. She caught his hand, not so much to make him stop as to prevent herself from falling. And still holding on like that, she followed him into his apartment.

When she left it was already very late. In the darkness she felt for the knob and looked down. There, very close, was the lift—she was on the landing of the first floor. Then she walked down the stairs, opened the door to the street, and stood there for a while. The few streetlamps had been turned down, and there was no one either to her left or to her right.

She set out on foot. She passed no more than a dozen people, two policemen, a few motorcars, and one high farmer's cart loaded with cauliflowers on its way to the Central Market. She walked for nearly an hour. As she was walking over the bridge she stopped. The Seine, bloated by the rain, looked as turgid as lard. Zhenya crossed herself and leaned out over the water. At that moment someone rode by on a bicycle, and the rider's shadow passed over her. She straightened up and walked on. When she got home she saw that it was four o'clock.

She took off her hat but kept her coat on and cautiously entered her aunt's room in her stocking feet. The old lady's breathing was heavy and regular. In the darkness Zhenya walked over to the bedside table, opened the drawer, and rummaged around in it, but whatever she was looking for she didn't find. Taking the drawer with her, she went into the kitchen, turned on the light, and started searching again. She came up with various medications: strophanthus, aspirin, and finally what she'd been looking for—the Veronal. But there were only eight tablets left in the glass vial. Then with the help of two kitchen towels and the bread knife she sealed up the door, extinguished the light, and turned on the gas.

"God," she thought as she sat in front of the burner and looked out unblinkingly through the curtainless window where the sky, red from the lights, seemingly filled with smoke, hung low over the earth. "God, if You exist, make me afraid, make me come to my senses. If You exist and if my soul wants it, make it so that at least my body turns back, holds me back from sin. If You exist, help me at least to react, even if it's only as an animal reacts. . . ."

But then, while she held her mouth to the hissing rubber tap, what Zhenya felt was not disgust: she felt an even more passionate desire for death. And in truth, her broken body and her consciousness began to call out for extinction and darkness. In fact her soul, far from separating itself from her body, embraced it even more firmly, helping it along, moving down through the ringing of bells and the explosion of rockets into the white, vanishing, melting Milky Way. For one single minute her body and soul found themselves united in a miraculous whole. With unwieldy force, life boxed Zhenya once more about the ears, and everything went out in an oblivion that held no visions.

IV

"CONGRATULATE ME," said Alexei Georgievich. "Today I closed—or nearly closed—a deal I've been chasing for three weeks."

A mustached middle-aged man wearing a high collar bent over toward him, and there were more murmurings in the adjoining windows.

"Bring out the champagne," someone said.

Astashev was already nodding to the right and left.

"Without fail. Today. Not only that"—he stopped short for a second—"today I made contacts—"

"Gentlemen, he's going to be a director," exclaimed someone sitting behind a desk under a lamp.

"But I have no desire whatsoever to be a director," Astashev laughed happily. "I'm utterly content with my fate."

He turned on his heel and walked out between the desks, treating everyone he passed to cigarettes, which he had bought for just this purpose. Feeling light and sure of foot, he set out to roam the streets, to look at ties in shopwindows. It was cloudy and cold, but today he was so full of himself that he noticed neither the weather nor the women. In a small seventh-floor office on the Champs-Élysées, where the only furniture consisted of an empty desk, a chair for the owner, and a leather armchair for a visitor, he had finally met the businessman's son, a Russian, but one who no longer spoke Russian, and he had promised to slip a million-dollar policy under his father's nose for his signature at an opportune moment.

Astashev had immediately adopted the tone of a hardened conspirator, keeping quiet when the ocher-powdered secretary entered abruptly. And when a celebrated pilot had appeared without being announced—a large fellow dressed in a garish coat, a tough man who, shortly before, had signed a contract in that office for a role in a film, and whose presence so affected the little room that even the voices seemed to change in tone—Alexei got up to go.

"Shouldn't you take out some insurance as well?" the director asked. "After all, you're probably going to take a nosedive before anyone else. It's strange you haven't broken your neck already."

The pilot tossed two large light-colored gloves on the desk.

"The company insures us," he said, throwing a quick glance at Astashev.

"That doesn't make any difference," he replied. "This is neither the time nor the place, but allow me to submit that your company insures you officially, as one of a group, but you could also do the same thing in an individual capacity. It's always more enjoyable to act as an individual. In my opinion, it's even more enjoyable to enter paradise as a traveler at your own risk than as part of a group excursion."

"Rubbish! You have to pay insane prices for this individualism of yours."

"People who fly pay eleven percent more than those of us who just creep along the ground."

The director burst out laughing.

"He's trying to reassure you. Listen, give him your address. He'll stop by and give you a little tête-à-tête explanation of what awaits you in the next world."

"I never talk about the next world," Astashev said cheerfully. "This one's enough for me. We're living in the capital of the world, not the desert."

The pilot took a calling card out of a wide, patent-leather wallet, and while fumbling with some photographs, handed it to Astashev.

"Stop by . . . sometime," he said nonchalantly. "I live quite far out, though, in the suburbs. You have to take the train."

Alexei Georgievich thanked them both and bowed low as he did so.

He was so at ease and so happy, he felt so fresh, young, and confident, that when he sipped his Chartreuse at the bar where he was treating eight or so employees from the insurance company, he became even more cheerful and charming. He had had a good, tasty lunch, and by about two he was feeling that he had had enough for one day. Now he would arrange some minor diversion for himself, relax, and recuperate his strength before going to the suburbs the next morning to see the pilot. He never put anything off until later. He was always hot on the trail of something new.

Three hours later he was at Xenia Andreevna's. He had spent those three hours at a certain house where he had been merely an observer, not a participant, and that had taken more than enough out of him for today. They knew him at that house, which was expensive and only open during the daytime. When he appeared the doorman asked whether he wished the left door or the right. Behind the left door there were women; behind the right, an armchair and a screen. He alternated. Today it was his turn for the screen.

Xenia Andreevna was never at home at this hour, however. The servant opened the door for him, and he walked into the living room, took off his shoes, put his feet up on the sofa, picked up the newspaper, and ordered a cup of tea with lemon for himself. It was the evening paper, which he read for lack of anything better to do, and strangely, whether because of the state of his digestion or from the length of time he had sat in that stuffy and perfectly silent darkness, there was nothing in it that caught his interest, and drowsiness hovered quite close at hand.

He read the paper every day, and always with the same feeling: OK then, let's see what they've done now. What are they all worked up about today? Any news that concerned Russia aroused ridicule in him. So, gentlemen, you're still around? Then when he came upon photographs in which one man wearing a first-rate pair of army boots greeted thousands wearing the same boots, something inside him shivered secretly and happily. That was exactly how he imagined power should be, and like that only: the personal and ultimate source of knowledge and authority.

And then he dreamed, and his dreams—as with many people who don't know how to dream properly—

were abstract and clumsy, far removed from the reality in which he lived. He dreamed of order—of a man who could hold in his hands all of Europe, and thus the whole world as well. And then he, Astashev, would get himself a pair of those smart shiny boots, which would stand as a mark of distinction for people adhering to a great discipline. He would prove indispensable to the world, much more indispensable than now, because now everyone was equal: healthy and sick, scramblers and losers alike. But then there would be just Astashevs. Astashevs, Astashevs, and more Astashevs.

His eyes ran over the page: a mining engineer in a fit of dementia had slit his wife's and two children's throats; the dog show had opened; subterranean tremors had been felt on Formosa; the rising cost of electricity; a ministerial crisis in Belgium; the suicide of one Mademoiselle du Pont: her neighbors' attention was drawn by the strong smell of gas, and when they broke down the door . . . In a note she asked them to forgive her for the inconvenience and wrote that she was dying out of unrequited love.

When he woke up it was already completely dark in the room. Xenia Andreevna had not yet returned. He put his shoes on and wrote on a scrap of paper:

"Mamenka, how about going out somewhere and having a good time? Put on your most ravishingly low-cut dress. I'll come by at eight."

And since he had absolutely nothing to do, he went by Klavdia Ivanovna's, whom he hadn't seen in all this time.

Klavdia Ivanovna was lying in her bed. Her teeth

ached, and she had a fever. The room hadn't been tidied, and there was nothing good for tea.

"You know, Mama," he said, sitting by the bed. "I hate to see you ill. Really, we could have sat a while and had a nice cozy chat." He felt that his good mood had actually begun to slip even before this, even before his nap on the sofa.

"Five days you haven't been here," she said, warming her puffy cheek with her hand. "Are you well? Who have you been with? Have you been eating properly?"

He was suddenly sad and didn't answer right away.

"Has it really been five days? Mama, I don't even notice how the time flies. It makes me a little sad. My youth will just pass me by like that—if it hasn't already! Why on earth have I started feeling so terrible? I was in such a great mood before. It's you that's had this effect on me. When you're ill everything else seems wrong. You're not getting up, Mama? Really, if you'd just drink some tea. . . ."

She shook her head.

"It's because you're still single, Alyosha."

He undid the two lower buttons of his vest, rested his elbows on his knees, and propped his face on his hands.

"What, get married?" he asked with derision, but there was a serious note in his voice, and Klavdia Iva-novna's heart started beating faster under the covers. "Marry some modest young thing in love up to her ears? A Russian girl, they'll tell me. Yes, of course, but pure, nevertheless, awash with virtue. Goes around in the same dress for two years. Has a job."

"Alyoshenka," Klavdia Ivanovna moaned softly, afraid of frightening him off.

"She and I could build ourselves a little nest. After all, now I can . . . thank God! If not now, then when? I deserve it. Mama, you'll laugh, but we would have the most freckle-faced children—both of us so fair." He raised his head, touched the lamp burning on the night-stand, and rocked on his chair.

"All that just popped into my head—idle dreams! More for you than myself. We could all move in together, and I'd give up all my bachelor pleasures. What man doesn't have dreams from time to time? We could have a maid, a poker-faced old maid. She'd do everything for us, and none of us would ever have to lift a finger again, right?"

Klavdia Ivanovna raised herself on her thin elbow and let a tear fall on her pillow.

"Are you in love, Alyosha?"

He looked at her, and suddenly a harsh, dry shadow crossed his light eyes.

"Mama, you can't stop living in your fantasies, can you?" he said, and stood up. "What am I, a schoolboy? If I'm going to marry, then there should at least be a dowry so that you, and we, and all of us could live in style."

He was especially put out just now that he had said anything to her about a life as a threesome. That would mean giving up Xenia Andreevna for good, and that, of course, was out of the question.

He left very quickly, with a heavy heart, recalling the note he had left for Xenia Andreevna and picturing where he might take her. There, in the living room, which was draped with silk scarves and pieces of oriental fabric, sat Vyazminitinov and Evgraf Evgrafovich playing piquet. Mamenka was still not back. He took a turn of the room, ate a pear, and without saying good-bye left once again, leaving his briefcase and umbrella in a prominent spot in the hall.

Mama Klavdia Ivanovna. Mamenka Xenia Andreevna. A successfully transacted bit of business, a hearty lunch, the films in that house he knew, money tucked away in the bank, a few thoughts about the fate of Europe, and a possible ticket to any one of a number of evening establishments where the doorman would greet him at the entrance with a bow. That was his life. He had a right to say: "It's me, thank God." Once in a while it all wore a little thin, but then that didn't happen more than once in five years, after all. True, the perfected mechanism, those creatures that wore those exquisite stiff sleek boots, knew no inner conflict their entire lives, and that meant that he, Astashev, was a representative of a period of change. What could he do? We have to console ourselves with the fact that everything is relative and the individual of the transitional period is an advanced creature in comparison with Mademoiselle du Pont, who died of unrequited love, or with the sculptor Engel, who eats nothing but rabbit food. If in moments of groundless melancholy we can't turn to the people of the future (the degenerate Slavic soul lacks any real space-age energy), and if there still aren't, if they haven't thought up yet, associations for people like him, advanced people ("and there are lots of us, lots and lots of us, lots more than you think!") to march and sing in chorus, then we can turn to people from the past, who in those moments are somehow so troubling, and irritating, and essential.

The evening was cold and damp, and the city's stones and lights were frozen in the deep twilight of the streets. Oh, those boulevards, which led to the edge of the city, which he now walked along as their master, and which he at one time trod with the thought of dying in rags, poor and humiliated.

"Nothing special, gentlemen, nothing special," he mumbled, striding with a spring in his step and already making out Engel's dark house in the distance. "You're a bohemian," Astashev prepared himself to say, "and I'm a bohemian when I have to be. So it's all right to drop in on you at this late hour, isn't it?"

"Thank you for coming by. Thank you," Engel said joyously when he recognized his visitor. He held on to his hand for a long time. "Welcome. Won't you come in and sit a while? You look tired. Did you come on foot?"

They both walked into the studio.

"I'm very happy to see you, my dear man," said Engel, "although I don't have any need of you at all now. None at all."

Astashev spoke quickly:

"You took out insurance with someone else?"

"Sort of. But not insurance. I straightened myself out. Sit down, anywhere. Relax."

A big swarthy man in a heavily creased, dusty black jacket and gray-striped trousers was stretched out on the sofa. He wasn't sleeping, but apparently he had just woken up.

"The artist Kharin. Came in from Florence today," said Engel. "Mishenka, please sleep. We aren't going to bother you."

The artist Kharin shifted around for a minute or so, found a comfortable position, and was still.

They sat down on two stools right by the window, in which both of them were reflected, and Astashev rested his puffy hands on his knees because he had nowhere else to put them.

"It came to me gradually. Maybe it's not even over yet, but the one hint has already made things much easier. Don't think that I've taken to frequenting church, confessing, taking communion, hanging up icons. No. But now I know that God is necessary. Prayer is necessary. Otherwise it can't be done."

"My congratulations," said Astashev. "I have an old mama. I must tell her about you."

Engel wrapped his smock around himself, huddled up, and slapped his pockets, feeling for a smoke.

"I'm so grateful to you for coming by to see me. If you only knew what went on inside me after the first time! I was minding my own business and suddenly you show up—like the archangel's trumpet. Now I know that death is like passion. You can't explain it; you have to feel it. Some people live to old age and never discover that; others might grow up knowing it. So it came to me at the age of thirty-eight. *What*, you ask, came to me? That's something I can't answer. The words are all so trite—'the awareness of inevitability,' 'the certainty of one's own end'—and all that implies. Let me make one more comparison: 'She kept on whispering: I'm yours.' That's from a love song, and we don't pay attention to it anymore. But if you really think it over!"

"And she, full of passion," added Astashev. "I heard it on a record."

"It seems to me that here is the crux of all human wisdom—the sense of death, the idea of the end. Because you can understand everything except for that. You can accept everything except for that. These thoughts of mine nearly drove me out of this window once. But my instinct was correct. When you were here last time, though, I already knew that it's impossible without God, but I still couldn't say so. Now I'm happy."

"From the bottom of my heart, I congratulate you. Evidently even your health has improved since then. Your color seems much better."

Engel smiled; his mammoth teeth seemed to make his head lean forward.

"The small hope—weighing no more than an eyelash perhaps—of not dying, of fixing something, of resolving something, of seeing someone, of running into them . . . someone dear whom you cannot recall without tears. But the main thing is being, being, carrying on in some way. Now I know what that is. For me that eyelash outweighs the universe, and even the doubts themselves seem like bliss to me in comparison with how I was living before."

"So you still do have your doubts all the same?"

Engel squeezed his two bony hands into two dark fists and brought them up to his chest.

"Oh, not like before."

Astashev shuffled his feet under his stool.

"I'll be going now, if you don't mind," he said. "I stopped by for a light, as the saying goes, and walked in on an auto-da-fé."

"Yes!" Engel exclaimed joyfully. "Go now! I don't need anything more from you at all."

Astashev stood up. Still wearing his coat and carrying his bowler he walked through the studio, slowly looking around, as if reluctant to leave. On the table lay a thick earthenware platter with a shiny dark green glaze.

"A cunning thing," said Alexei Georgievich pensively.

"Would you like me to give it to you?" Engel was already hugging the dish to his skinny chest. "I was wanting to give you something as a remembrance all along. As a souvenir. Take this. It's not worth anything, but it's very pretty. You could put something on it."

Astashev didn't refuse. With the platter under his arm, he walked out, having said good-bye to Engel and bowed silently to the back of the artist Kharin.

On the street he breathed freely. He had felt as though he was suffocating all evening. Only now did he realize that he had started feeling suffocated and out of sorts in the twilight of the afternoon's films, and ever since then, all day and by now well into the evening, he had been carrying around that choked feeling, that melancholy, inside him. One definitely had to arrange some kind of retreat for oneself in life. He'd been at it ten years already, and now it was time: either piquet with Vyazminitinov, or fishing, or conjugal bliss, or something else to fill up his spare time.

"I've always developed harmoniously," he thought. "And at forty this natural thought has occurred to me. One can't just go through life like a beast of burden: occasional women; office gossip; my lady mamenka and her cavaliers. Enough. I've been missing something, and it's been eating away at me for two days now, ever since that night with Zhenechka. She wouldn't take any money. A sweet girl. She was so frightened!"

He walked and walked, carrying his unwrapped green platter the way officials carry papers to be signed. Walking felt pleasant. The doctor had advised him to walk as much as possible to fight off the fat. This evening walking mechanically brought back his equilibrium, but he still didn't feel like going home. For the third time that day he set out for Xenia Andreevna's. It was already too late to go out, but he could sit up with her until midnight so that he would finally feel like sleeping.

He rang twice. Steps rang out in the distance, her steps, heavy but still quick; even her house slippers had French heels. She opened the door a crack.

"You? What has happened?"

"I can't sleep for some reason. Let me in. I left my umbrella here. Here's a platter for you as a present. You could put something on it."

Dressed in brightly flowered silk pajamas that flowed and glimmered, she led him through the dark apartment to her bedroom, sat down on the bed, and lit a cigarette.

"I was getting ready for bed. I've just got back. Imagine, that young girl (fool that I am, I thought she was innocent!) had an *ami* and killed herself yesterday."

He was standing over her. He looked her in the eye

and pretended he didn't understand, surprising himself that he understood right away. Why? After all, it was inexplicable, mysterious. How could he have guessed that Xenia Andreevna was talking about her?

"No, she poisoned herself with gas. The owner of the cinema said that the night before some gentleman came by for her. She was living with him—that's clear. Maybe she was pregnant? Maybe he was tired of her. My God, what scoundrels you all are!"

He asked quickly: "What gentleman? Are they looking for him?"

"No one knows who. Why look for him?"

"Was there a note?"

He didn't understand what was going on inside him. He felt liberated from a two-day nightmare: brooding, his conscience, dreams, sadness. Once again he was utterly free, absolutely tranquil, light of body and firm of soul.

"Sit here. Don't look, my hair's a mess. Anyway, to me you're not a man. I've even taken my teeth out. . . . You know, her aunt got so upset that she sent for me. What, they didn't have anyone closer or something? Her mother didn't even show up all day."

"The bitch," said Alexei Georgievich calmly.

"It's a good thing I ran into Yuli Fyodorovich on the street. I took him along. He took care of everything. Her aunt wanted to lodge a complaint, but what was there to do if she was found in the kitchen with a pipe in her mouth, the gas pipe, that is. My hands are cold even now."

"Calm down," he said loudly and firmly. "That person misled both of us. If she was so sensitive, why did she wear lipstick and nail polish and sew buttons on her dress? It's illogical, unreasonable."

"Her lover must have left her."

"Mamenka, what are you saying! What, no lover ever left you? If women are going to poison themselves because they've been abandoned, the human race will come to an end. You have to know how to live, how to survive: bravely, beautifully."

"You're all scoundrels," she repeated with affected coarseness.

He kissed both her hands, which now, without her rings, were unrecognizably old. Then he walked over to her vanity table. Since childhood he had felt a strange attraction to all items of the feminine dressing table, and now he dabbed himself with perfume and lipstick, ran a brush through his hair and a powder puff over his chin, sniffed some cream, touched her scissors.

"I know people," he said, cleaning his nails. "Oh, how well I know them, Mamenka! Everything is always their fault. They deserve what they get. I could talk about it to a Tolstoy or a Dostoyevsky, but we don't have anyone to compare with them these days. It's not worth dirtying your hands with the ones we do have."

Hanging on to her headboard with both hands and swinging her bare blue-tinged feet, she watched him.

"In my opinion, suicide is the most unforgivable act there is." He stuck his fingers through the gap in his vest, thrusting out his chest. "Something that should be strictly prohibited. To destroy everything that's come before! And, have you noticed, Mamenka, it's always out of some selfish cowardice: Oh, there's no way I can pay off my gambling debt! Oh, he offered me neither his heart nor his hand and took advantage of my feminine weakness!"

He stopped and looked at himself in the mirror. She waited for him to go on. Her sallow face, greased for the night, her low-slung breasts, her hair, which had recently become copper, and her still lively, still flashing eyes, despite the bags, were perfectly motionless. All of a sudden she cracked her knuckles and said in a muffled voice:

"Alyosha, how I love you! So intelligent, so profound and elegant. I can imagine how many females you have hanging around your neck!"

For a minute he felt a searing pride in his chest, and then, when it went away, he jumped up and plumped her pillows.

"Go to bed. You're exhausted. Don't worry about the women. I don't allow them to hang. Sweet dreams."

Lazily wrapping herself up in a shawl and yawning with her empty mouth, she saw him to the door.

So he went. Umbrella, briefcase. His soft hands swung from side to side, back and forth. His brisk legs pressed down on the stones. Through the darkness of the streets, through the gloom of the city, he walked toward the sound sleep of the Astashevs. Then, the next morning, once again—a call on the pilot in the suburbs, in the sun and the wind, wearing his freshly brushed bowler. Onward, onward, with a spring in his steady step—citizen, taxpayer, consumer (but no soldier!)—past people and over borders, carrying a flimsy passport in one pocket, a pen in the other, through the fog, through the heat, through the gray drizzle, one, two, left, right, crawling like a shadow over everything he encountered, handing out cigarettes, hinting, reminding, bowing low, leaving a trail, already a little flabby, already balding, with gold in his broadest of smiles, already breathing just a little more heavily, jiggling the pale fat of his baby cheeks as he walked, up stairs, down side streets, along thoroughfares where cars raced, over rails where trains passed, and on, past cemeteries, women, monuments, sunsets.

The Tattered Cloak

I

MY SISTER'S NAME WAS ARIADNA. I was nine that unforgettable, snowy, hungry winter when she finished school and became a grown-up. That was the year my mother died, too, in one of Petersburg's cold, desolate clinics. In the space of two months our whole life changed, and so did we.

There had been a modest but comfortable apartment, a maid who never let me out of the door without inspecting me first, my eccentric father, and my soft-spoken, invalid mother, who seemed to be barely alive after all her protracted illnesses. There had been the family's good name and its struggle to survive. And suddenly all of that was gone, all the color and light. After the second operation there was a quiet funeral. Ariadna knotted her hair at her nape and pinned a piece of crepe to her hat. Papa turned gray, skinny, and became utterly mad, but he was a happy madman whose laughter often turned to tears. The servant was let go, and strangers moved in with us. I started running out to the cooperative and to the bread distribution center on the way to the

Warsaw Railway Station, where sometimes you could get milk.

That long winter of 1920 brought the three of us together in one room, which had once been the dining room. In the middle of this room stood a cast-iron stove. Our life revolved around that stove, which gave out a slow, heavy warmth in the evenings. Father groaned and chuckled and told jokes behind his screen. At that time they still made me laugh, but Ariadna didn't even smile with her eyes. He dressed and undressed behind that screen, read, slept, and muttered to himself. Sometimes when we were in that room it seemed as if Ariadna and I were the only people in the entire world. Especially in the evenings, when she and I went to bed on the deep leather sofa that had been in Father's study. Various pieces of furniture had been brought in from each room. We lay with our heads at opposite ends, each covered up with her own blanket. And as everything died down and the last flame flickered behind the grate, chasing and shaking the shadows on the white wall, I fell asleep hugging her knees.

I warmed them. I held them close, close to my strong childish chest. I had conversations with them, conversations I couldn't have with Ariadna herself. I told them stories; I whispered my dreams to them; I called them pet names. She would stir in her sleep, shift away from me, and come back again. A white spot from some light— maybe the streetlamp or the moon—flickered in the corner of the ceiling above Father's screen. I cried softly; I laughed from happiness. I feared life and believed in it. I wanted something grand and yet felt very small. I always came first, and no one needed me.

The long, almost seamless night merged into a long, almost seamless day. We went to bed when it was still light and awoke to bright May sunshine. Yes, she was grown-up now. That year she grew up. Her arms were gently rounded, and her slender face was longer. She was so skinny that when she undressed to bathe (and I stood on a stool and poured water over her) I could see all her bones move beneath her skin. Her pink-blue breasts moved, too, either vanishing completely (for instance, when she raised her arm) or reappearing (when she leaned over).

On the evenings Father was not at home we were especially quiet and industrious. We took baths, washed out our shirts and slips, shampooed and trimmed each other's hair, made over old dresses, darned stockings. Sometimes we dug into a trunk and came up with an old jacket or a funny old-fashioned cape, and Ariadna would try it on and walk around the room looking at herself in the mirrors. Then she would forget she was wearing it and without taking it off proceed to think up new hairdos for herself and for me, attach buckles to a worn-out pair of shoes, or play with faded ribbons. She tried to picture the wondrous masked ball in her imminent future. Her life was about to start. Not this dull, miserable, half-starved life but another life, a life that had yet to begin. She would put her arm out to one side, throw her head back, and deliver a magnificent, non-sensical monologue that would make tears glisten in her eyes and roll down my cheeks. No matter what she did then—and she was eighteen that summer—it meant just one thing: somewhere there was life. Somewhere there was the rapture of happiness and the tyranny of fate, and you had to be ready for anything when the doors to the light- and music-filled ballroom were flung open.

Usually Father came home from work late and ate a bowl of kasha, washing it down with black tea. No bread, no sugar. Sometimes we were both asleep by then, and he woke us up with his heavy boots, the soles tied on with string, which were forever just about to come apart. Every so often he would walk over to our sofa and look at Ariadna, at me, and back at Ariadna. She would open her light blue eyes, slip her hand with its transparent little ring between her cheek and the pillow, and say, "Oh, Papa!" in a kind of doleful reproach. But he was ready to settle into his easy chair and trundle out one of his strange stories, which more often than not began like this:

"Mark Twain once said to me, 'Listen, mister, I forget your name and patronymic. . . .' "

In September Ariadna got a job in a museum, and once again I was alone for entire days at a stretch.

Indefatigable, I slaved away from the moment she walked out the door. I washed the floor, stood in lines, picked up our rations, cooked, and did the laundry. Sometimes when I couldn't lift the big kettle of borscht or the caldron of boiling linen I asked old Countess Rydnitskaya, whose hair was cut short like a man's and who always had a pipe clenched between her teeth, to come in from the next room and help me. In each room of our apartment—there were five altogether—a separate family lived with its own stove and laundry and children. Only the Countess lived by herself. She was waiting for permission to go back home, but her papers still had not come.

After breakfast Father went to work, and I went back to my scrubbing and mopping, holding my childish imagination in check between tough dried fish and moldy millet. Then I went to see the Countess and listen to her stories of a gay, lavish, fairy-tale world of mustached men, lace stoles, fur muffs, and the Virgin Mary.

At six Ariadna and I had our supper.

"If only you'd read some Pushkin," she told me. "It would be good to send you to school. We could pay the Countess to make dinner for us."

Then I knew that this muddled life of mine was about to end, that I was going to start learning. At ten I was strong, my hands red, my voice rough. I wore a wool cap with earflaps and felt boots, and the sole purpose of my childish existence was to lay my hands on something edible and bring it home.

When Ariadna came home from work she undressed, sat down at the table, and, looking straight ahead, began telling me about her day. She worked in a back room of the museum where books were kept and there was always something being packed or unpacked, far from where the pictures were hanging and people walked about. Her rations were quite good: tobacco, herring, sometimes lard or groats. I had to take the sled when I went to pick them up. How I harnessed myself to it! How briskly I tramped over the icy pavement, across the steep bridge over the Ekaterinsky Canal, pulling at my nose and tossing my braid behind my ear!

I already knew Georgy Serafimovich, her boss, and Vera Sergeevna, her co-worker, and the other museum workers, as they were now called, who came to see

Ariadna from time to time—Professor Maximov, the paleontologist Grize, and the poet Andrei Zvonkov. I had a very precise picture in my mind of the big room where Ariadna sat next to a tall window and made entries in an oversize ledger in her round, back-slanting script. Vera Sergeevna sat opposite and wore a silk top. Everyone was in love with her. She knew every writer in Petersburg and went to the theater every night. And Georgy Serafimovich in his cap and galoshes—he was well educated and never satisfied with anything—crawled among the boxes of antiquities, forever cursing and threatening to go to Moscow and lodge a complaint.

At the time it seemed to me that the life we were leading, that everyone around us was leading, in this, the only city in the world (because I had no conception of other cities), that this life of ours with its constant, gnawing hunger, its cold, its torn sheets, and its hole-filled shoes, the black soot of the stoves and the gloom in the streets, the ice, the dread of winding up an orphan, of prison, of beggary, the separations, and the hospitals, was the only life there was. Just as I couldn't imagine an orange or a seashore, which I'd never seen, so I couldn't believe then that there were such things as frivolous presents, aimless walks, spending money, or peace and quiet.

Meanwhile, Countess Rydnitskaya visited us from time to time and told Ariadna and me stories about fur muffs and lace stoles. She grieved over us—over me because I'd never know "life's golden dawning," as she put it, and over Ariadna because her life was slipping by without that vague poetry which the Countess held so dear.

"My poor little girls," she would say, puffing away at her pipe. "My poor spring flowers."

Ariadna, saddened by this, chewed on her sparkling ring. But I guffawed just as crudely and loudly as I did at my father's jokes, though I did have a feeling (which I never admitted to anyone) that in part she was right, not completely, but a little. That feeling made me afraid that my laughter would turn into tears.

Two young girls visited us as well, the Dyukova sisters, Lyuda and Tata. They were big, buxom, pretty girls, Ariadna's friends from school. At first they didn't trust me and made me cover my ears at the most interesting parts, but eventually they got used to me.

"That Sasha! Oh, that Sasha!" they chorused, and even Ariadna chimed in sometimes: "Oh, that Sasha of mine!"

And that "Oh" referred to my fearlessness, to my smart rejoinders, to my acquisitive eyes and my strong hands, which latched on tight to anything and everything.

She was many times better than Lyuda or Tata, my Ariadna, with her big eyes, pale hair, fragile build, and her heart which was like nobody else's, or so it seemed to me at the time. Listening to their conversations, usually conducted in alternating whispers and laughter, it dawned on me that one of the Dyukovas was planning to get married, that is, planning to move out of her parents' house, away from her sister, and live with some stranger, having registered with him first, of course, at the commissariat. And what was the reason behind this whole calamity? Her love for that stranger, who apparently was not so young, and his love for her, which they spoke of chiefly in whispers on our couch. It also dawned on me that the other Dyukova was in love with someone too and was running up against extraordinary obstacles to being united with him. The thought that Ariadna might marry someday and leave us, leave me alone with my father, alone to the cheerless gloom of my life, horrified me. I started to keep special watch over her, and what I saw frightened me.

What I saw was creeping indifference toward us, as if her thoughts were otherwise occupied. She came home later and left earlier. She started going out in the evening, and she never told me what she did. She started sleeping differently—her breathing couldn't fool me. Even her face looked different.

I remember one of the first Sundays of the New Year of 1922. We were all still together. Father was writing something at his desk, and from time to time he would look calmly in our direction and say something mad, and we would exchange bewildered looks. We were sitting on the couch—Ariadna in the middle, Lyuda and Tata to either side of her, and I on one side or the other trying to perch on an arm, but they kept pushing me off and once even set me down on the floor.

"There are animals, girls," said Papa, "who can pull their intestines out through their own navels and play beautiful melodies on them."

I looked at Ariadna.

"Why do you keep looking at me?" she demanded. "Lyuda, give her a poke. Why does she keep looking at me that way? If only you'd read some Pushkin! When you screw your eyes up your face looks so plain. You're going to be so ugly when you grow up!"

Tata laughed, wound my braid around her hand, and said:

"Ugly but practical—and very mad."

"Practical and mad, like her late lamented father." Papa raised a cold-blooded voice from behind his paper.

But I kept watching her, and fear of the future—hers and mine—gripped me, a fear which I could share with no one. I tried to squeeze in between them again, and finally they let me, tickled me, covered my face with a cushion. And I kept trying to figure out why I loved her so much. Why was I so afraid of losing her? Why did I want to be near her always?

I remember that evening. It was the evening before that amazing night when we were finally alone. Father snored behind his screen, the stove had gone out long before, and the room was cold. The upright piano on which Lyuda had banged out a Chopin waltz had been left open and showed its white keys, and every so often something would shift in the stack of dirty dishes. (I didn't have the energy to wash all those cups and saucers so late.)

I hugged her cold skinny legs and asked softly:

"Do you like them? Do you like them a lot?"

"Who? The Dyukovas?"

"Do you tell them *everything*?"

She stirred.

"I don't tell anyone everything."

"I'd like someone to tell everything to. Wouldn't you?"

I could tell she was tempted to brush me off with a joke, a tease, but she refrained.

"Tell me everything," she said.

"I can't. I will if you will too."

Suddenly she reached under the blanket and gave my fingers a gentle squeeze.

"Why aren't you older, Sasha?" she said almost out loud. "You'd be my best, my closest friend."

I gasped and froze.

"What about now?"

"Now all I've got is Tata and Lyuda. Later, only much later, I'll have you. Oh, I don't know. Maybe it's better like this. You know, there are times in your life when you don't need girlfriends."

"Don't you need me?"

"You're my sister. All of a sudden you start needing something completely different, something special and serious. Everything else seems so childish."

I sat up in bed.

"Are you in love?" I cried out in horror. Tears gushed down my face and hands.

"Calm down! What's come over you! You'll wake Papa. Come here. Lie down next to me."

I crawled over to her, and we were still for a while. She'd never asked me to lie next to her before. I was so happy that way, so untroubled—even in the darkest corners deep down inside. Right then I wanted only one thing: for that night to go on forever. A warmth came from Ariadna, a dear soapy fragrance from her neck, and something sweet-smelling from her hair. She lay stretched out next to me in her long, high-collared, long-sleeved nightgown, and I could feel her shoulder, her knee.

"Tell me who he is," I said, swooning from bliss and terror.

"Who is he? Oh, that's not so easy to say," she replied as if to herself, for herself. "He works in the theater. He wants to write for the theater. He wants to be a director. But he's married, so we're just going to live together."

I didn't really understand what she was saying, but I didn't want to interrupt to ask.

"Papa will never allow it, naturally. He doesn't have a real job or a ration card. Anyway, he's kind of odd, very special, and terribly ugly. You'll see."

"Does he love you?"

She sighed a broken sigh.

"Yes, Sasha—" And suddenly she pulled away from me. "He loves me, and I love him. And we've decided to be together."

When we were both quiet you could hear her heart and mine pounding in counterpoint under the blanket.

We fell asleep together, and that night I had a dream.

I forget what the dream was about, but it left a mood, an anxiety connected with it, a melancholy that ran all through it, from the first time the stranger appeared in our room, between the stove and screen, to when he vanished in the unfamiliar back streets of a city that looked like Petersburg. I lost the point of the dream, although probably there wasn't one, as in most dreams. All that remained of it was a strange aftertaste, a mysterious knot that weighs on me to this very day. That man, who in my dreams was called Ariadna's husband and around whom the whole complicated mechanism of my childish dreaming revolved, was bound up in some incomprehensible way with our entire existence, with the collapse of Russia, with the hard, brutal, grievous things that happened in our waking hours. It was as if he bore some inexplicable and horrible relation to Mama's death, and the cold, and the hunger, and my older brother's recent execution, and Countess Rydnitskaya's troubles.

His name was Sergei Sergeevich Samoilov, and when I saw him for the first time it was dark—the dark of winter that had begun long before and would end much later—and Ariadna was getting ready to go to a concert, tying the strings of her hood in front of the mirror. Papa watched her silently and morosely, but she was all rosy, in full bloom, telling first him and then me one silly thing after another and stomping around in her felt boots. When the bell finally rang in the hall she told us in a low voice that her friend, Sergei Samoilov, had come for her. He was Andrei Zvonkov's friend, a poet, and a good friend of Vera Sergeevna.

"A beau?" asked Papa, and there was something nasty in his face.

At this first meeting it suddenly became clear to me how much Ariadna had broken away from our father's and mother's military background into that rootless avant-garde associated with the university, museums, literary gatherings, and experimental theaters. The conjunction of all our misfortunes, great and small, had led her to the expanses of a different life, had led her to Samoilov, and Papa seemed to understand that then, too. Smiling, she greeted Samoilov and introduced him to Father. I stood motionless behind the stove, in the corner near the cupboard, and watched them, completely absorbed.

Samoilov was nearly thirty then. He was blond, round-shouldered, and red-nosed. His teeth were bad, and there was an intelligent look in his bright eyes. He was a young man with no sign of breeding or of any awareness of other people. He had a way of speaking without listening to anyone else and of coming and going when he wanted to. He didn't maintain the proper physical distance between himself and other people, and there was something obstinate in his hiked-up shoulders and sloping forehead. He wore a thick gray quilted vest and quilted coat and did not remove his peaked cap right away. He stood there and waited for Ariadna to pull on her mittens.

"I must warn you quite frankly," my father told him after a minute had passed, "so that you are under no false impression: one of her eyes is glass. My poor Ariadna, what a nasty thing happened to her in her childhood! But it's so well done that you can't tell which one isn't real."

Samoilov looked at him with curiosity.

"So, then, and what do you do, Comrade Samsonov?" Papa asked, smiling sweetly all of a sudden, all ready to sit in his chair and have a cozy chat.

But Samoilov and Ariadna were all set to go out. Her face was unrecognizable. It shone.

"I'm thinking about putting on some little plays, various kinds of plays, in a theater I know, and take it to the people," Samoilov replied in all seriousness. "I'm trying my hand at all kinds of comic skits. I'm giving my all—and I've not done too badly, even if I do say so myself. I adore any kind of poetic presentation."

I was standing in my corner, behind the cupboard, and looked at him, wide-eyed.

"But who is this? A little girl or a little boy?" he asked suddenly, when he saw me, and pointed a finger in my direction.

"A girl," I answered loudly.

"So, you must be Irochka or Kirochka, right?" he continued without the slightest softening in his voice.

"No, I'm Sasha," I said again, firmly.

"How do you do, Sasha!" he exclaimed simply and with a sudden curtness. He walked over to me very quickly and shook my hand. A minute later they were both gone.

"How do you do, Samoilov," I said proudly, but I don't know whether he heard me. Father didn't look in my direction. He picked up a fragile blue glass that we kept by the washbasin where we brushed our teeth and threw it at the mirror over the mantel. There was a terrible crash. The glass flew into tiny pieces, showering the entire room, but somehow the mirror was left intact, and everything looked the same in it: the murk, the lamp clouded in smokiness, our silvery wallpaper, the slanted closed door. Then Father went behind his screen, lay down on his bed, and started laughing very loudly—or crying. I could never tell his laughing from his crying. But later that night the mirror shattered.

For a long time I couldn't sleep. Countess Rydnitskaya sat by my feet and knit a scarf, a lilac scarf with tassels. I watched her and felt like crying and telling her all about it, but I was brave and said nothing.

"So, my wonderful little girl," said the Countess, "that evening, for the first time, he and I went to the islands. The driver waited downstairs. I was wearing a gauze dress the color of champagne with an open neck and a diamond and amethyst pendant. At that time women wore curls on top of a chignon. Each curl was perfumed, and a comb was stuck in on top, a very very fancy carved comb, and with paste jewels as well."

She left and for a long time I stared at the place where she had sat and I waited for Ariadna. But I fell asleep before she came in. I woke up when I felt someone getting in with me under the blanket. Her hands were shaking, and so was her whisper.

"Sasha, Sasha," she whispered. "Time to sleep, Sasha. Are you asleep? Why not? You have to sleep. Give me a hug, Sasha. What's wrong? Don't mind me. I don't know what's happening to me either."

But I wasn't going to hug her anymore, and I wasn't going to cry with her. That night I had hardened, and I even experienced a certain satisfaction from feeling harder. I curled up and moved closer to the wall, feigning sleep.

In the daytime everything was the same as ever: laundry, cleaning, standing in lines, going out to buy sugar from the dealers in the third courtyard of a building on Marat Street, carrying firewood up from the cellar, where someone was pilfering it, and my tears over the missing logs, the harsh, cold, unbearably rough, dark life, the third winter—the longest, the saddest. In the daytime everything was just the same: "If only you'd read some Pushkin," and Father's soft hand resting on the table as he wrote or ate or just sat and stared into space. But at night everything was different. Ariadna went out almost every day, or rather, she no longer came home after work.

Instead she came in late, when we were both already asleep, and sometimes I didn't even wake up when she came in.

But once, in early March (I remember, it was the first thaw; I'd caught a cold and was staying at home with a muffler wound around my neck), on one of those evenings when Father wasn't home, Samoilov came to see Ariadna again, for the second and last time. He wasn't alone. With him were Zvonkov and Vera Sergeevna, and the four of them drank tea, which I heated on the stove, ate black bread, smoked, and talked.

There was a semblance of coziness in our room that evening. The shattered mirror had been replaced by a bright cheerful picture, which Ariadna had been given by an artist friend. There was a new homemade shade on the lamp. A clean tablecloth was spread on the table, and there was a big dried pink flower in the vase—you couldn't tell whether it was real or imitation.

"This is Sasha," Ariadna told each one of them in turn, pointing to me, and I clumsily stuck out my red hand.

Later I quietly undressed and lay down, and the guests paid no attention to me, shouted, nibbled on crusts of bread with their tea, recited poems, argued. It was as if Ariadna were her old self again, though the cigarette in her slender hand and a peculiar curl over one ear were a surprise that made my heart contract. Tall, flat-chested, slant-eyed, but nonetheless in her own way beautiful, Vera Sergeevna spoke least of all, but it was clear to me that she was in charge of the conversation. Zvonkov and Samoilov used the familiar "you" with each other. Zvonkov recited several poems, and I figured out that they were all his own. He read them in a singsong voice, which made the poems sound wonderful to me, and when he stopped, Samoilov started to talk about something, also in a slightly singsong tone—and then it got quiet and they all listened to him, but he broke off without finishing, saying that God hadn't given him an ear, hadn't given him the gift. He could invent anything at all, but he couldn't rhyme two lines. At the same time, he clearly had something on his mind that he wanted to bring to life, that tormented him, that had been maturing, perhaps for a long time, an image for which he had already found a name: the tattered cloak.

"It was dug out of an old trunk that had taken root in the floor of Grandfather's house. It smelled of camphor and looked terribly big to us, but in the old days men must have been more substantial than we are. See, it's full of holes! It's completely out of fashion. But although it's badly moth-eaten, it's still splendid. You could wrap yourself up in it from head to toe and keep out the cold. It needs an airing. It's been lying too long at the bottom of the trunk.

"Many years ago our fathers, in the forests of Manchuria, at the approaches to Port Arthur, wrapped you and me up in this cloak. We were children, and we were cold out on the Korean steppes. Our fathers never came back. Our mothers came back with us alone. Our gray-eyed, fair-haired mothers raised us, and when Russia's troubles came they couldn't bear the summers or the winters. We buried them and set plain wooden crosses over them.

"We've seen a lot. We've never been afraid. But a lot more lies ahead of us. We've forgotten our prayers, and life has stolen away our hopes. Nothing will ever bring them back. You've wrapped your dainty feet up in this old cloak so many times, and I've draped it over myself more than once, trying to cheer you up by pretending I was Childe Harold of old. Tell me, wasn't this the cloak Joseph wrapped round Mary and the infant on their journey into Egypt? Or maybe it's Don Quixote's cloak? Or perhaps it belongs to the god himself, Cervantes? Remember how we wrapped his wounded arm in it and covered his blinded eyes with it, and how we ran after him, weeping, but by then he couldn't see us? Or is this the cloak of Lear struggling through the storm we've known so well for so long?

"Now times are different. I must go one way, and you another. We'll rip this old cloak in two. It's gone out of style anyway. It reminds me of an old-fashioned pelerine, but that's all right. I'm leaving for good, for the open spaces of my gloomy and cruel land, not because I love it but because for me there is no other road. Farewell!

"You take the other half of this two-thousand-year-old garment of ours. You run away from here, from me, from us. Run and don't look back, my sweet one, my love. Run over the seas and the mountains, run to other lands. Do not fear loneliness, do not fear your orphanhood. Live like a bird, perhaps the wind. Safeguard your young and tender life. Run away—to Africa, Australia, Asia. Pick one of the two Americas. Run away from these sad and awful places—

The tattered cloak to shield
Your young and lovely face."

I'd probably started a fever. I listened to Samoilov's high-pitched voice. He rocked ever so slightly as he spoke, sometimes trying to couch a line in iambic trimeter. I remember him saying: "There is no other road," and then, at the end, "one of the two Americas." But he couldn't write verse, and naturally his poem would never be written. Nonetheless, in the semidark of that room so full of smoke and heat, it somehow did take on a precise form for a few moments because after Samoilov fell silent his three listeners and the fourth (which was myself) could still hear the flow and rhythm of his unrealized poem inside us.

"That's good," said Zvonkov, "very good. Why don't you give it to me?"

"It's yours. Do what you like with it," Samoilov responded.

Then there was a silence that seemed endless to me, when I could hear a pounding and ringing in my ears.

It was the stinging wind cutting me in the face. I see Petersburg of those years like a sketch traced in the snow. By a steep stone footbridge at the juncture of two frozen canals I see a big poster tacked up: In this theater, Samoilov's play is being performed for the two-thousandth time. The wind whips the poster, and it tears, like the old cloak. Through the holes in the cloak you can see the red sunset. A poem about a red sunset is being recited in a smoke-filled room. Someone is garbling it—deliberately, insisting on his mistakes, and pale, slant-eyed Vera Sergeevna is correcting Zvonkov, but he is insistent:

> But we the heirs of Blok
> Are helpless to forget.

What are we helpless to forget? The cold clinic where Mama died? Or the dense, gray, claylike hunk of our daily bread? Or that green and lonely star over Senate Square last May? And I take that star to sleep with me as if I'd filched it.

Later that night I opened my eyes. The light was on in the room. Father was standing in his shirt and underclothes, hanging on to the screen and saying something in a very loud voice. Ariadna was sitting at the table, tousled and pink, her arms stretched across the table. There was indescribable disarray in the room. I stirred and closed my eyes again.

"If his intentions are honorable, he shouldn't be furtive. Let him come. Let him marry you," said Father, evidently repeating the same words for the tenth time. "Where did you get involved with him? Where are you running off to? What kind of man is he, anyway? No, answer me, what kind of man is he? An actor? A stage-hand? An acrobat, maybe? Does he work on a trapeze? Has anyone bothered to explain to me who it is I'm dealing with?"

She snatched a breath, as if for him.

"I'm going to go and live with him soon," she said calmly. "We're going to live together, as he's married."

Father let out an "Ah!" and it became very quiet

in the room. That frightened me. I opened my eyes and sat up on the bed. At that moment I felt no more love for anyone in the world, and Ariadna seemed like a total stranger to me. Stunned by that revelation, I looked around me and burst into noisy tears.

She had noticed the change in me. The next evening—the last evening of her life with us—she and I found ourselves alone together, like old times, and she gathered her things into a canvas duffel bag and barely spoke to me. She avoided me, not explaining her departure, as if it should all have been clear to me without that. I was standing by the window.

"How can you go out in that snow?" I asked.

Fat wet flakes were falling on the street.

"That's OK, it's not far," she replied. "What time is it?"

It was ten to ten.

"Give this letter to Papa."

I felt something powerful stir inside me.

"Aren't you ever going to come here again?" I asked. "But what about me?"

"Enough, enough. Don't be such an idiot. You're going to come and visit me."

"That's not true. That's never going to happen."

Suddenly she sat down and hid her face in her hands.

"I realized," she said, as if she were trying to justify herself for something, at the same time aware that I was the wrong person to listen to words like that, "I realized that this isn't life." She indicated our room. "Not you, not him." She pointed to the screen. "Life is something absolutely, totally different. It's nothing like this."

"It's Samoilov and his tattered cloak," I said rudely.

She smiled.

"Yes, it's the tattered cloak. Someday you'll remember me, and those words, and that whole evening, won't you, Sasha?"

"Don't go," I said, barely audibly. "Don't go, Ariadna. Make it be different."

"I can't."

I couldn't understand her. I sobbed at the cold windowsill, and she kissed my hair and held me close. I don't remember what happened after that: saying goodbye, her leaving me alone to the light of the lamp burning in the ceiling, the heartbreaking silence. Father came home later than usual. I jumped up to meet him. He stopped short, two steps away from me.

"A letter," I said. "You have a letter from her, Papa."

"Ah!" he said abruptly. "And what might this letter be about?"

I felt my whole face tremble under his gaze.

"She's gone, Papa," I stated finally.

"Ah! So why read a letter? If that's all, then there's nothing to read. It's the fact itself that's important. The fact is known. To hell with the letter."

He kicked open the grating and thrust the letter into the burning stove. Without removing his cap, galoshes, or snowy overcoat, he went behind the screen, sprawled on his bed, and was silent.

For a few days we hid our misfortune from everyone, but Countess Rydnitskaya finally came to see us.

"One must never do things like that," she said, puffing on her pipe. "Youth is flowers and love. Youth is beauty. This vulgar, crude life we lead is tearing off all the petals, killing off the tender shoots. Your father's tragedy simply defies description."

I didn't understand a word she said, and that bothered me.

Ariadna lived nearby, on Razyezhaya, and I ran into her once or twice that year. She wore a velvet ribbon around her neck and a homemade leather hat. Each time she kissed me happily and excitedly and questioned me about our lives, and whether I was going to school, and did I remember her (as if I could forget her, as if I were five instead of eleven). She had lost a certain sensitivity to me and talked to me in the way that adults who aren't used to children talk to them. I began to hold back with her as well. I wanted to let her know that I wasn't the same little girl I'd been when I'd slept with her on our only sofa, that I was going to school, that I read books, that I had tasted life and understood quite a lot already. So we stood on the corner by the stationery shop and were deeply insincere with one another.

Later I did in fact start school. Ariadna moved across the river. And a year after that Papa's sister sent for us from France. Dressed in government-issue shoes, coats sewn from soldiers' greatcoats, and shirts cut out of old sheets, we went to Paris, carrying a basket of tinware and a bundle of strapped-together pillows.

II

PARIS. PARIS. There is something silken and elegant about that word, something carefree, something made for a dance, something brilliant and festive like champagne. Everything there is beautiful, gay, and a little drunk, and festooned with lace. A petticoat rustles at every step; there's a ringing in your ears and a flashing in your eyes at the mention of that name. I'm going to Paris. We've come to Paris. We're going to live in Paris. But what I saw my first day resembled neither silk nor lace nor champagne.

Imagine that a man has landed on the moon. He's expecting to see a majestic and menacing wasteland, dead mountains, stone chasms, a special sky. And suddenly he notices that he's looking at the stucco wall of his neighbor's house, it's raining, and the courtyard stinks. When I looked out the window of our Paris apartment it seemed to me that everything was exactly as it had been at our old place: that feeling of being on the edge of a big city along with a multitude of poverty-stricken people, chiefly women, and chiefly old women at that; a quiet murky street with the smoking chimney of a commercial laundry and a blue locksmith's sign; over the sign an open window with a torn tulle curtain and behind that an old man inserting a set of false teeth in his wide wet mouth. Above it all there is a narrow stripe: a swatch of the local sky,

gray and low. There, around the corner, and farther—
the same street again, desolate and impoverished, where
an ugly little girl who looks a little like me is walking (or
is that me walking with my butcher bag?). A hunk of
beef juts out of the bag, red and solid. A worker passes
with a bottle of wine in the bulging pocket of his patched
jacket. And then nothing, no one. All you hear is the
pounding from the artificial sausage-casing factory. From
time to time the din increases, which means they've
opened the door to the street, and then the whole block,
including our house, starts to smell of something rotten
and astringent.

I lived on that street not one year, not three, not
five, not even ten. I lived there for sixteen years of my
life, looking out of those windows, breathing in the black
fumes from the factory chimney. Those years were utterly
indistinguishable: the swing of a pendulum, from spring
to summer and from autumn to winter, forming a constant rectangle of time, in the cell of which I listened
with equal docility to the noise of the factory and the
hush of Sunday. During those years things withered,
rusted, and faded around me; the locksmith's azure sign
turned a duller blue. On the other hand, some things
were renewed, scrubbed clean, freshly painted. But in
our apartment—inside our house, where a Strauss waltz
played on the radio day after day, where the ubiquitous
cat played with her shadow day after day, where my
father and I slept in our cramped room and put out
folding cots end to end, like corpses in Russia, night after
night—nothing ever changed. Everything held fast somehow, intending, surely, to disintegrate someday, perhaps

after we were gone. Only we ourselves changed. Father's sister Varvara, who had sent for us and who seemed at first a fresh, forty-year-old woman who never lacked either work or a lover, in those years became an old woman, still doing daywork, going to other people's kitchens to wash dishes or to mop floors. Her friends still came by in the evenings as they always had, but her lieutenants and captains were not as bold or assiduously groomed and pomaded as they had once been. No, they were old and meek, like Varvara herself, and they had the same big rough worker's hands.

During the first seven years Father worked as a guard in a garage, and after that as a delivery boy in a pastry shop. Now he was out of work. In fact, he wasn't fit to work anymore, and he had stopped trying to find a job. His stories were as mad as ever, without beginning or end, his laugh was more like a sob than ever, and he still liked to pull your leg. Only now at the end of each story there came a tearful address to me: "My child Cordelia! Daughter of mine!" And when I wasn't there, he said it into space, to where I ought to have been.

I, of course, changed more than anyone. I had been thirteen and I became twenty-nine. My whole youth was behind me, and I had nothing to show for it. Having been a plain little girl, angular and muscular, I became a plain young woman, stocky and pale. It didn't take long for me to lose what youthfulness I'd had, my freshness and high-cheekboned purity. Although quite healthy, I suddenly started to resemble my sickly mother, and my hands, once so deft, became large and white, like the hands of a peasant woman who has just given birth.

I had been thirteen and now I was almost thirty.

But sometimes it seemed to me that I was just the same as before, that I had never learned anything, never mastered anything, never discovered anything here, that everything I had inside me I'd already had in me there: my knowledge of the world, the despair of loneliness, my secret lofty sentiments, my tears, my thoughts, and the fortitude I hid from everyone. All those things I had brought with me, all those things had been given to me back in Russia, and I remained what I had always been.

Meanwhile, my life had worked out no worse or better than other lives. That voracious scramble for a bite to eat and a warm corner had ended. In this new city you could live like a human being: work, earn your keep, make ends meet. At first I went to school, but after a few years I had to give it up for lack of time. I had to help out at home. Varvara was sewing then, and for quite a while I worked for her. It was from her that I learned to iron, sew, and work buttonholes, and in return she made me a dress once a year, a new dress out of some thick wool which I lovingly and secretly admired for months before getting to put it on.

When I turned twenty, I started working as a presser in the commercial laundry on the corner. By that time things had taken a turn for the worse for Varvara. One sad winter Sunday just before Christmas she went out to wait tables in a neighborhood Russian restaurant and shortly afterward took a regular job there. But a few months later she slipped and broke her leg while carrying a plate of oysters, and she was crippled for the rest of her life. That was when she started doing daywork in private homes.

And I became a presser. In the course of nine years

I ironed other people's sheets every day from morning till night, learning to stand on my feet for ten hours at a stretch on a daily basis. I got a regular wage, and since by then I already knew that all pressers and laundresses put money aside—and not just them, but shopgirls and clerks and actors and even ministers—I too started saving. I liked this idea, of which I had had no conception before: save part of the money you earn by the sweat of your brow and then use that money to . . . but what exactly I would do with it I did not yet know.

At first I liked the wartime air of my aunt's apartment, so unlike that of our Petersburg caves. In the evenings, when guests sat at the tea table and all talked about how the next day they would sally forth and do battle, it seemed to me that the dispositions had already been made, that we were all bivouacked. "The general has ordered the troops to assemble." "The gentlemen of the staff have decided." "The hussars are now on regimental leave." That was all I heard. And I was surprised that these people with gray faces and rough hands didn't wear plumes and blue and lavender greatcoats, didn't click their spurs or rattle their sabers. They had their own closely knit, uniquely agreeable life: the Maria Ivanovnas, Evgenia Lvovnas, and Irina Alexandrovnas didn't hang around with other men. They had their dances and parties, their raffles, their traditional dinners, prayers, and masses for the dead, at which they prayed piously, vigorously thrusting out their bemedaled chests and joining in with the church choir. But more important were those intoxicatingly pointless conversations—which mattered only to them—about the retreat from Ekaterinoslav,

the surrender of Perekop, and the evacuation of Sevas-
topol, and Varvara, whose husband had been a bugler in
the hussars and had died from wounds on the way to
Constantinople in 1919, was one of the few living links
in that rusty, odd-sounding chain.

Nine years. No, I can't believe it. Do things really
happen like that? Why? Why, though I had committed
no crime, did I end up standing at an ironing board for
nine years lifting a heavy iron? The first few days I came
home and cried all night at the impossibility of fulfilling
my own destiny. Then I stopped crying and came to the
conclusion that the people around me were right: my
work was clean and my job steady; my documents were
in order; and my wage was sufficient for me to live in
the way I was expected to. After all, I had no education,
no looks, and no talent, so what else could I possibly be
good for?

And I saved. Never in all those years did I buy myself
a single extra or unnecessary item. All the stockings, shoes,
dresses, and underwear I wore were the plainest possible,
and I went for years without buying gloves or a hat. I
brought enough into the house for myself and Father,
and the little left over I kept in a thick book on the shelf
above my bed, a cookbook that no one had used in a
long time. I heard about people putting money away for
an operation, for their teeth, for a trip to the seashore,
for a new sideboard, or simply for their old age. From
the very outset I got the idea of going to Italy one day.
I didn't know quite what I was going to see in Italy—
paintings, or cities, or just its dark nights and orange
groves, the cypresses in its cemeteries. But I had a feeling

one day my dream would come true. All by myself I would go to Italy, Genoa, Rome. Why? To see what I had never ever seen.

In all those years only one single time was I able to get away from that life. That was five years ago, when Cavalry Captain Golubenko proposed to me. Captain Golubenko, one of the most valorous of Varvara's visitors, was over forty and owned an electrical supply store. He was a dark, hirsute, lively man, at one time quite the daredevil and dragon slayer, but now his passion was balalaika orchestras, Russian cooking, and singing at the table.

"You can sit at the cash register," he said. "My partner Vasily Karlovich Perlovsky and I will carry you on our arms."

I was supposed to pay for the privilege of sitting rather than standing for the rest of my life, and pay with my freedom.

"Thank you for the honor," I said, as gently as possible, but it still came out rudely, "but I must decline."

Where did I ever come up with that horrible word?

The next day Varvara asked me:

"Answer three questions for me, please. One, why did you refuse Golubenko? Two, what bastard are you sleeping with? And three, do you have any intention of ever settling down with a husband and, if so, what kind?"

"My child Cordelia! Daughter of mine!"

I thought conscientiously for a minute or two.

"One," I said, "because Golubenko is poor. Two, I'm not sleeping with any bastard. And three, I won't marry anyone who's not rich."

That said, I went to the corner and turned my back to both of them, took the cookbook off the shelf, and counted my money. I had 3,370 francs.

Varvara went into the next room and there made that characteristic sound I knew so well: not exactly laughing, but not exactly crying either. It was something she and Father had in common. They looked alike, too. She called to me from the next room. Had I ever experienced any sort of love?

"What's love?" I asked. And suddenly I remembered Ariadna, and instead of going to Italy I felt like sending her all my savings.

All the time I'd lived in Paris one memory had lived on inside me; it breathed, changed shape, grew, intensified, subsided, melted, and burst into life again. It gave me no rest. Often it made me happy; it let me know that there can be genuine and kind relations between people. It showed me the joy of intimacy with someone who until then had been a stranger but who touched your heart for eternity and was reflected in that heart, where he remained. This memory was very brief. It was a voice that once said to me gravely and kindly: "How do you do, Sasha!" It was a look that once fell on me and had become stuck there. There were nights in my miserable existence when I lived for this memory, lighting upon and dwelling on it, sometimes gaily, sometimes tearfully.

It seemed to me that ever since my childhood I'd been a little in love with Ariadna, and now I could be in love with her husband. It seemed to me that I was unconsciously looking to compete with her and imitate her, or else that all this was just my curiosity about her life, about their fate, curiosity about his unrealized poetry, which certainly ought to have had a continuation. Gradually and imperceptibly the image of Samoilov became linked inside me with everything unattainable and wonderful in life, things I could only guess at, the world as it might have been but wasn't for me, people as they might have been but as I would never know them, my secret conjectures that apart from everyday reality there was something else—an image, a melody. As if in the darkest, most brutish years of my existence the beauty and poetry of the world winked at me as they raced past and instantly vanished. No matter that Samoilov himself was ugly and not very kind, and had no talent for composing poems (we hadn't heard anything here of his having made a name for himself, had we?). Through him I had caught a glimpse of something, the enchantment of another world flashed before me at a time when there seemed no possibility of any kind of enchantment in the world. There was also the warmth of the man who had leaned toward me for a moment when all around me was cold and miserable and people were frightened and mistrustful. His "How do you do, Sasha!" and his advice to "live like a bird, perhaps the wind," not to be afraid of anything, to wrap ourselves up in the two-thousand-year-old cloak, our cloak, albeit ripped in two, remained with me throughout my Paris life. I won't hide the fact that the actual memory of his face and voice faded over the years and lost its childish power, but everything that that face, that voice, had once awakened was alive. It lived on and sometimes blossomed within me.

This memory possessed no solidity or continuity. In

my small, awkward soul it was sometimes absent for
weeks and then suddenly stung me for no apparent reason,
or began weakly, looming dreamily in my thoughts, and
then it was gone. On especially lonely nights, when my
father slept soundly near to me with his eyes wide open,
talking to himself (that was the only way he slept these
days) and on the other side of the wall Varvara's guests—
they were all gray now, bald, toothless, and wheezy—
drank and sang (vodka, a guitar) with the same women
friends (some long since grandmothers) at a Christmas
party, or later, in the spring, it would descend upon me,
uncoil, cast a spell over me, and leave me in blissful thrall,
on the verge of tears.

It was late August 1939, and of the three of us I
was the only one who had a job. Father sat for days on
end at the table and laid out hands of solitaire, paced
from room to room hugging the walls, looked with fixed
eyes but didn't see, listened but didn't hear. Coming upon
the evening paper in a corner, he would read it for a
long time and then say, barely mustering up the words:
"We can't give in. We'll simply have to fight. We'll all
go. The main thing is showing some muscle."

Varvara, mumbling away, mended and darned,
washed and cooked; she was always out of work in August
but could never reconcile herself to the fact. She was
always grumbling, always cursing the summer and her
own uselessness. A Strauss waltz boomed over the radio.
It was hot, dull, and dusty in the deserted city, and there
I was standing and ironing, standing and ironing by a
white wall, by a white table, wearing a white apron,
alongside others exactly like me, old and young, puffed

up and dried out, taciturn and talkative pressers who, like me, earned four francs an hour.

Time stood still. The warm smell of starched linen lingered static among us. The heat of the stove where the irons were heated, the red flush of our faces, the hissing of the irons, their quick tap on the edge of the board, and at quiet moments, the ticking of the clock over the boss's desk. All this was static; certainly it had been like that for many years, and it was likely to remain so forever. We cleaned up in the laundry at six-thirty, and at seven we went home. Staggering with weariness, dragging my swollen feet, I covered the few hundred paces that separated me from home. Women poured out of the sausage-casing factory toward me, and each of them was like me in some way, or so it seemed at the time.

They poured out toward me that day their faces different, transformed by fear and worry. A radio snarled from a small café, but no one stopped to listen. Each already knew what she would hear.

"Here it comes again," someone said, hanging out the window, and the man standing on the street below replied: "Here it comes again. It'll be the same thing all over again."

The men's dismay and the women's terror made them all look alike. The old were tossed back into life, and the onrush of emotions made them young again; the young were transported by despair, which aged their pinched, darkened faces. The hot evening overhead came to a complete halt and stopped breathing, and on our street, in the twilight, someone wept loudly in the entryway of a large gray apartment house.

In the evening after supper I went outside again, and for three evenings—through Sunday—I went for a walk. At the corner of the rue Vaugirard, under the group of plane trees that grew there (there had been plans for a square, but they were dropped), a handful of Varvara's friends clustered and spoke quietly in Russian: Musya Meshcherskaya, Petrov, von Moor, Uncle Drozd in his navy coveralls, Madame Churchurazova and her feeble-minded daughter (both bareheaded and in slippers), Vasya Vostronosov, Petya Poleshatov, and others, they too looking either a little older or a little younger. They called each other by their first names and called me Alexandra Evgenievna, as if I were from a different regiment. For three evenings we stood there, and on Sunday I circled through the sobbing, moaning, shouting streets and ended up at the train station, where no one paid anyone any attention, no one reacted to anyone else, and people, drunk with grief, crushed one another in the moving crowd and farewell embraces, stuffing themselves into the heavy, overloaded trains.

But the sky was still exactly the same. And I had the feeling then that a new page was not being turned that evening. No, it was as if someone had gone back through half the book, whipping back through more than twenty-five years with a swish and with a heavy hand dragging all of us back into dreadful, boring repetitions. We had fallen into the same trap. The shutter had snapped shut. Only a moment ago this or that had both been possible, and now it was finished—it had crushed us, knocked us down, and slammed shut.

Like everyone else that winter, I was stuck in my lonely indifference. I had less and less opportunity to save, being the sole breadwinner in the house now. Father was ill, Varvara was getting old and almost never went out to do daywork, she was so busy with Father and the house. Like the true breadwinner that I was, I came home from work to find everything done for me. What kind of Italy could there be now anyway? What kind of dreams could anyone have at all? They withered in the airless expanse of my continuous twilight. For two decades half-childish thoughts had been enough for me. When Ariadna left us, ever since the last time I saw Samoilov, it was as if a star had gone out but its light had been traveling toward me from an infinitely long way away. Now I knew, according to the precise law whereby all things come to an end, that the light would go out.

It was during the June catastrophe that Papa died, as if he couldn't bear what was going on, although what did it matter to him, and vice versa? Then I took the money out of the cookbook. About half of what was there went toward his funeral. Varvara, hot and puffy faced, disheveled, unwashed, stood there and took the bills in her outstretched hand, struck dumb. Then she sat down on my bed and her tears gushed—not over Father but over me, as I understood her, through her sob-laced words:

"She saved! She saved! How did she find the will-power? She hasn't got a warm coat for the winter and never takes a holiday, but she saved! What are you, French or something? Where did you get that? There you have it, the younger generation. Machines, not people. No passion or abandon, nothing but reason and calculation. But us, what about us? Yes, we certainly did know how to live! We never gave a thought to tomorrow and burned our candles at both ends. Never put anything in a bank. They're different now. They know about rainy days. When I was your age I ran fast and loose. Well, you won't have to bury your father in a common grave after all. She saved! Hear that, Evgeny, my friend? That Sasha of ours saved!"

He lay in a ray of sunshine, and there was something noble in his face now that had somehow been lacking before. A light edging ran between his eyelids and his tightly bound mouth. His legs were tied together, too, as were his hands. The effect was that of an ancient mummy. "My child Cordelia! Daughter of mine!" he had whispered to me the evening before, and that memory made me cry, because every time he said that I knew he was remembering Ariadna. On his chest we found a baptismal cross and a worn locket that held two photographs—my mother and Ariadna—probably put there back in Russia. I put the locket on, along with the cross, and for a few days it annoyed, as it caught at my brassiere.

His funeral was quite out of the ordinary. One bright sunny morning a hearse, a nag, and two attendants from the bureau appeared. They loaded the coffin onto the hearse with the help of the concierge, and then both of them sat up front and suggested that Varvara and I sit on the sides, which we did. We rode at a jog-trot, holding on to the coffin and tucking our feet underneath us and the whole time thanking God that everything had worked out as it had. There wasn't a soul on the streets of Paris, if you didn't count German guards. For some reason I remember especially well the square at the Church Montrouge, where there was no one to the right or the left, ahead or behind. The avenue du Maine was blank all the way to the horizon, and the avenue d'Orléans was pristine. All the doors and all the shops were closed. It seemed to me that there were people standing in windows pointing at us. At the Port d'Orléans two German soldiers wearing full battle dress and shifting from foot to foot asked for our pass, after which we jog-trotted on. The boulevard Peripherique, absolutely devoid of human life to the right and left, reminded me of a movie I'd seen many years before in which a scientist blanketed Paris in instantaneous sleep, everything ground to a halt, and only the lovers on the uppermost platform of the Eiffel Tower escaped.

The shutdown at the laundry lasted exactly eleven days, after which everything started in again—with the difference that now we were doing laundry for German soldiers rather than private clients. Soap and lye were requisitioned, as was fuel, and the linen was dropped off and taken away by truck.

We blundered into a winter without bread, lard, wool, or coal. Simple everyday household items around us gradually started to wear out and break down, but there was nothing to replace them with. The matches wouldn't light anymore—as in Russia once upon a time— a sure sign of impending disaster. Now it was just the two of us, Varvara and I, and when I came home in the evening there were two places set at our three-legged kitchen table. We sat opposite one another. She, nearly gray, heavy and lame, but still outlining her eyes in dark pencil, was beginning to be ashamed of her harmless little pleasures: drinking, smoking, sitting with von Moor, who was himself now quite bald and very ragged, for an evening by a darkened lampshade. Skinny but broad in the bones, with hair of indeterminate color and a crudely asymmetrical face (the left side was a little smaller than the right), I always dressed in the same dark green skirt and gray top, leafed through a library book (Varvara's taste—a novel based on the lives of counts and princes), or shuffled an old deck of cards to lay out the only solitaire I knew before Petrov and von Moor came and sat down to a game of hearts.

Although her dark pudgy fingers were swollen from the cold, Varvara still raised her little finger high when she held her cup of some suspicious concoction that smelled vaguely of chamomile and pepper. The saccharin in it fizzed because of the baking soda, and ragged slices of stale bread spread with apple butter completed the refreshments. Usually everyone crowded into the tiny kitchen, where it was warmer because there was gas. It was there, when the guests had gone, that we undressed, washed up as best we could over the gray basin, and ran, each to her own icy bed, where a hot-water bottle rolled around under the covers.

The guests emerged onto a dark staircase, struck matches, and clapped their sides looking for a flashlight, only to find it and discover that the battery was dead— the property of all batteries, lamps, and lighters in bad times. They emerged into the dark gloom of the street, where there wasn't a single light, into the urban gloom of the street, into the urban autumn night that was like a night in the forest or the fields—no fire, no voices, no shadows. When there was a moon, people were a little bolder. They took bigger steps and crossed the pavement with glad hearts. When it was raining you couldn't hear people coming, and sometimes two of you would collide head-on: a stranger's repulsive warmth would touch your face; a stranger's weight would graze your body. When snow fell after the New Year it was brighter for a few nights from the white patches and the starry reflections. And you had to chide yourself, stepping around the drifts, groping around the corners of buildings, not to misjudge the intersection, that this was Paris—silk, lace, champagne—not Oboyan or Cheboksary torn between Whites and Reds, not 1920 but 1940, 1941, 1942, and the earth was revolving around the sun as before.

Even the conversation reminded me of my Petersburg childhood. If on a lofty theme, then it was inevitably about the fact that nine-tenths of mankind were always half-starved so we Parisians were only getting our fair share. If not, then it was about where you could get oil and when they would start distributing potatoes. Hitherto indissoluble knots unraveled with ease. The words "arrest" and "deportation" were bandied back and forth like small change. And in that shattered, hungry, cold life, any light of memory, any ray of hope, died inside me.

That winter many people left, some to work in Germany, others to fight in Russia, others illegally to the South. Neither Musya Meshcherskaya, the gypsy with dangling earrings, nor Petya Poleshatov, that bore, liar, and glutton, nor Uncle Drozd, the Saint George's cross holder and cabdriver, were among our number any longer. Petrov and von Moor kept coming, however. Both worked in a repair shop attached to a garage the Germans had requisitioned, and they brought either a head of cabbage, or a kilo of sugar, or simply a counterfeit bread ration card, all of which I paid for. If my wages didn't cover it, I took more money out of the cookbook.

Varvara limped from the kitchen to the bedrooms, sprinkling cigarette ashes in the Lenten rutabaga pudding. The guitar Petrov loved to hold—he didn't play—hung right there in the kitchen. All three of them sat around the table on creaky chairs surrounded by brown walls and toasted each other with a little "native booze," munched on pickles, and drank eight cups of tea apiece. After she had had something to drink and smoke, Varvara laughed playfully, and they called her "Barbishonchik," as they had forty years before. They even pretended to be jealous of one another. In any event, they took turns hugging her around the waist, squeezing her leg under the table, and kissing her rough pudgy fingers. Von Moor wielded notably greater rights over her than Petrov did. Meaningful, emotion-laden allusions sometimes popped up between her and von Moor, allusions that made Petrov sulk and strum the guitar strings.

"Come out here! We would be honored by your presence!" they both exclaimed.

I had nowhere to hide in that chilly apartment, so I joined them in the kitchen because it was warm there.

"Alexandra Evgenievna, don't condemn us for behaving like children. As a certain Spaniard once said, passion is life."

I sat down between them. And scrawny little Petrov, with his awful thick lips and sunflower-yellow eyes, kissed me on the shoulder, pretending to be drunk. Varvara, outraged, slapped him on the hand with her heavily perfumed and slightly grubby handkerchief.

There were two bottles on the table. Varvara liked to put old envelopes under them to protect the oilcloth. But this time, placed ingenuously underneath the bottle of red *ordinaire*, was an unopened letter addressed to me, and when I saw it it was already spotted with wine.

"Forgive me, Sasha. It's my fault, my fault!" cried Varvara. "It's been there two days already, hidden under the bread. I kept forgetting to tell you."

"The gas company?" von Moor showed interest and gave a loud laugh.

"The tax collector," Petrov replied and solicitously passed me a dirty fork to open the envelope.

The letter was very short. The longer you wait, the shorter the letter is. Actually, it ought to have consisted of one simple appeal: so many years. . . .

"Dear Alexandra Evgenievna, I would like to see you. I've known for a long time that you are in Paris, too. Once I even caught a glimpse of you (two years ago). However, I don't know how you feel about me. Perhaps not entirely friendly? I will wait for you this coming Saturday in the café on your corner at about nine. I have something to say to you. I have a small request for you. It's a matter of my conscience. In case you don't remember me, I'm your sister Ariadna's husband, Sergei Samoilov."

I read the letter ten times over, and from it I realized two essential things: first, that Ariadna was no longer with him; and second, that he had been in Paris for a long time but had never given me a thought until now.

Samoilov's letter in my hand, I left the kitchen, went to my room, and sat there in the dark and cold for rather a long time. I was amazed that I had felt no presentiment. You would have expected a hard frost and pitch blackness; famine, terror; matches that didn't light; and grass growing in the streets come spring. Who could turn up to complete a picture like that if not he? But the letter was a total surprise. I turned on the radio very softly and spun the dial without seeing. Suddenly someone said gently and with all the conviction the human voice is capable of:

"You're still here? You're still here? But I swear to you, they're waiting for you. Everything's all set for your arrival. The orange trees are blooming in the gardens, and from the windows of the white villa you can see to the bottom of the sea. And you know, in the evening dark blue dragonflies like you've never seen flit around the garden. It's time for you to go. It's time!"

A moment's silence. The thunder of applause. And, apparently, the heavy rustle of a falling curtain.

He had seen me two years before, but until now he hadn't given me a single thought.

But why should he think of me? Why should he remember that his wild, slender, bright-eyed wife had any relatives—a crazy father who had been adamantly opposed to him, and the boy or girl sibling of uncertain age whom Ariadna herself had abandoned so easily, whose letters she didn't answer, and who had never played any role in her life whatsoever. They were people of another world, and they doubtless would have been stunned had they learned that Ariadna became a minor actress, at first acting in minor but avant-garde foreign dramas and later in homegrown political plays. Together the two had knocked around the theaters, first in Petersburg and later in the Crimea. She kept aiming for the Tairov, but there never happened to be an opening for them in Moscow, and for several years they lived in Simferopol, where they acted until Ariadna contracted typhoid fever and died. Then (that was in 1928) he moved in with his sister in Tver, where he was arrested in some factory incident which his sister's husband had been mixed up in. He served a short prison term, four months altogether, and there was even a trial, after which he was sent to a camp on the White Sea Canal. There he met real political exiles, sectarians for the most part—Anabaptists, Old Believers, and Seventh-Day Adventists. And finally—through the snow, forests, a virgin Karelian birch grove, past a lake of such beauty and calm that he knew he had to go back someday, past border guards—from a distance, when they were buried in the snowdrifts, their helmets looked like dog heads and their bent sabers stuck out from under their greatcoats like tails—past all that, from snowdrift to snowdrift, carrying a hunk of stolen bread under his shirt, until he reached a hut that stood on stilts and had whimsical lintels, vermilion shutters, and blue smoke coming from its lacquered chimney, where a little flag popped in the wind—a Finnish police station. Did you think it was the toy house in the fairy tale where the gingerbread dwarf lived?

"Two years of Helsinki and five years of Berlin, first as a truck driver, then as a magician, then as a cabdriver. I moved to Paris, but I won't stay here forever. No, no. I might leave very soon. There's nothing to keep me here. Where will I go? East. East, naturally. I don't like oceans or islands. I like firm ground. That's why I'm in such a hurry. That is, I could have before, but there wasn't this real ne-necess—"

Only at this point did I notice his way of speaking without finishing his words.

"I'll explain my reason presently. This is very important to me. This is a request. . . . This . . ."

He encircled and gripped the little round table our beer was on.

He had been plain, pale-faced, red-nosed, and his smile had been bleak. He was exactly the same, but his intelligent, sparkling eyes still cut right through me.

But apart from that his outward appearance had taken on that Russian shabbiness I knew so well. It was a special shabbiness that began and ended with our life abroad. Like fate, it missed a few—the dandies and the hell-raisers—and absorbed all the others, with their shiny clothes, frayed cuffs, worn ties, and dingy handkerchiefs. Despite the fact that Samoilov looked more like an actor or a messenger than a former officer who was now a machine operator at Renault, his shabbiness was no different from the shabbiness of Varvara's friends.

"I look at your sweater," I said, "and it seems like the same one as before. Do you remember 'The Tattered Cloak'?"

He shook his head. "I never wore any cloak."

"I'm not saying you wore one. You made it up.

Remember, there was a part about Don Quixote and Lear?"

He looked attentively into my face, and suddenly something happened in his, something flared in his memory.

"That wasn't me, that was Zvonkov who thought that up. I had this comrade, he died in Siberia."

"But no, that was you. I know. I'm sure. Have you really forgotten? It was an old-fashioned pelerine, and it was too far gone to mend."

We both fell silent. I thought about Ariadna, about her translucent face, about her breasts, which glowed when she bathed in the tub. About that night she left us, tying the ribbons on her hood and taking a bundle on her arm, an age-old peasant woman motion. And I thought about Samoilov, about the fact that he had lived two-thirds of his life and that this meeting held some special meaning for him. And also about how when he looked at me he didn't see me.

I never get upset, I'm generally very calm, but that evening I got terribly upset, as if something depended on this meeting, and my agitation interfered with my listening. I can recall the dim light of the lamp in the smelly café, the spots of dampness along the walls, and Samoilov, of course, who turned out to be shorter than I had thought. In my childhood he had seemed tall.

"I called you here on what is for me a very important matter, Alexandra Evgenievna," he said, and he smiled at me in a new way, with his whole mouth. "I would like to ask your father's forgiveness. The kind of forgiveness that is given when people repent. Could you help me do that?"

My face must have registered astonishment.

"I've sinned against him, sinned greatly. I took his daughter away from him. It was worse than stealing. I nearly killed him. The longer I put it off the more it torments me."

Then I laughed right in his face.

"Do you really believe that nonsense? You must be out of your mind! Are there really people who believe that nonsense?"

He let go of the table, which he had been clutching all that time.

"I don't know what to say to that. Perhaps I'd do better to say nothing. Or to say that yes, there are people like that, who believe. You're foolish to imagine they don't. You know yourself that there are quite a few of them."

I reached for the old worn-out cigarette case from which he had just taken a cigarette.

"It's amazing," I said, raising and lowering my shoulders, "amazing, Sergei Sergeevich, that you think about things like that and talk about things like that. And you want to repent. Only my father—"

But he cut in.

"In the North, in the camp, I met people like that. . . . I could tell you—"

A disturbance broke out in the small café where we were sitting. They were looking for someone's umbrella. We too had to get up. The waiter crawled under the benches on his hands and knees. A shaggy dog dozing by the extinguished stove started growling and opened his purulent eyes, and the curtain over the door (a torn billiard cloth) fluttered without letting the lavender light of the lamps escape when someone went in or out. It reeked of cheap red wine, as do all little Paris cafés, and your feet scuffled softly over the wet sawdust on the unswept floor. Wherever you looked your eye fell on wet rags, which from time to time that same waiter used to mop up puddles that had formed in the corners.

Samoilov's hands were large and clean, and he wore a slim wedding band on his skinny ring finger. I thought: "Where did that ring come from? And just what does he do?"

After a pause he suddenly asked:

"Am I keeping you? You must be busy. Couldn't I see your father? I want, I have to ask his for——"

I replied:

"My father is dead."

He remained seated, frozen. At that moment I realized that one could never find out what he was thinking, what he was feeling, from his eyes, his vivid, intelligent, eyes.

"What do you know," he said slowly, softly. "In that case, forgive me for disturbing you needlessly."

That was all. He put down a stack of change—for the beer that he and I had drunk. Our handshake was firm and brief, and after that he turned left and I right. And it was so dark that no one could have seen my face.

The kitchen that night was full of smoke and fumes because Varvara was frying pancakes. Petrov, von Moor, and Vasya Vostronosov, who was back from Brittany on leave (he had a scar over half his face, and still remembered General Wrangel), were sitting there and were already on their third apiece. I sat down with them immediately, crowding in. I had a drink and was soon laughing at how von Moor wrapped his pancake on his fork. And when I laughed like that, I could tell that my laugh was beginning to sound like a cry—the very image of Papa's and Varvara's. It runs in the family. And the vague feeling that I was powerless to do anything about my life made me laugh even louder. But it was better to laugh like that, with everyone around, than to cry alone into a stiff pillow, under a thin striped blanket, in a room that was unheated all winter. After all, this was my life.

Our possessions are becoming more and more fragile. Each is the last: there won't be another. People grow transparent, and when they leave I have the feeling that they are just about to come back. Everything is disappearing: bread, paper, soap, thread, kerosene. The world is going to hell, but among it all a blessed light is burning quietly for me—not from the star, which went out a long time ago, but from a new source, like a fog filled with the trembling light of stars.

I can't explain when or how it came back. I no longer have my old ability to perceive with the unerring perspicacity of a child, the flair I once had. But I know that in our gloomy life, as I get duller and weaker, I am picking it up once again with special strength, special fervor. What it is that is being revived in the face of everything (as it was twenty years ago) inside me might— very approximately and clumsily—be called a search for grandeur, a thirst for wisdom, love, and truth, although all those words are just part of one infinite thing that I seem to skirt without actually seeing. What kind of grandeur could visit a life of such poverty and vulgarity? What kind of wisdom is there in my work at the laundry or in my evenings spent in my aunt's kitchen? Where in my life is love, which has never touched me? And can I really be affected by truth, to which I never gave a moment's thought? Like twenty years ago, though, the sterile receptivity of my soul is becoming keener, as it is destined to be perhaps twice or three times altogether in a human life. And involuntarily I begin to think that one day, maybe in 1960, I will be faced once again with an experience that is something like it.

But where will Samoilov be then, and how exactly will he give me the signal?

The Black Pestilence

I

THE EARRINGS HAD BEEN at the municipal pawnshop for nine years. Much had happened in the world, events had taken place which had dazzled and shaken mankind. But the earrings remained in their numbered box, and for nine years I had paid interest on them. When your money is in the bank, everyone knows that it isn't actually there but circulating in the capitalist stream, returning as the need arises. But earrings, old clothes, gramophones, and silver spoons lie there while you pay interest, and later, should you stop paying it, they slip away forever.

The municipal pawnshop in Paris is one of the most repugnant places I know. It stinks of disinfectant, the walls are painted gray, there are two rows of benches. Everyone knows why people come there. The clerk in the gray jacket takes the item, gives it a number, carries it away, and a few minutes later calls out:

"Twenty-three! Seven hundred."

That means they are giving you seven hundred francs for whatever it is you've brought. You walk up to the window and collect your money, unless the sum is too small, and then you ask them to give you back your property and you go away. There's nowhere to go, though.

Sometimes when you pawn a valuable you can ask them to go up a little, but here only gold, platinum, and diamonds are considered precious. Rubies, emeralds, and sapphires are described as colored stones and they fetch next to nothing. Pearls fetch nothing at all—they have a way of dying when separated from their owner.

Side by side on the long benches people sit awaiting sentence. Nine years ago I sat there too, between a woman who had brought four old sheets, and got nothing for them, and a man with a beard, who looked like Lenin. He had brought some ancient book, and they offered him two hundred francs for it. He tried to explain that it was a 1747 edition, but the shout rang out:

"Yes or no?"

And he said, "Yes."

For the earrings, as I had expected, they gave me a wad of money. Each held a diamond the size of a small button, and both were of the purest white. Usually the municipal pawnshop gives one-third of the value, and I thought: "Yes, that's right, how many times did she tell me that if the earrings were sold, two people could live on them for half a year or so; that meant that by myself I could live on them for an entire year."

The money was spent that very day to pay the bills for her hospital and funeral. Only one bill was left unpaid: the last two blood transfusions. I had to sell her little gold watch. The jeweler who bought it told me to come back in a week.

"If I sell the watch for a good price," he said, "you'll get a little more."

When I came back a week later, he said:

"I owe you another ten percent. I sold the watch yesterday, and well. I never make more than twenty percent. That's my rule."

I thanked him.

"I like rules," he added, with an embarrassed smile. "Some people find them tiresome. But I think to live without rules would be despicable."

That was nine years ago. During that time I never had the money to redeem the earrings. And now I had decided to leave, to go to America. I'm not a particularly decisive character, but I told myself: "The time has come, you can't go on living like this." My visa had arrived a week before and my place on the boat had already been reserved. I now needed money for the ticket and for the first months of my new life. The solution was to sell the earrings. Every sum had been carefully calculated; I don't like sitting around in the evenings with a pencil in my hand, doing calculations, but I know that everyone does, so I did too. That arithmetic was a small part of a great truth: know thyself.

In order to sell the earrings I had to redeem them. As for redeeming them myself, that was out of the question. So I went back to the jeweler.

He examined the pawnshop ticket closely.

"Yes, I've handled this kind of thing before," he said, "and I'll redeem your earrings tomorrow morning. Usually they give one-third the value. It looks like these could be sold for good money. Come by tomorrow, at midday."

I arrived the next day. There was no one in the shop, but behind the curtain that separated the store from the workshop I could sense a presence. I coughed and began to inspect the rings and brooches under the glass; the whole shop ticked away with clocks, large and small.

He came out, holding open a velvet case lined in white satin.

"I have some bad news for you," he said. "If I'd known, I wouldn't have bothered. One stone is worthless. It has the black pestilence. Here, you can see for yourself."

He put a large glass lens against my eye, and I bent over the case. And as I looked at the stone, which was completely black, the earth seemed to cave in beneath my feet; a chasm was opening up and I was flying headlong into it, buildings were crashing down around me, San Francisco, Messina, Lisbon—earthquake scenes from old films which had somehow stuck in my memory.

"This couldn't have happened in nine years. This takes a million years," said the jeweler, and there was something mournful in his voice, in his gray head tilted to one side. "I don't understand how they could have made such a mistake. They never make mistakes. They have an expert there. Possibly he looked at the good stone and not at the other. You'd do well if you managed to get the same money that they were pawned for. To reimburse me. I can't sell these earrings."

"You can't? But who can?"

"That is going to take some thinking. You're in big trouble."

"When do you need your money back?"

He looked at me over his glasses.

"Put yourself in my position," he said in his even voice. "I redeemed your item, I took a sum of money out of my pocket. I would like to have it by this evening. As a matter of fact, I'm taking a risk, as you might not come back at all."

He brought me the telephone book and I started to search through it for the addresses of the jewelers that he recommended.

"Sell them to whoever offers you the most," he said. "There's Oginson. Sometimes he gives a good price."

"Oginson . . . O . . ." I began to flip through the book, forward and back. Everything in my mind was getting hazy. "How odd, N comes right after M. There's no O for some reason."

"O comes after N," he said patiently.

"O comes after N," I muttered. "There's no O in this book at all. Obviously the pages must have been torn out."

"That's impossible," he said sadly. "O was always there."

"Does it come before or after P?"

"Look right after N!" he shouted, suddenly afraid.

I found Oginson. We both calmed down.

"You know what else I would do if I were you?" he said. "I would go back to the pawnshop and try to pawn them for the original price, if they'll give it."

I thanked him for his advice, and put the glass lens in my eye one more time. Millions of years. A black pestilence. The stone sat fast in its gold prongs.

"I hope," said the jeweler, "that you don't suspect me of switching your stone?"

"No," I replied. "That hadn't occurred to me."

"That would be despicable"—and he walked to the corner—"I have rules."

"I swear to you the thought hadn't crossed my mind!"

"I believe you. And they couldn't have done it at the pawnshop. They seal the box immediately, no one can get to it."

We looked at each other.

"You know," he said, "sometimes in life there's a fact with no explanation, a question with no answer. It's rare, but it happens. Once I was sitting in my room and a letter disappeared from my desk. It was worth a lot of money. It was never found. No one could have taken it, no one came in. But it vanished. Yes, the more I think about it, the more I'm convinced that their expert had to have looked at the other stone."

Messina and Lisbon, I thought, and the vanishing letter *O*, and it was all a nightmare. Just that morning everything had seemed so simple, and now the journey seemed inconceivable. But there was no time to lose. I wrapped the case up in my handkerchief.

"Don't lose it," said the jeweler. "And please, bring the money today."

I went back to the pawnshop. There was a crowd of people in that squalid place. They gave me a number—604—and I sat down, between a woman with an old blanket on her knees, which had clearly been given back to her, and who was evidently at a loss for what to do now, and a very smartly dressed older man who looked like Nicholas the Second. I saw that he had brought a tortoiseshell fan.

"I can't think of any place in the world that is more vile," I thought.

"Six-oh-four!" they shouted from the window.

This time they looked at both stones and the sum offered was half the original.

"This is a misunderstanding," I said, upset. "These earrings were redeemed this morning. You had given much more for them."

The man in the gray jacket looked at me for a second, went behind the partition, and came back with the case.

"You're getting money for one stone," he said, and I saw that he had a cataract in one eye. "The other's worthless. You can take it back."

The stones were just like his eyes: one was completely worthless.

I passed through halls, up and down stairs, across courtyards. I saw five or six jewelers that day. No one would give me anything for the second earring, and they wouldn't give me enough for the first to allow me to pay off my debt. It was almost six o'clock when I finally reached Oginson's. It was a private apartment, not a shop, and a woman opened the door, which was locked by a chain.

"Who are you?"

I didn't know what to say.

"Who sent you?"

I explained. She went away, her slippers scuffing. A fairly long time passed. Finally, the door opened and

I was led down a long, dark passageway into a long, dark study. A fat man sat motionless behind a perfectly bare, smoothly polished desk. Two canaries chirped in their cage, by the window, directly over his head.

He was fat, pale, and old, immobile, and throughout our conversation he was reflected like a block of marble in the smooth surface of that vast bare desk.

"How much do you want?" he asked, having examined the stones, moving only his wrists. I named the figure I owed. He focused on some point beyond me.

"You'd have a hard time getting that much for one stone, and then only if it were remade into a ring," he said. "I don't need the other one."

A silence ensued. The canaries shook their cage. The noise of the street filtered through the closed windows. There was a smell of dust and tobacco. I was trembling inside.

He examined the earrings once more.

"This pestilence," he said slowly, "has been in it from the very beginning. Before man even existed, this plague was already in it."

I took a breath.

"But I'll give you your price. And I've changed my mind. I'll take the second stone, too."

He took his wallet out of his pocket, and counted out the money. I said a loud "Good-bye!" as I walked out, but he didn't answer. On the street I stood for a moment, in shock: both Messina and Lisbon had rolled over me but I was still alive. I dropped off the money, returned home, hungry and tired, and collapsed on the bed and lay absolutely still until it was dark. If someone had given me a bomb that evening and said: "Throw it

at whomever you want," I would have thrown it at . . .
whom would I have thrown it at? The first jeweler? The
second jeweler? The man in the gray jacket? Mr. Oginson?
The municipal pawnshop's expert? No, I told myself. I
would have thrown it at that horrible hall which reeks
of disinfectant, I would have thrown it at the entrance,
at the sign: LIBERTÉ, ÉGALITÉ, FRATERNITÉ. But, as my
fellow lodger, a man without profession, Michel Néron,
says, "Russians always manage to land on their feet, however tricky the circumstances. Russians are just plain
lucky."

"Lucky at what?" I cried out later that night when
he dropped by. "How? At what?"

But he, of course, didn't know what to say; as he
didn't like shouting, he shrugged his shoulders, walked
out without a word, and went to his room.

The next day was Saturday, and when Sunday came
I had time to think through what I should do. If I tried
to sell all the things that belonged to me, instead of giving
them away, I would only be able to get together about
a quarter of what I needed to pay for the ticket. That
much was clear without doing any calculations. Where
was I to get the rest? In my mind, I ran through my
possessions. Even if I were to sell everything, leaving just
the clothes on my back, my razor, and my toothbrush—
it wouldn't be enough. There was no solution. I even
started to consider going tomorrow morning to cancel
my boat ticket. There wasn't anyone to borrow that kind
of money from either. To write to Druzhin in Chicago
would have been absolutely pointless, for one very simple
reason, which I won't mention now.

"There are two engagement rings," I counted, "and

books, and clothes, and a radio, old, but still good." The day stretched on and on and I had to come to some kind of decision. In fact it seemed at moments as if everything had already been decided, and that there was nothing left to do, except to stop thinking about it.

Between five and six o'clock the hall clerk knocked at my door: "Someone's asking for you downstairs," he said. "Some young lady."

I smoothed my hair, put on a jacket, and went down, feeling no curiosity at all. A young woman I didn't know was waiting for me on the lower landing. She was wearing trousers and had a cigarette in her mouth. There was no one around. A radio was wailing somewhere.

"How do you do," she said in Russian, extending her hand. "My name is Alya Ivanova. May I come up?"

"How do you do," I replied. "My room is a mess, forgive me. If you like, we can go up."

Twice, she glanced rapidly at me, and then glanced once again as if my face were unusual in some way, although my looks are rather ordinary.

When we walked into the room, she looked around at the walls, the furniture, and sat down on the only chair, by the window. I sat down on the bed.

"I don't know how to explain all this to you," she said, looking at me with intense black eyes. Her face was slender, with a tinge of ill health, but you could see her energy and strength in her hands. "I found out that you're going to America. Don't ask who told me. There's a man who sells addresses. He knows about everyone who's leaving. You go to him, he takes out a sheet of paper, and there it is, by arrondissement. That's for when you want to rent a room."

I replied quickly:

"What does this have to do with me? Go and ask downstairs, ask the landlady."

She put out her cigarette.

"If I ask the landlady, she'll either give it to whoever's next on her list, or else she'll give it to me for a rent that's three times more than yours. Your rent is cheap and they can't raise it. If I move in here with you and stay a month, the room would stay mine at the same rent. I could move in tomorrow morning."

"But as you can see, there's only one bed here."

"That doesn't matter. I can sleep on the couch."

In the corner, near the washstand, was a three-legged sofa, barely big enough for a child to sleep on.

"Haven't you ever heard of making money this way? According to the law, I have to live here with you for at least a month in order for the room to be mine. It will be awkward for you, I know, I'll be in your way, but what's to be done? I'll be paying you for it."

I coughed.

"I'll pay you part of the money tomorrow, when I move in, and the rest, let's say, in two weeks. We're both taking a risk: you might kick me out; I might not pay you the last part. I've been told that some people bring in a third party, a witness; if you want, I'm happy to do that. But in my opinion it's better to handle this sort of business without witnesses. Maybe we could do it all on trust?"

She fell silent but kept her eyes on me. Evidently she was waiting for me to say that you shouldn't do anything on trust. I said:

"You paid to find out my address, and you're planning to pay me. Why, if you're rich, are you looking for a cheap room?"

"You're funny!" She smiled and I saw how pretty she looked with a smile. Her eyes shone even more brightly. "I don't have a lot of money, but by giving you five thousand francs now, later I'll pay six hundred a month. At present I don't have my own place and I pay two thousand. Do you see?"

For five thousand francs, I could at least try and work something out, I thought.

"Right now I don't have my own place," she repeated, and all of a sudden a shadow flitted across her face. "I can't stay there any longer. I have to leave."

I got up, walked around the room, and sat down on the bed again.

"Let's talk about this as calmly as possible," I said. "Suppose I stay here for another month, which is more or less what I was planning to do. You would stay here, with me sleeping on the couch, of course, not you. We could also put the mattress on the floor, which would actually be even more comfortable. One without a mattress on the bed; the other on the mattress on the floor. When do you go out in the morning?"

"I don't."

"Don't you work?"

"I work in the evenings."

"Well, that works out even better. You would get in late, I'd already be asleep. In the morning I'd leave— and you'd be asleep."

"Why are you so concerned about sleeping?" she asked. "I've slept on the ground in summer camps since

I was a child, in a sleeping bag, in a tent with everyone piled up together. I'm not worried about that at all. I thought you'd be more interested in putting it all down on paper. I do want to say one thing: this is strictly an arrangement between you and me."

"But you and I are making an illegal deal, so there's nothing to put down on paper."

"Illegal? Pardon me, but there's nothing illegal about this deal. You're not passing me off as a sister, or as a wife. You're not deceiving anyone. We live together for a month, and then you leave—we aren't obliged to say that it's forever. I'll keep the room, and a year from when you leave, it will automatically transfer to my name."

"Couldn't you move in just before I move out?"

"So that they could throw me out the next day?"

She opened her purse and showed me a wad of notes.

"Here's two thousand, which you'll get tomorrow. I'll pay you the other two thousand in two weeks' time and one thousand just before you leave. That's how it's done, apparently."

I stood up, walked over to her, and surprised myself by saying:

"I want the whole five thousand this week. I have to pay for my ticket. I can't wait."

That didn't frighten her in the slightest; it even seemed to please her.

"Fine," she said. "So be it. I had no idea you were so greedy."

And she smiled, looking at me fearlessly.

"Come on, if you have the time, let's have some

coffee," I said, unable to sit like that any longer looking at her. We went downstairs and out on the street. By the door, on the pavement, stood the landlady, Madame Beauvaux, and as we walked past her Alya Ivanova calmly placed her hand on my shoulder, as is the custom with Parisian women, announcing to her and to the passersby and to the whole city that I was her property, her captive.

We sat down at a table in a café, and Alya, having barely sipped her coffee, went to make a phone call. The phone booth was three steps away from me, and I could hear fragments of the conversation: she was talking with someone called Zina and telling her that "he" was asking for the entire amount by next week. She asked her to ask Jeannot what he thought, what she should do. Then, evidently in answer to a question, she replied: "No, he's clearly honest. Absolutely! But he insists."

We sat there for half an hour. She smoked, thoughtfully and quietly. I looked at her: her body seemed very long, as if she had been stretched. Her hair was smooth and short, her ears narrow, her face an even oval, and her neck a little bit too long. Her complexion, white or pale, was exceptionally pure and clear, and her whole being gave the impression of clarity, there was never a trace of hidden meaning, ambiguity, or enigma in her eyes or in her smile. That impression came, no doubt, from her clear black eyes, from the way she looked at things around her and, at times, at me.

My conscience was anything but easy, though. I felt embarrassed at the thought of taking her money. The month I faced living with her in a single room first seemed wretchedly inconvenient in the simplest everyday sense—

no sleep, no privacy, constantly feeling cramped and in-hibited—and then seemed suddenly easy, silly even. In any case, it was going to be unlike anything else I'd ex-perienced.

She moved in the following day. She had one suit-case, old, black, and tattered. In order not to embarrass me, the only thing she took out was a flashy theatrical costume, a wide raspberry-colored tulle skirt with a se-quined bodice. It had to be hung on the door, on the hook, and nearly filled the room. Together we dragged the mattress onto the floor and each of us made our own bed (she had brought two sheets and a small pillow), after which she washed up, changed her clothes, penciled her eyes, and dressed in that raspberry skirt, trying not to crush it, sat down on the edge of the chair, and told me that she danced at the Empire, that she had two numbers in the show, that she had been working with a partner for four years already, and at one time they'd even appeared in the Casino de Paris. Ten years before, while still in her teens, she had studied with Olga Osi-povna and had thought she would be a ballerina, but "fate" had decided differently.

"Who's your partner?" I asked.

"My partner broke my finger three months ago, but I can't get rid of him: they'd fire us both. We're no use without each other."

"Did he break it on purpose or by accident?"

"On purpose, of course, and it was during a per-formance! He didn't like something, he's so nervous and touchy. He grabbed me after catching me in a leap and broke my little finger out of spite. I was in the hospital three days after that. They wanted to operate, but I got by."

She extended the little finger on her left hand and examined it closely.

"Crooked?"

"No, I don't think so."

"Well, I think so," she said, and she frowned. The corners of her mouth drooped, but a minute later she was smiling at me.

"I'll leave the costume at the Empire, I'll set it up, otherwise it's going to clutter up your room. Nice costume? You like it? Goncharova designed it for me."

When she had gone and I was left alone, a thousand thoughts assailed me. The sensation of humiliation, impotence, of all my human worthlessness and weakness gripped me. I felt—for the umpteenth time—my disgraceful inability to wake myself up, to regenerate, to live like other people. What would Druzhin say if he knew? It was a pity that I couldn't write to him about it! Then I considered everything from the perspective of Michel Néron, from the standpoint of a sober and sensible man. Yesterday a fine precious stone was switched on me for a bad one, and today someone moved into my room. Yesterday I made no attempt to complain, and today I didn't drive her out. Some people are like steel springs, as resilient as tennis balls. It was quite clear that Alya wasn't going to pay me anything, and that the whole deal with Oginson had been fixed up beforehand.

But that only lasted for one moment, and then my thoughts took a new tack: the old wooden screens that closed off the washstand and the stool with the spirit lamp, the skillet, and the teakettle were going to play a leading role in our future life together. They were easy to move and set up, to shift this way and that; however, as the first few days showed, I was the only one who had any need of screens. Alya didn't need them at all: accustomed in theaters to dressing and undressing wherever and in front of whomever she had to, she shed her clothing calmly and without a hint of embarrassment, down to her little black knickers and narrow black brassiere, and went to wash herself. And her body, on which each muscle was developed and which fed her by its artistry, was just like her face: pure, clear, and yet slightly incorporeal.

On Wednesday morning she gave me the money, and I paid for my ticket. The two engagement rings made up the balance. By the end of the first week, our life together had already taken on a reassuringly routine aspect; the only thing which preoccupied me was the thought of having taken money for something that, in essence, did not belong to me. I got up in the morning at seven o'clock while Alya slept soundly, her face to the wall; at eight I left (at the time I was working for an architect selecting colored tiles for mosaics and sometimes I even did sketches for those mosaics, which earned me the description of "artist"). I got back at eight-thirty in the evening, having put in overtime, since the work was there. When I came in, having eaten already, Alya usually wasn't there. Everything in the room had been carefully tidied, the mattress had been pushed under the bed, a glass of anemones stood on the table, and her beads hung from a nail by the window. The coffeepot was full of coffee; I heated it up and drank it, went to bed at twelve o'clock, and had usually dozed off before her return. She came in at about one and when she turned on the table lamp immediately blocked off the light.

About ten days before my departure, I woke up in the night and saw her sitting in her old robe at the table, eating a chocolate bar and some bread and reading a book. The lamp was shaded with something dark blue. The blue light fell on her bare leg, on her long, extended, pale instep. She couldn't tear herself away from the book. And her profile, bent so attentively over the page, her tiny black head, the sight of her long gaunt hand raking her hair, for some reason suddenly made my heart ache; I experienced a strange happiness from the fact that she was there, and so close to me.

"Time to sleep," I said softly.

She started, removed her hand, smiled.

"How are you doing down there on the floor? Can't you sleep?"

"I'm fine. I love it on the floor. But, what do you care about me? Why do you ask?"

Still smiling, she continued to read, and I shut my eyes and began listening to the sounds that reached me: the occasional scraping of her chair; the pages of her book being turned; her chocolate bar between her teeth; and little by little, in that harmony of sounds that oscillated around me, I began to fall asleep. Only one thought, somewhere deep down in my conscience, poisoned my happiness: her money.

A few days later, as I was leaving the office, during lunch, I ran into Attorney N., whom I hadn't seen for a long time. We were both delighted.

"You've been sent to me by fate," I told him. "You know, only yesterday I was thinking about you. I wanted to stop by for some advice."

We went to get some lunch together, and I let him talk about himself. He complained about some relatives of his wife's with whom he had some tangled financial relations. Then, having exhausted that theme, he asked me about my "case."

"Or better yet, maybe we should go back to my office?"

It turned out to be quite close by, and there, to the constant ringing of telephones, I told him about Alya and asked him whether they would evict her from my room or let her stay after I left.

"They have to let her stay," he said. "She's absolutely right. Good for her. No one can kick her out, nor can they raise the rent. She's been clever. And you, my dear friend, have been had. I could have found you a much better customer. Why didn't you come to me?"

"I had no idea. And you don't think it was dishonorable on my part to take her money?"

"Dishonorable? What a word! Everyone does that nowadays. You'd simply be a fool if you let a chance like that slip. And she was lucky. Incredibly lucky. You can't imagine the things that happen. Right now I've got a case coming to trial: the person didn't move out. A month passed, another, a third, and the two of them are still living there. I tell her (in this case she was supposed to have left and he to have stayed), I tell her: 'Madame, you gave your word'—in addition to her word, of course, I had seen both her passport and her ticket—'and now you sit there as if you were pinned down. You took the money but you haven't gone anywhere!' And she says to me: 'Where am I supposed to go? I like it here, I've got no place to go, we're getting along fine.' That's what she thinks, but he's taking her to court. Quite possibly my mother-in-law thinks we're getting along fine, too."

Then came the last Sunday. On Sunday Alya had matinees, so she left at one o'clock, came back at four, and at eight went out again. On Sunday we always had dinner together. I waited for her and we set out for the restaurant on the corner, where we had "our" little table. A fat waitress brought us our food while humming a tune, and an accordion player came, a gray-haired Hungarian, and played, seated on a stool the proprietor brought out for him.

"Alya," I said, "this is our last Sunday. I sail on Thursday. Are you satisfied?"

The question amazed her.

"Satisfied?" she echoed. "I can't answer that. Sure, this is what I wanted when I came to see you. But on the other hand, I've grown rather close to you. It's been very cozy, even if the room's small. Maybe you'll reconsider and stay?"

I was so surprised that words failed me.

"Don't stay," she continued, and even sighed. "Your Druzhin is waiting for you there. Even his name says so—it comes from *druzhba*, 'friendship.' "

I looked at her and said, trying to pretend that what I said should not be taken entirely seriously:

"He's been waiting a long time, he can wait a little longer. I warn you, Alya, I'm going to send you back all the money you gave me. It will be easy, as soon as I start working, in four months, maybe even in three. That money has been on my mind night and day, and I can't go on like this. I'll send it to you as soon as I can."

The joke didn't come across, and she replied solemnly:

"You don't owe me anything, Evgenii Petrovich. There's no point in your worrying about that. Before, I was renting a fine, big room, but it was beyond my means. And they had four children in the apartment and the whole situation was very hard."

"Noisy?"

"Not noisy. I just felt sorry for them. The father and mother were getting a divorce, and the children were on their own all day long. No one taught them, and how they wanted to learn! The oldest boy was already twelve, and the girl ten. They literally swallowed whole everything I told them, and what do I know? When I studied with Olga Osipovna, I never had any time to read a book, and then I had to make money, to struggle, and I was in no mood for reading. I'm completely uneducated, I know absolutely nothing, but those children simply clung to me, they wanted to know everything, and there was not a single book in the whole house. I used to cry over it. They had never been to school, and their parents didn't care. All day long they talked with each other—they didn't have any toys, not even the little ones—they did nothing but discuss things: Why this? Why that? And do you know what I did? I reported them to the police. And then I had to leave."

"Who did you report?"

"The parents. You know, there's a law: parents are

required to send their children to school. Otherwise there's a fine and they force them to send the children to school. So I went to the police station and reported them. At first I wanted to send an anonymous letter to the police chief, but then I decided, I have to be brave, I'll go myself. I said, 'All four of them are exceptional, they never fight or break anything. They teach each other arithmetic on their fingers, they've worked out their own system, and all they do for hours on end is ask: Why is there thunder? Why are there stars? What's beyond the stars? How many years do dogs live? Who was Napoleon? Do something to help,' I said. So the police chief thanked me, and, can you imagine, they did everything they were supposed to, and not long ago three of them started school and the fourth is in kindergarten, and all four are at the head of their class. How happy they must be!"

I didn't say anything.

"Do you think it was bad to report them to the police?" she asked, frowning.

I still said nothing. Finally I said the first thing that came into my head.

"If someone gave me a bomb and said: 'Throw it at anyone you like,' I would blow up the entire planet."

"Who would give you a bomb, Evgenii Petrovich?" she said, very seriously. "And what kind of a bomb would it have to be, anyway, to blow up the planet?"

Four days later I left. Alya went to see me off at the station. I told the landlady: "My girlfriend is staying, and I'm going." She winked (she had a habit of winking; it must have been a tic) and replied:

"It doesn't matter to me who lives there, just as long as they pay."

"Ah," I said, "in that respect she's even better than I am: the first of the month is sacred to her."

We shook hands.

When the train left and Alya waved her handkerchief at me, I thought I saw something unfamiliar cross her face, something I had never seen in it, a flash of sadness, and seriousness, and a clouding of her clarity—I don't know the words to describe it. So much happens in life that has no description, no name. So many questions are left, in the end, without answers (for example: Is it all right to report people to the police?). There are so many things that cannot be explained. The pestilence that I've had inside me for the last million years . . .

Michel Néron came to the station, too. He was indifferent toward Alya; he had two girlfriends of his own. He waved his handkerchief as well. And for a little while my two friends, the two witnesses to my lonely Paris life, kept even with the window I was leaning out of and told me:

"Write, Zhenya, write to us about how it's going. And help us to get out of here. Don't be selfish, you hear?"

II

SOMETIMES IN MAY, after two or three warm summery days, the weather suddenly turns cold and rainy. The trees, like the birds who have only just returned to their nests, see time standing still, if not going backward.

The leaves, which have barely emerged, do not unfurl but wait, like the tips of little brushes. The bird, having chirped timidly earlier in the day, now cowers under a ledge, waiting for the bad weather to pass. Outside the rain falls without cease for a whole week; the sky rests on the house; the wind carries clouds; it's cold. And passersby on the street smell of camphor and naphthalene, having once again taken out the warm vests, jackets, and coats that had been laid away for the following autumn.

The smell of camphor and naphthalene, as everyone knows, is death to love. Perhaps some of the mothballs, some of the moth crystals, don't get cleaned out of the cuffs, perhaps people pull their warm things out of cupboards so hastily that they don't turn out all the pockets. Here and there on the streets there's a whiff of naphthalene, and houses smell of camphor. And since both of them are death to love, no one that May (which seems more like November) thinks of love, no one understands love, and there are even some who are not far from condemning it, either in themselves or in other people.

But Lev Lvovich Kalyagin had not felt the effects of the weather for a long time: he hardly ever left the house, and never looked out of the window. In his house, winter and summer, the temperature was always the same, controlled automatically; the light was always the same, and only when he went outside—very rarely and with much trepidation—did he inquire as to the month, the day of the week, and the temperature, Celsius and Fahrenheit.

I worked for him for about a year. I did not find him immediately upon arriving in New York. For a whole month I shuttled around town, looking for work. The last of Alya's money was running out and my hotel presented me with a bill that I couldn't pay. It was then that I saw an advertisement in the paper: "Secretary wanted."

He received me standing at first, but toward the end of our interview he sat down and indicated an armchair to me with his rubber-tipped cane.

He had the gaze of an eagle and a quavering voice. He said:

"Your duties, Arsenii Petrovich . . ."

"Evgenii."

". . . will include typing my correspondence in two languages and keeping accurate track of my affairs. I have two litigations in progress, one here and one in Europe. My wife is living in Switzerland, and I pay all her bills. I'm writing my memoirs. It is essential that my archives be sorted out, that everything is numbered and put into folders. . . . My daughter lives with me but she has refused to help me. My situation, Arsenii Petrovich . . ."

"Evgenii."

". . . is a difficult one. On the one hand, there is so much still to be done—I have an obligation to posterity. On the other, there's no way of knowing how much time I have left to do it in. That is, no one has any way of knowing—it's the secret of destiny!"

With a majestic sweep, he turned his hawklike profile toward me.

"And now, if you're not in a hurry, I would like to ask you"—suddenly he made a strange sound, like a whimper—"I'd like to ask you to iron a handkerchief for me, my favorite one. I washed it myself, but life never taught me how to iron. And Ludmila, my daughter, she's getting divorced, which does not suit her temperament."

Somewhere in the apartment on the other side of the wall there was the sound of movement, a door slammed, and another, quick steps rang out, and a woman of about thirty-five walked into the room. She was short, with a hard but vaguely attractive face. She looked at us both and without saying anything, an expression of profound contempt on her face, turned on her heels, walked out, and slammed the door after her.

Kalyagin paid no attention whatsoever to the commotion.

"I'll tell you something else: I feel bad about troubling you, but I absolutely have to have a button sewn on. It's been three days"—again he whimpered—"since I've been without that button. It's an embarrassment. But to thread a needle—no, when we were young we weren't taught that! I remember everything I was ever taught, but needling a thread . . ."

"Threading a needle."

". . . was not considered an appropriate subject."

The door opposite opened quietly, Ludmila Lvovna poked her head in and said:

"Have you ever taught me anything?"

Kalyagin smiled guiltily.

"Allow me to introduce you. This is my daughter."

"How do you do." She walked in and stood in the middle of the room. I stood as well.

"Don't get up. I don't want to disturb you. I only want to say that you shouldn't believe everything that people tell you. Has he reached the part about 'serving the Tsar' yet? No? Then you've still got lots of fun in store."

"Don't pester us, please," said Kalyagin, not in the least angry.

"One chapter of his memoirs is going to be called, 'How I Wore a Red Ribbon in 1917.'" Suddenly she looked me up and down. "Of course, no one now will ever know whether that's true or false."

She walked out and slammed the door shut again. Kalyagin looked at me.

"You see," he said, "that's what she's like. Just like her mother."

My job began that very day. First I sewed on his button, then I ironed his handkerchief, and later I sat down at the desk and began looking through his papers. His wife wrote to him often, almost every letter included a request for money, and all of them began more or less like this: "Yesterday Daisy and I read and reread your last letter. It hurts Daisy so much that you don't like her! Often she only has to hear your name and she starts to cry (you didn't even remember her birthday!). Poor thing, she has no one in the world but me. Once again we are forced to move from this hotel and find another. Write poste restante. No one wants us to stay on anywhere. . . ." Then there were business letters: a lawyer writing from London about interest-bearing securities; a letter from Geneva about selling some property; there were numerous letters from distant relatives all over the world: from Formosa, from the Canary Islands, from Persia— one asked for money to patent an invention, another for money for his son's education, yet another for money to go to Paris. And finally there was a file for the papers on the factories in which Kalyagin invested his capital. In a week I already knew all of it by heart. On my way out I sometimes had to put iodine on his waist; he believed that iodine was a universal panacea. His body was well groomed, a touch yellow, with large birthmarks.

After four months I sent the money I owed to Alya in Paris, and I felt the time had come to start saving money for the move to Chicago. I thought of Druzhin. I kept a clear picture of him in my mind at all times; you could say that I never let him out of my sight. In the evenings I thought about him, and sometimes I felt a need to tell someone about him.

At first I didn't see Ludmila Lvovna at all. She lived on the upper floor of the apartment, where I never ventured. In the mornings an old Irishwoman came in to wash the dishes from the previous evening, straighten the rooms, and prepare dinner. Kalyagin had dinner at midday alone, in the big dining room; the maid served him, cleared, and left. She must have thought he was deaf, because from the study I often heard her shouting at him:

"Your supper is in the icebox. You only have to heat it up. Heat the blue pot on the stove and pour the contents into the white bowl, then pour what's in the glass cup over it all. All right?"

Kalyagin answered:

"All right. I'm not deaf."

"I shout so that you don't do it backward. Then there's stewed fruit for you. Old people shouldn't eat raw fruit. The doctor said you don't have enough fauna in your intestines."

"I hear you."

"Good-bye."

In the early days I would go out, eat a sandwich, drink some coffee. Later Kalyagin said I should have dinner with him, and then in the evening, before going, I usually poured what was in the blue pot into the white bowl—or vice versa, which pleased him greatly.

It was six months after I'd come to the Kalyagins that I had my first conversation with Ludmila Lvovna. That day Lev Lvovich had gone out to a formal dinner with his old classmates (or perhaps they were from his regiment, I can't remember exactly). I spent an hour or two with him while he prepared himself, put him finally in a taxi, and, going back, went into his bedroom intending to put his closet and dresser drawers in order. He had been asking me to do that for a long time.

She walked in wearing hat and gloves and sat down by the door, on a chair. Her face was dry, and her eyes had that hardness I had already noticed. In a sharp, mocking voice she said:

"You can tell right away: European. No American would let herself go from being a secretary to a cook, then a laundress, then a servant."

"If you think that I'd be insulted by that, then you're wrong. I'm docile by nature, and I'm not bothered about being a cook or a servant."

My reply surprised her, and she said nothing for a few moments. I folded Kalyagin's shirts neatly.

"How much is he paying you?"

"Excuse me," I said, "but that's between us. It's none of your business."

She narrowed her eyes.

"You don't realize who you're dealing with," she said, and she shook the tip of her foot. "My parents are both mad, lonely, and unhappy. They made me mad, lonely, and unhappy too. But they don't admit it and I do."

I continued to open and shut the dresser drawers.

"They're living in a dreamworld. They're sleep-walkers," she went on. "And I lived like a sleepwalker until I realized that one day you're a sleepwalker and the next you're taken away. All their generation is sick and irresponsible. Look at what they've done to the world. And if you tell them to think it all through—who they are, what they've done with themselves, their lives, their children—they try to wriggle out of it as much as they can and then they cry."

"But they aren't all as unhappy as that," I replied, still uncertain as to how I should act with her, whether to keep up her conversation or stay out of it. "Sometimes they're very happy and even, in their own way, happier than you or I."

She opened her large handbag and the room suddenly smelled of perfume; she took out cigarettes and matches and lit up. "But I absolutely do not consider happiness the be-all and end-all of life. What counts is the sense of responsibility and logic. And they don't know the first thing about that! They don't know what they're doing. Maybe the Kingdom of Heaven will open up to them because of it, but personally I wouldn't encourage all those meek and simple people. They've already wrecked enough."

"Pardon me," I interrupted her, "but you said that

your parents are lonely, unhappy people. If I've understood it, your mother isn't lonely: she has a companion
or a relative with her, doesn't she?"

"You mean Daisy?"

"Yes."

Ludmila Lvovna looked at me coldly. "That's her
Pekingese."

At that moment the phone rang and I went into
the study. When I returned Ludmila Lvovna was already
gone. The room smelled of perfume, and a cigarette butt
smoldered in the ashtray. I stood there a few minutes,
listened for a door shutting somewhere, but this time she
had vanished without a sound.

Every evening, as I left for my hotel, I thought about
how, despite my complete solitude in this city, I was no
worse (and no better) off here than I'd been previously.
From time to time, as I had for the last ten years, I would
occasionally dream the dream that haunted me and had
become one of the secret cornerstones of my life. It is
almost impossible to relate it in words. Nothing happens
in it. I move noiselessly in a thick, yellowish fog, as if on
wheels, without motion, without making a sound. The
sensation of a scorched desert. The sensation of speech-
lessness and the absence of time. On my path I sometimes
come across strange plants, gray, grayish-yellow, like
everything that surrounds me, like me. Perhaps I've been
swaddled? Or am I a wooden doll with unarticulated arms
and legs? The plants are thorny, dry, and mute; they are
motionless. Slowly I glide between them. Ahead everything is just the same. . . .

I told myself that my life here was temporary, that

I had finally made an effort, a decision, a resolution, had surmounted various obstacles, exercised my will, and, perhaps, found a way to slip out of my quasi existence. Nevertheless, I was more and more convinced that I was a simple being, comparable to something halfway between ABC and quantum theory.

Lev Lvovich also lay somewhere between those two poles: he comprised several elements. One of them was his attachment to a certain middle-aged lady, whom he never introduced to me but of whom he spoke more than once:

"There was a time when I was considered quite a connoisseur with regard to the female sex, the personification, so to speak, of the demand which engenders supply. Now I am abandoned by everybody and I sometimes feel a need to hold her warm hands in mine. My hands are always ice-cold, it's very unpleasant, and I want to warm them up, I want to feel a live woman near to me. You understand me, of course. Passions, jealousies, romanticism, that's all over now, but the poor orphan needs a woman's protection."

Whenever this need became urgent he asked me to put him through to her on the telephone. She had a long first name, a long patronymic, and a long, double-barreled surname, and he would say tenderly into the telephone: "I miss my angel. I'm freezing, your orphan is cold. Have pity on a helpless sufferer who already has one foot in the grave."

Another element was his two friends. The first was called Pavel Pavlovich, and he belonged to that chapter in Kalyagin's memoirs which Ludmila Lvovna referred to as "serving the Tsar." The other was called Peter Petrovich, and he belonged to the next chapter, which was referred to, once again in Ludmila's words, as "How I Wore a Red Ribbon in 1917."

The third element to Kalyagin was the Russian church: he went either with Pavel Pavlovich to one or with Peter Petrovich to another, and sometimes, when he was too lazy to travel very far, to yet a third where they did something in a different way than in the first two. He returned from church, as he himself put it, pacified, looking rather less hawkish. Once in a moment of peace and, apparently, mercy, he inquired whether I *too*, like certain others, considered Stalin to be the Peter the Great of our time.

For a split second I decided the hour had come for us to go our separate ways, that it was time to send him, his wife, his lawyers, and his memoirs to the devil, but five minutes later he had already forgotten his question—his memory was failing by the day—and never again did the subject of politics come up between us.

Two weeks after my first conversation with Ludmila Lvovna, I found a note from her on my desk: "If you're free this evening, come up and see me." I went up after six. She was wearing a light, pastel dress, sandals, and a large pearl necklace, and although her face was as hard as ever, she smiled and played hostess, walking nimbly around the room, perching from time to time on the sofa and on the arm of a chair. I sat and thought how surprising it was that she and I should suddenly have so much to talk about. At the same time, our silences, in which we would both camouflage ourselves now and then, quickly became easy, calm, delightful even.

Thinking back to that first evening, I try to find in

it something that might have hinted at what was to follow, and I find it above all in the very fact of her inviting me upstairs. Why do that? Probably out of boredom and curiosity. I cannot believe that Ludmila's love for me— a love that was not returned, naturally—had begun before that point. I was impressed by her eyes: gray, with a blueness around the pupil, candid eyes, with a forthright gaze that she never took off me. We immediately began talking about people's faces, about how they had changed over the last twenty years, about what they had looked like a hundred years ago, and a thousand years ago. ("It may be that a thousand years ago they were more like us now than in Schiller's time," she said.)

"Your face is rather unusual," she remarked. "I mean, its shape, there's something about it that's not quite . . . I can't find the word." And right then the expression on her own face softened; goodness and humor animated it.

"What do you mean! No one's ever said that to me before!" I exclaimed (which was the absolute truth) and accidentally knocked over my glass. Fortunately, it was nearly empty. Suddenly I felt that the time had come to start talking about Druzhin. "I have a friend in Chicago. Now there's a face for you! You can't look at that face without laughing."

The conversation did not, as one might expect, stop there, did not shift from the general to the specific and then turn to something else. No, we lingered there. I mentioned Druzhin and she wanted to find out who he was.

"To begin with," I said, and suddenly I knew that

I was just about to make her laugh, "to begin with, he has no idea, but he bears an uncanny resemblance to a horse." As I had foreseen, Ludmila Lvovna burst out laughing. "And then, to tell you the truth, he has an entire theory: he only likes people who remind him of horses. He thinks they're nobler."

"Doesn't he see himself?" she managed to say, through her laughter.

"No."

"Where are those people?"

"He looks for them. At one time he dreamed of forming a secret society of horse faces."

After prolonged laughter a silence fell over her. And we looked at one another for a few minutes without speaking. For some reason it seemed to me that it was precisely at that moment that a change began to take place in her. It was amazing how the outlines of her cheekbones and jaw softened, how her forthright gaze suddenly acquired a tenderness and flexibility, a light even, and sadness. Her thin hands suddenly unfolded, and I saw her beautiful fingers, which I had a great desire to squeeze, to intertwine together with mine and then press to my face. I didn't move.

I remember she started talking about herself. Her great-grandfather had spent his entire life in bed. That was how she put it: "My great-grandfather spent his entire life in bed, and from time to time his serfs turned him over. On a Turkish sofa. My grandfather married three times: the first time to a Gubkina, the second to a Ve-ryovkina, and the third to a Stolovshchikova. The family business prospered; their factories spewed smoke all over

Russia. My father . . . what did my father ever do? I don't think he ever did anything. And he found out that it was possible to live like that. Oh, my youth, my innocence! I got married six years ago, and now I'm in the process of getting a divorce. My husband left me, he said: 'I don't understand what's happening, but living with you is impossible. You have absolutely no sense of humor. A woman has to have at least some sense of humor.' I have no idea what that meant, do you?"

Music was playing on the radio. There was a stack of books on the table, and I wanted to read each and every one; another stack next to it had color reproductions that I wanted to look through. To sit next to her, reading books, listening to the soft string quintet on the radio, watching her sweet-smelling hair all fall to one side of her tilted face. She was talking about how *paradise* meant "garden" in some language I didn't know, that she had read about it somewhere, and hell, probably, was a boring room in some government institution where people waited; you know, there are places like that in courts, pawnshops, train stations. . . . It seemed to me that I'd heard that, too, about a big gray room painted in oil paint, with benches, where the windows are never opened, where it smells of disinfectant. I was sure that I had been there myself, that she was talking about something I knew well.

"That tired old legend—about how paradise is deadly boring and hell is full of interesting people, all of whom you know—ought to be ditched. In paradise Socrates and Homer converse and anyone can listen in, and in hell there's nothing but tedious bureaucracy and loathsome officials."

"With a cataract in one eye," I put in.

"With a cataract in one eye," she echoed. "And the hour hand doesn't budge for millions of years."

"Whereupon a tiny little window closes."

"Whereupon a tiny little window closes and then there's absolutely nowhere to go. And in paradise . . ."

". . . horses stand in clean stalls, dark bay, light bay, roan, black, dappled," I slipped in.

". . . dappled, and so clean that you want to rest your cheek against their smooth sides. And everyone has a face a little bit like yours—" She suddenly broke off, as if she somehow had frightened herself into silence.

"Why like mine?" I asked, surprised.

"I don't know," she said shyly, and she cut the conversation short.

She had never been to Chicago, and she had only a vague impression of it, and although I had never been there either, I told her that once Druzhin had written to me about it.

"First of all, there are some places which have been created by Piranesi."

"You don't say!"

"I assure you," I continued, and my voice rang with the firmest conviction. "It seems that there is a Piranesi at work there, but not the famous one, the museum one, but a descendant, his double, closer to us, our contemporary. This one, ours, works in steel instead, the same steel that is used for bolts or rails, that's been in the forge at the same time as automobile parts, taking from them something that the other Piranesi, the museum one, never knew. You see it especially in those stormy gloomy neighborhoods that run south from the northern reaches of the river, passing by several train stations, hugging the canal on two sides and getting lost between Goose Island and the wharves. On those narrow streets, from roofs to pavements, there are staircases, on the outside, fire escapes, like broken lines in the air, against a sky that is white in the day or red at night. Those stairs make you think of the reverse side of life, of buildings, of the city, they make you think of the flies backstage in a gigantic theater. Once in a while motionless figures sleep on them, hunched and hanging like black sacks, and it's as though these sleeping people hadn't lain down on the steel by chance but had battled for their sleep in a drunken brawl, or haggled for it in a drunken quarrel. Those gloomy neighborhoods are part of the city, they are like veins running through the city, narrow in the north, where they struggle to reach the Gold Coast and creep nearly all the way to the Loop, and broad near the harbor and also where they head south toward the factories, the granaries, and the slaughterhouses."

"Have you ever been there?" she asked, looking at me in amazement.

"No, I haven't."

"How do you know all that?"

I didn't answer.

"Tell me more."

"I'll tell you about the river. It's a highly original river. At one time it passed under sixty bridges before emptying out into the lake, but now it's the other way around, it flows out of the lake and through canals and rivers to the Mississippi Valley. The water is so turgid and filthy that no one would ever drown themselves in it. On one bank there's a forbidding hulk of a prison; on the other, like ships emerging from the fog that comes in from the lake, stand the tallest buildings in the world. There's no particular logic: North Avenue runs from east to west. The West Side runs from north to south. The southern part of town is called the East Side; and the sun, which rises from out of the water, also seems to set in the water; when it sets in the west, red reflections fall on the water to the east. Fogs travel north, sailing past a magnificent lake that's like the Mediterranean for this hemisphere, but at the same time it's also the great water-way 'from the Varangians to the Greeks,' that is, from the Gulf of Saint Lawrence to the Caribbean, and from Labrador to the West Indies, and the Chicago shore lies along this great waterway."

"Did you make that up yourself?"

"I don't think so, no."

At that moment the clock on the mantelpiece chimed softly, just as it does in the Moscow Art Theatre, during the third act of *A Month in the Country*. I jumped up. Had I already been here with her for four hours? We had talked for twenty minutes about heaven and hell and an hour and a half about Chicago. Even if one counted another half hour for her story about her grandfather, that still didn't add up to four hours. Where had the time gone?

"Where has the time gone?" I exclaimed. "Where?"

"I didn't take it, I swear I didn't take anything away from you. Don't shout like that. If someone heard you they'd think you were being robbed."

"Forgive me. Now you will never invite me back again. . . ."

She laughed.

"I think," she said, "your horse-faced Druzhin has written you some very extraordinary letters. Come again. Or have you already told me all you know?"

"Oh no. I've got a lot more to tell."

Now we both laughed, and I left. "Where did she get a clock like that?" I thought on my way home. "Probably an inheritance from her grandfather."

I thought about her, and her femininity, which she hid as if it were something to be safeguarded in secret, not for everyone. It was being safeguarded, and now it was being shown to me, I thought. Why? What was I supposed to do with it?

A week later she and I were at a concert, in a new hall that had opened in a museum building, paneled in dark wood. "It's like sitting inside a contrabassoon," she said, laughing. She was high-spirited that evening, high-spirited and elegant, almost too elegant. People were looking at her and admiring her.

I took her home and went upstairs. She immediately switched on the radio, and once again I heard the exact same music I had heard the first time, as if I had never left her at all.

"So how are things in Chicago?" she asked, settling into the corner of the sofa.

I slowly shifted my eyes from the radio to the clock, from the clock to her.

"People there are out on the streets day and night, as if they had nothing better to do. And they have two types of faces: some have perpetual concern in their eyes, whereas the others have a special sleepiness and limpness. The streets run on and on until they finally turn into notches two or three feet wide, though even then they have names. Nothing grand or melodious, but names just the same. Real streets there are called Bonaparte, Goethe, Byron, Dante, Mozart, and Cicero. But I can't tell you anything about them, I can tell you only about the notches. These have barbershops where tramps get their hair cut for free—the student barbers practice their art on them. You run a great risk of someone building 'stairs' on the back of your head, but tramps are brave and— all is flux!—life goes on and it grows out and a week later you're a human being again. Besides the barbershops there are also lots of little shops where you can pawn things and drink up the proceeds. Once a man pawned his wooden leg and then hopped from bar to bar. There are charitable institutions, of course, that look after the homeless and the drunks. For instance, there's the Low-Cost Sanitorium for Alcoholics, that's what's written on the sign; there are children's shelters for minors named after David Copperfield. And of course there's the Salvation Army—God grant it health!—you can always tell them by their drum; the slang for them is Sally. You go straight from the pavement into a big room where people are singing in unison:

> How wondrously the world is made:
> Water enough for all to drink,
> Bread enough for all to eat.
> Glory be to God, I sing.
> More wondrous still in heaven.

There are places where you first have to sing in the chorus and then you can go wash up and have a bowl of soup, and also get your mattress. It's called the four S's: salvation, soap, soup, and sleep. There are others, three *S*'s, where there's only salvation, soap, and sleep. There are some even more involved combinations, too, but it's not worth going into. It's already late and I should be going."

She stood up, watching thoughtfully as I stubbed out my cigarette and walked to the door.

"If you like we could go to the country next Sunday," she said, standing between me and the door. "That is, if the weather's good."

"If I like," I repeated. "Of course I'd like. Would you?"

"Isn't it obvious that I do?" she said, and she smiled.

"I'm the only one she smiles at like that," I thought, and I kissed her hand and left.

It was summer, the honeysuckle was blooming and fragrant, and we were sitting looking out over the water, above the bay, where hundreds of sailboats were rocking on the waves, racing far away and turning back again. I looked in her face for the expression that had been there that first time I saw her in Kalyagin's study, but I didn't find it, although it had been there, it had come out so markedly then, in that scene she staged at her first introduction to me, and that meant it could come back again. But each time we got together she pushed that old self farther and farther away, her look, her voice, her movements—everything was reborn before my very eyes, and it was no longer a smile but a very youthful, quiet, almost childlike laughter, carefree and lucid, that now accompanied our long conversations. And I kept looking into her face and thinking that it had been conceived of as stern, that its foundation was hard, but how it was being transformed into something quite different.

"It seems to me," she said, first sipping coffee from her cup, then cutting up a pear with a knife and offering me a small piece on a fork, "that there is no Chicago. Wait, let me explain it to you. There's a strange, scary, immense city that you know a lot about but that neither you nor I will ever see. Instead, it's as if you and I both were already living there."

"You might not see it, perhaps, but I certainly will."

She didn't respond.

"I'm going there very soon, there's nothing keeping me here."

She looked in a strange way.

"Why don't you take me with you?" she asked in dead seriousness.

I laughed. "What would you do there?"

She turned to the large dark blue mirror that hung on the wall over our table and examined herself closely.

"No, I don't have a horse face," she said sadly. "Have you noticed how as women get older they look more and more like either fishes or birds or trained dogs? I think in twenty years or so I'll fall into the third category."

"You've got a long way to go to old age," I said, laughing.

But she didn't laugh.

"Tell me, Evgenii Petrovich," she said, having suddenly decided something. "If I had a horse face, would you take me with you?"

She was speaking in all seriousness, but I didn't know what to say to her, I was suddenly gripped by a silence that I couldn't break.

In the evening we sat on the dunes, listened to the sea, lay back, and looked at the sky.

"No," she said suddenly, "I don't believe that the stars are so far away, millions of light-years. That simply doesn't mean anything. One day they'll discover that they're much closer, and everything that used to seem infinite and immense will suddenly turn out to be quite small and much closer."

"In Paris," I said, "there are sometimes street fairs: a circus, freaks, acrobats, fortune-tellers, archery. Once an enterprising, self-taught astronomer set himself up in a booth. The barker (there are still barkers over there, like a hundred years ago) shouted into the megaphone: 'Hey, you, come on in, see the stars for fifty centimes. You live like moles, you don't believe in God, you have no feeling for beauty—at least take a look at the stars!' "

Now she laughed merrily, raised herself up on one elbow, saw that I was sitting up and looking at her, cautiously pushed me down on my back, laughing all the while, lifted my face to the sky, grabbing me by the chin, and repeated:

"At least take a look at the stars!"

I put one arm under my head and started to look at the sky.

"Those barkers are amazing people—failed public speakers or something." I started talking again, lying on my back. "Now in Chicago—"

"Yes, in Chicago. . . . What in Chicago?"

"There failed orators give entire speeches. One of them will get up on an empty soapbox at some inter-section where there's a scraggly broom growing instead of a tree and start to give a speech, for instance, about effective poverty: how to extort the maximum amount of money from passersby with the least expenditure of energy. It's a science in itself! Or here's another one—about finding free entertainment."

"There's no such thing!"

"You can take a walk in the park and admire nature, you can listen to a wind orchestra in the city parks for free, you can find an old newspaper and read it from cover to cover, old newspapers being more interesting than new ones. You can compose a ballad and sing it on some corner and people will listen to it all the way through—that's just how people are. You can attend free courses to learn which mushrooms are poisonous and which aren't, and when the Australian aborigines devised a calendar. You can stop in at a museum once in a while, and if there aren't any, then you can go to the harbor and admire the outdoor tattooing. You can also spend an hour or two standing underneath a staircase admiring women's legs. But the best entertainment of all is the health questionnaire."

"What kind of questionnaire?"

"Health statistics. It's great fun. They give you a questionnaire and you write whatever you want. How many times a week do you have dinner? How many times do you sleep outside? How many times a week do you wash—and a box where you put an X: with hot water, with cold water. Do you accept charity? When was the last time you worked? Once a man wrote: 'Forty-two years ago.' Why aren't you working? 'I don't want to!' Some write: 'I want to work but only on condition that I do what I like, because otherwise life isn't worth living.' And the young lady asks you: 'So what would you like to do?' And the man says: 'I'd like to raise flags.' 'What kind of flags?' 'National flags that they raise on holidays. I'm a specialist in flag raising and I'm very partial to holidays. And I'm not going to do anything else.' "

There was a long silence. With her, it never weighed heavily.

"You know, Evgenii Petrovich," she said after a while, "with you I feel quite different. No one would ever recognize me now. It's because you're not in the least bit afraid of me. You can't imagine the happiness when someone isn't afraid of you."

"Why are people afraid of you?"

"Ask them. I think I already told you that my husband left me because I had no sense of humor whatsoever, that I was too conniving and cold for him. He even admitted that sometimes—not that he was afraid of me but that he was wary. Can you understand that?"

"I think so."

She put out her hand and placed it on mine. We were both lying on the sand looking up.

"He also said once: 'You live as if a tiny clockwork system were running inside you day and night, and you know I like to listen to the nightingales once in a while, and make mistakes.' I thought a great deal about that."

She took her hand away from mine and turned on her side, resting her head on her elbow, looking at me, and smoothing the fine sand with her deeply tanned hand. The sand was like snow under her fingers.

"I feel I want to listen to you and to tell you about myself," she said after a pause. "And I treasure every minute with you. Before I met you I always thought I knew myself, my limits, so to speak, well. Everyone has their limits, after all, don't you agree?"

"Yes."

"But I suddenly realized that I don't know myself at all. And instead of feeling lost, mixed up, insecure, I feel happy. And I feel like telling you about that."

Again, we were silent for a long time, thinking our own thoughts, and she moved closer to me, soundlessly, and put her head on my arm, by my elbow, and was still. Then she asked:

"Is it too heavy?"

I answered:

"No, keep it that way."

Later we went to the car and raced back to town along a broad, moonlit highway. She loved driving fast and was calm and confident about it. Pulling up in front of my door, she held out her hand. My eyes met hers.

"You can be very beautiful sometimes," I said, "and good. When you want to."

"I always want to . . . now," she replied.

The car drove off; I went inside.

Summer was coming to an end. Everything that bloomed in the parks and squares had long since bloomed and burned up in the sun. It smelled of gas and dust. Every city has its own smell. Paris smells of gas, tar, and face powder; Berlin, when I was younger, smelled of gas, cigar, and dog; New York smells of gas, dust, and soup, especially on hot days and hot nights, which can only be broken by a sudden thunderstorm or a hurricane from Labrador or the Caribbean. Time was starting to pass more and more quickly, and a fresh wind was blowing in from the ocean, as Lev Lvovich Kalyagin learned from reading the newspapers.

We saw each other almost every day now. I would go upstairs to see Ludmila Lvovna and have dinner with her. To the whirring of the fan we listened to Bach and Mozart on the radio, or talked. Sometimes we took a walk or a drive somewhere. We already had our favorite spots in Central Park; when we crossed on the diagonal and came out at the other end, music was playing and couples were dancing around in a circle at the open-air restaurant. Here, where no one knew us and we knew no one, we often sat until late in the night.

One evening when the weather was especially close and it seemed that the humid September day would never end, she suggested we drive down to the sea, to the very edge of the city, and there board a boat that went to an island—a twenty-minute trip altogether, and we could make it two, even three times, until night fell and there was some respite. I remember we reached the edge of the city, the tip, very quickly. The sun was beginning to set, the streetlights were being turned on. Three ferries were docked, ready to sail, and we boarded one of them and immediately were struck by the carefree feeling you have when you're sailing without knowing where or when you'll be back: a rare feeling, to which you can almost never afford to succumb.

"Maybe we should ask where we're going anyway?" I said when we had sat down in the wicker chairs, and the boat, having sounded its horn and let out a cloud of black smoke, began moving away from shore.

"It doesn't matter. It's too late now."

We sat at the bow and could not see the city we were leaving behind. Before us was the sea, a hot, windless, orange-gray evening; to the right, beyond the black hulks of the factories, the sun was setting and the bridges, smokestacks, and buildings at first dissolved in the incandescent smoke-tinged air, and then, when the sun had set, all this seemed to arrange itself in a row on the horizon, against the background of the sunset, like a menacing black army, but gradually disappearing from view, merging with the darkening sky. It was quickly growing dark. Gulls hid, vanished, and flew out overhead once again. We could hear the waves slapping around us, the engines running in the depth of the ship. Our chairs had been moved, we were sitting side by side, she slightly forward of me, leaning into the woven chair back, looking ahead and thinking about something, and I was looking at her, at her hair, at the contours of her head and neck, now so familiar and somehow oddly close to me. Suddenly she said:

"You know, we're not going the right way at all!"

"And just where were we thinking of going?"

"I don't know. Only we're going somewhere entirely different. We're turning around. Interesting, will we go back or will they take us somewhere and leave us?"

At that moment the ticket taker came up; we bought two tickets and found out that the ship was making a big circuit, circling the island, stopping twice, and returning back at around midnight.

"How nice," she said. "How nice."

"You know in Chicago there are children," I said, watching the shores slip farther and farther away from us and the air darken, "who don't steal, don't beg, and don't sell their bodies. They play cards, day in and day out."

She turned to look at me.

"They set themselves up in a vacant area, where a building has been torn down, on a pile of rubble, put a collapsed legless couch there, or bring an old mattress from some nearby dump, and gamble around the clock for four, sometimes five days. They have skinny faces and tightly pursed lips. Sometimes they actually have children. Rarely, though. And the old men just *sit there*. By a chain link fence, under a tree, near statues, and, naturally, in specially designated places. They just sit there. For which a small fee is exacted, but sometimes not even that. The old people just sit. They have a few distractions and that's it. That's how the days, months, and years go by. And they go on sitting there. Their only pleasure is in choosing where to sit. Here, if you want. There, if you want. And choosing where to sleep: in the night shelters there are sleeping cells on two levels, and they're all identical so far as I can tell, but they choose all the same. The cell locks from the inside. They can hook the latch from the inside, you understand, not from the outside! They can also choose what to eat: kidney beans, peas, green beans, sweet corn. No one is forcing them. Each one has his own jar, not an official ration, but of his own choosing, individually eaten, protected by that latch. His own bed and his own jar."

"Was he ever there himself?" she asked, narrowing her eyes slightly.

"Who?"

"You know, your friend, the horsey one."

"N-no. He wasn't. He's just interested. He's lived there a long time, and he's always been intrigued by oddities. It's too late for him to change now. Not him."

"Are there really people like that?"

"Not only that, he says that it reverberates somehow with a deep chord in his soul."

"I understand."

"Sometimes he expresses himself oddly. You have to put the chords of his soul in quotes."

"I understand that, too."

The boat sailed on and on, night was falling, blue-black, lit up, all with a hint of salt and smoke.

"I'd like to take a look at his letters. . . ."

I didn't meet her eyes, I started looking to the right; the water was sparkling and playing there.

She and I both immediately forgot the names of the places where we were going. They didn't mean anything to us. When it got completely dark and the shores disappeared, she turned toward me and said:

"Tell me now, at last, about yourself, about your life. You evidently aren't going to take me with you to Chicago. All right, let's leave it at that. Have you always been on your own?"

"No," I replied. "Not always. But for the last ten years I have."

"And before that?"

The moment I had thought of so many times in recent weeks had come, and with an effort I spoke the words:

"Before that I was married. I was married for fifteen years. I was happy."

Ludmila Lvovna sat up very tense and straight in

her chair. Even in the darkness I could see the anxiety in her face, as the contours seemed to sharpen. Her eyes grew larger.

"And I thought, Evgenii Petrovich, that you had never had relations with a woman."

I was silent and thought how this trip to nowhere might turn out to be the last time we spent together.

"Why don't you say something," she continued. "You were married, you were happy. Is that really all, a happy man?"

The last two words sounded devoid of all meaning. I couldn't utter a single word in response: my old thoughts, difficult thoughts about myself, returned with new force, thoughts about my inability to forget and be reconciled, to change inside, to become strong; the terrible crack that had lived in me for millions of years.

"You are, in fact, a happy man," she said in a new voice (or was that her former, old voice, which she had spoken in at one time and then stopped), "the first happy man I've ever met. There has been grief, of course, how could there not? It happens to everyone. But then, you see, you lived as you wanted, you reconciled yourself, you forgot. You flit around the world as free as a bird, you don't love anyone, you don't want to love anyone. You don't suffer, you don't want to suffer. And I, I must confess, thought that you were someone special, solitary in a special way, the kind of person who is always looking for something, who doesn't know where to go, or who to trust. . . . You fooled me!" There was a jeering in her voice.

But I wasn't sure whether she was joking or serious. I answered barely audibly:

"If you were to give me a bomb I'd——"

She laughed. "You? A bomb? You'd give it right back, very politely, frightened out of your wits. Better if someone gave me a bomb. I know who I'd throw it at."

"Who?"

"You, of course."

It was night all around. We were sailing on the open sea; it was the ocean, a mysterious nighttime passage. Below, on the lower deck, an orchestra was playing softly and an invisible black woman sang the blues in a low voice that was no longer young. At these latitudes it had the same resonance as our gypsy songs.

She was sitting facing me now, her elbows on the arms of my chair, her face close to mine.

"Marry me, Evgenii Petrovich," she said, as if she couldn't stop herself, as if she were being swept along. "Marry me for all time. Can't you see how good I feel with you? And you know why? Because I become someone else when I'm with you, someone new, someone real, someone I've probably never been with anyone else. I'm *funny*, especially right now, this very moment, don't say no, because now I realize what that means. Utterly defenseless and still funny! I become someone different because you're the kind of person I've never met before in my life. What kind of person are you? I'll tell you: In the first place, you're not afraid of anyone, including me. In the second place——you're very happy. Yes, yes, don't interrupt me: happy, and free, and honest. You don't mind me discussing you as if I were talking about some third person? I could use the third person: he's honest, and vigorous, and . . ."

This suddenly became unbearable.

"Ludmila Lvovna," I said. "Be quiet. I have no idea how you've managed to deceive yourself to such an extent. I'm weak, good-for-nothing; I'm racked with indecision; I lack what everyone else has—the ability to die inside and come back to life. I don't like life or people, and I'm afraid of them, like most people are, probably even more than most people. I'm not free, I haven't really enjoyed anything for a long time, and I'm not honest because I didn't tell you anything about myself for so long, and now, when I do, it's so difficult."

"Tell me just one thing," she asked quickly, interrupting me. "Can I go on loving you?"

In that instant she saw my face and took my hand.

"Keep quiet, don't answer. I understand. Forgive me for tormenting you."

I took her hand and kissed it. I was so grateful to her for withdrawing her question. What would I have answered her?

A few minutes later she had calmed down completely. I went below to bring her some iced coffee. She drank it and played with the straw. We stood amid the lights of some dock, then once again departed into the black night. And at moments it smelled as salty as the real ocean, so that it seemed as if we were sailing to Portugal.

But by midnight we were back.

"Still," she said, holding on to me as we walked down the ramp, "how nice it was. How nice! And neither of us has the slightest idea where we were. It's just as if the whole world belonged to me, everything in it but you."

But something in her face had changed, I noticed, as her movements had, and her voice. Once again that hard, angular, stern foundation showed through, a solid shape emerged that became her face. It was as if she didn't feel well. I didn't see her smile again that night.

A week later, I was in Chicago.

III

FIRST — AN UNFAMILIAR TRAIN STATION, the feeling that I'd arrived at the very center of something, whereas in fact it was anything but the center, the center was far away, perhaps to the right and perhaps to the left; we had arrived somewhere off, to one side. But that's hard to believe: in a strange city it always seems as though the center is wherever you happen to be right at that moment. Then—the charm of posters, a blue, pink, green world, an imitation of reality that is too precise to be true. The better the imitation, the less you believe in it, the less you recognize the world in which you were born and are going to die, where so much is left unfinished, unspoken, unappreciated. The more unreal the depiction, the more it affects us. The spaces of a train station. A white day breaks through the windows. A crowd. A child eats ice cream. The dog wants some too, but doesn't get any. Someone's suitcases all piled up. It's a shame, dog, but there's nothing you can do. The taxi stand on the street. I have the address written down right here. The street has a fine name, but of course not Cicero or Byron. They say there are three theories as to why Byron was in such a hurry to get to Greece that time, but I think there was a fourth reason. There's only one theory as to why I'm here right now. (And not only am I not Byron, I'm not even the dark horse; I come only fifth or eleventh, or three hundred eighty-sixth.)

I tell the driver the address. I'd like to hear how a man with a nape like that expresses himself, that is, which words he uses and where he keeps them. We are driving fast, and the center of the city, which for me had been the train station, goes with me: this corner, where some people are grabbing papers from a newsboy; this inter-section, where we've stopped for a red light. I imagine a life where it's all green lights, like emeralds, sprinkling life all the way to the horizon. And there, beyond the horizon, a turn, and again—the pointsman's wife stands with a green flag, just like in a children's cartoon. And there's no reason for it ever to end, unless she catches a bad chill, or some fatal tumor is suddenly discovered, and it has to be a fatal one.

It's very noisy, very crowded, but no noisier or more crowded than other cities. I've seen many of them in my time, big and little, and I've appreciated and loved them. At one time, both of us had loved them, but then they started collapsing around us one after another. After that we started to be a little afraid of them.

So I had arrived. I still can't make out anything but the bills in my hands, which are passing into the driver's. Then the change pours from his into mine and I climb out with my two suitcases. A woman opens the door.

I've never seen her before. She was once married to my cousin; he died a long time ago; now she's married to someone else. Six grown children: two of her own, two from her second husband by his first marriage, two of their own. She leads me through a series of strange rooms: a parrot in one, an aquarium in another, a cat in yet another. She offers me eggs and cold roast beef and takes me upstairs, to the neighbors, where a room has been rented for me.

"There are other tenants, but they're quiet," she said. "Nice people, educated."

"I'm quiet too," I tell her, and I see that she believes me and smiles. I'm trying to memorize her features so that I'll recognize her on the stairs or on the street, but for some reason I can't.

The room turns out to be better than I'd thought: light, warm, clean. The hallway smells of coffee. Next door a record player is playing softly. This is a place in which I could definitely live, and then we'd see, maybe we'd move on. . . . The teakettle would sing songs to me in the evenings, I would read books, write letters, go to the cinema, and meet the people who lived to the left and right of me. To the left I'd find someone who loved order, a harmonious life, discipline, when B follows from A and leads to C. A classicist! To the right I'd find someone who loved his nightmares, whims, and anarchy. (What are people like that called?) And I would vacillate between them and go to work and love in equal measure both my order and my nightmares. And the big Mediterranean lake would lie before me (this was when I took walks on the shore), and I would tell myself over and over that I had actually made an effort, I had found within myself the strength to resist, the will to pull myself out of the state I've been in for so many years.

How many years? Ten years had passed since she'd died, but nothing had gone, nothing was forgotten. Alya's clear face watched me leave with excruciating sorrow; Ludmila Lvovna threw her grandfather's antique clock on the floor. But what did I care whom Homer talked with in heaven? Once, on a train, many years ago, between Freiburg and Zurich, I heard a conversation in the corridor at night: an old colonel was telling an engineer from Schaffhausen about how his wounds wouldn't heal. Ten years had passed since that global madness had ended (the first, believe me, there will be others!), and his wounds still ached.

I was standing nearby and listening (in those days absolutely everything fascinated me). "Yes, young man," the colonel put his hand on my head, and for a whole minute, petrified, I tried to decide whether or not to take offense from my position as a fifteen-year-old passenger. "It won't heal up, the old stinker. It aches and aches, and I'll end up with gangrene."

For years now nothing in the world has mattered to me, but people don't like that. They stop noticing you, and the mirrors stop reflecting you, and the echo stops answering you. I'd like to get better, but I just can't. I can't shake off that black pestilence, I can't be resurrected. Millions of years have passed since the day she died. I fly somewhere I don't know; I spin; I live in places it seems I never went to. And I am a mirror which no longer reflects anything.

She had everything I hold dear in this solar system, all the rest was Neptune and Pluto. When she was by my side, I had no desire to look through interesting picture books. Music and the starry sky both reached me as if refracted through her. In her, the whole world revealed its lovable face, and all the rest was Neptune and Pluto.

From the window of my room I could see . . . here follows a detailed list that riveted me to that window, to that city, from the skyscraper to the blue trousers hung on the line. In the room there was the following furniture . . . another list; in this way I'll have objects all around me, and I'll be in the middle of them. If only I could retreat from this quasi life, back to my free, marvelous, immortal, just, shared life.

If only I could return to the world healthy, still strong, take up various interesting hobbies, marry, and have children. My wife would be quiet and meek; at night she'd shade the light of the lamp so that it wouldn't bother me; she'd economize on the house and look after sick kittens. Or maybe she'd be sharp and would make accurate, intelligent remarks, use expensive perfume, raise one eyebrow and narrow her eyes. Then the old colonel moaned on his berth on the other side of the partition, at the same time as I was calculating the speed of the new arctic icebreakers—the final fascination of my brief adolescence. I heard him grinding his teeth: "Damn knee!"

No, I don't have what I need to heal the loss, to reconcile myself to my nightmares, to adapt myself cleverly to my own catastrophe. A Personal Catastrophe. I don't care about the world's; I'm not interested in them anymore. I don't even know whether or not there have been any, these past few years. But it wasn't always like that: in the cellar of a certain building, in a certain city, at the other end of the world, where once we were buried, I lay on top of her, in order to cover her. "I am a King, I am a slave, I am a worm, I am God!" Together we shook, as did the cellar, and the entire building, until it collapsed on us. That was one of our most joyous and most terrifying nights of love.

Her whisper. Her moans. Her sob. Her cry—and one more. At that very second—a deafening thunderclap and the six-story building began to rock. The sixth and fifth stories flew up into the air. The fourth and third crumbled to earth, and the last two shuddered for a long while, sprinkling us with sand and plaster from the ceiling. Her eyes were still closed and two tears fell from under her eyelids, two tears of final bliss.

Then the cellar ceiling started to give way, but not the walls. Deafened by the thunder all around, I tasted plaster in my mouth, going down my throat. Pieces of plaster were falling around and upon me. My left elbow was broken. She was motionless beneath me. She was silent. A thin stream of blood began to trickle slowly out of her round ear, under my chin. I lost consciousness.

They came with stretchers. My love. My life. Mutilated. Silenced.

The doctors said there was nothing to be done. So did the jeweler: it's always been there and it always will be. "Nothing to be done"—what a familiar phrase. That's what the doctors said, only not to the old colonel but to me, when she was lying whiter than a pillowcase and only her eyes seemed alive. They were alive one more day after that. Then I had to close them.

I don't know whom to write to first: Alya or Ludmila. Alya asked me to write about myself and how I was getting on, which would be an awful lot easier to do. Ludmila asked me to write about Druzhin, and that's very hard. She must have guessed that there never was any Druzhin, that I dreamed him up, that I was going without knowing where I was heading. To nowhere, to see no one. That can happen: a person will be going somewhere where he doesn't know anyone, and there will turn out to be friends all around. With me it was the opposite. It all started one fine day when someone said to me: "Make an effort, Evgenii Petrovich. You can't go on living like this. It's not right. You've got to. . . ." Maybe it was Attorney N., that troubled soul? I wonder what's become of him.

I unpacked my bags, washed, and went out. The front door slapped me on the shoulder; it had been a long time since anyone had slapped me on the shoulder. Although Kalyagin had two evenings before. He'd said: "I never expected such peculiar behavior from you. You've put me in a tragic position. I'm too old to allow myself the luxury of changing secretaries." He went into his bedroom without shaking my hand. And then I walked to the door, trying not to go faster. There was no one there, no one in the whole house, in the whole world. I went down the empty stairs, walked down the empty street to the bus. And now once again I was in a wasteland: my room was empty, the street was completely empty, and this city was empty as well.

The crowds, however, went back and forth, the space was filled with lights, the trees rustled and bent over my head. Far far away tugboats moaned and bellowed, cars leapt out from underground and dashed back again, the thick gray sky swirled overhead. None of it quite resembled the descriptions in that old book I'd come across once on a certain bench, on a certain Left Bank boulevard, not far from the Pont du Sully, where I sat waiting for the barbershop to open. I remember there were pictures and a map of the city. It lay there forgotten by someone, as if it had been waiting for me. And I'd thought: "Good, I agree, dear little book, I agree to you, I'll live again and see whether something comes of all this, after all. Even the dead are resurrected so why shouldn't I, as I'm alive?" Only for that I had to do something, I had to make a decision, get moving, adapt, I had to invent cities, people, sorts of stories, my own life, fit in, walk in step, try to resemble other people. And it had to happen quickly, otherwise I'd turn into a vegetable.

I'll definitely write to Alya. She would have slept on my shoulder, lying in my arms, whereas I would have slept on Ludmila's shoulder—that's plain as day to everyone. I'll write to her, too. But, you know, I'm not going to write to anyone. I'd do better to spend my evenings walking the streets and searching for Druzhin—he has to be somewhere after all! I got so used to the idea of him that maybe I actually will find him in the end. I can see him clearly before me: reddish hair, thoughtful, a little sad, a white spot on his forehead, a thick mane of hair. We would have something to say to one another, something to discuss. If I don't find him, then I'll move on. It makes no difference to me where I live. And I like new impressions, they ease the pain, and doesn't everybody want that? Especially when there's a fear—good people—that you yourself might soon become Neptune or Pluto.

In Memory of Schliemann

THE BUS MARKED "Schliemann Square—Great
Fountains" moved off from the statue. It was over-
crowded, but I found a seat: I sat down by an open
window, stuffed my small canvas duffel bag under the
seat, tossed my hat on the shelf. It was a noisy, dusty
evening, hazy from the heat of the day; crowds were
walking through the streets, going from stuffy, hot offices
and workrooms to stuffy, hot city apartments, but I was
going out of town, as far as I could from Schliemann
Square, to Great Fountains.

These three days off hadn't just fallen into my lap;
I'd earned them. More than four hundred people worked
at the large agency where I'd been employed for two
years in the modest position of junior accounts clerk,
starting from the people no one ever saw and ending
with the man with the broom, whom everyone always
saw, since he spent entire days chasing papers and various
kinds of rubbish out from under our tables and chairs
and into a broad red dustpan. Work time there was
calculated by a special, complicated, poorly understood

method. For weeks they would seem to be cheating us, and suddenly they would come out with a bonus. I hadn't had a day of holiday all year and suddenly: "You have off Tuesday the fourth, Wednesday the fifth, and Thursday the sixth." This was the decision of the huge machine that issued our salaries and our bonuses, that calculated who had the right to be sick and for how long and who should get time off when. This machine looked like the mausoleums which used to be built in cemeteries for four generations of a family.

Before I had started at the job, they broke through the ceiling to the next floor for this machine and added bracing under the floor. The employees simply deferred to it: it never made a mistake. Out of it came my time off, out of it came my bonuses, out of it came a dismissal for one young lady with golden hair and jangling bracelets because she was always late.

But the machine couldn't have new ideas. And once, while I was looking down at it from the balcony that ran around the big hall where we all worked, a strange thought occurred to me: a way to increase work time by one twenty-fourth a day, that is, a way of doing something which the people I never saw would like.

This idea was the consequence of an idle game of my imagination. A game that bore neither cupidity nor a desire to curry favor. I couldn't have cared less about those ideals pursued by the inventors of the prison peephole or the time clocks that recorded how long an employee took for lunch. It simply occurred to me that if work were to start an hour earlier every day, then that could, so to speak, increase production—

without any perceptible harm. On Monday, say, the day would start at nine, on Tuesday at eight, on Wednesday at seven. A week later it would be starting at two in the morning. But since the entire city would have shifted over to this kind of accelerated life, then it wouldn't matter essentially; at the end of the year each individual would have gained about two weeks of life, which was not bad. As a consequence, satisfaction would be accorded not only to the exploiter but also to the exploited. After working for twenty-five years, the individual would be rewarded, so to speak, with an extra year of life.

The concepts "day" and "night" seem utterly outmoded to me. Now, when shops, restaurants, cinemas, and hospitals are open at night, when one-fifth of the inhabitants of large cities work at night, it would be very simple to shift over to new tracks. The old concepts about how you should sleep at night and work in the day made sense back when it was light in the day and dark at night, when it was noisy in the day and quiet at night. Why must we live as our ancestors did? Wouldn't it make more sense to shift over to continuous activity? And wouldn't it make more sense to start building *down* in parallel with building *up*, in order to save space, assuming that lighting, air-conditioning, and heating, and, of course, perfect ventilation could replace light and air?

It would follow to promulgate a law: when a twelve-story building is built, twelve floors plus, then twelve floors minus must be built as well, into the earth, where neon light, warm air, cold air, sea air, would be supplied continuously, imperceptibly, noiselessly. For ten or fifteen years or so it might not be altogether comfortable, until people adjusted to it, but then after that! When people met they could add a plus or minus sign to their name:

Petrov +
Sidorov —

This means that if you were Ivanov —, then you couldn't have anything to do with Petrov, you could never get together with him, but it would be fine to be with Sidorov. So once again—you've gained time.

My idea was running in my head for several weeks, like a well-oiled motor. I thought: "Instead of political speeches, prophecies, lengthy conversations over tea, long heart-to-hearts under a lamp, or leisurely strolls, we should give one another our final decisions of a public-moral or individual-psychological nature." For instance:

"Do good. It's often not at all profitable to do evil."

"If you take something, return it. But don't give anything up to anyone."

"Respect the healthy. Avoid the infirm."

"Forget the elderly. They won't be around long."

I remember, about a week ago, inspired by this idea, I called Didi and said I'd been missing her and would like to come over. This made her very happy, I heard her bracelets jangle into the receiver, and that very night I went over. She took a complicated dish which she'd probably slaved over for hours out of the oven, and it had puffed up, browned, spread out, and smelled of cheese. We sat down. Her girlfriend, with whom she shared the apartment, was playing the mandolin for us, self-taught. They had a whole shelf of teach-yourself books, and the girlfriend peered at the book as she played. I saw, by the way, that Didi, too, peered at a book she was holding in her left hand as she stirred something in a saucepan.

"Why were you always late for work? There, you see? Now they've fired you," I said rather dryly.

She looked around sadly. Her hair was so magnificent that I felt like pulling out the comb that held it and burying my face in it.

"Wait for the bus. Wait for the subway. The crowds. I couldn't make it," she said sadly.

"You should have got up earlier. The time will come when there will be plenty of room for everyone and no one will be crowded.

"The Bomb?" she asked timidly.

"Not the Bomb, a double life," I said. "Someday I'll explain it all to you. Nothing terrible. I could tell you right now, actually: there'd be just as much above ground as below, as much in the day as at night. And that would make for more time and space."

The mandolin strummed very softly; I felt good, peaceful, even rather happy with them. "Take your comb out," I said.

The girlfriend immediately stood up. She left the room, taking her mandolin and her instruction manual with her, and a minute later music began to play beyond the wall, starting from that same interrupted note. Exactly as if we were in Japan.

Nonetheless she did not take out her comb. At a distance her hair smelled to me like a mix of lily of the valley and roasted chestnuts, the kind they sell sometimes on street corners when autumn comes, and there was something autumnal in her burnished hair, too. It was during these moments that I got the idea of taking a trip with her out of town. Once I'd entered this enormous city where she and I lived I'd never left it. It was summer now, sultry, long, but shouldn't there be flowers somewhere, and leaves, and air, burnished as her hair?

"Let's go away somewhere," I said quietly.

"Where?" she asked, again with a sadness that implied there was nowhere to go.

But nothing ever came of this because a week later she found a job and our lives never coincided—as if she were a Plus and I were a Minus. Or vice versa.

The bus sped straight down the road. Hours passed. Outside the opened window passed houses, people, cars, signs, shops. I thought about Great Fountains, I thought about my three days, about the machine that had given them to me. It's never wrong, the senior accounts clerk told me, and that was right-true as well as right-fair.

I thought the sun had set, but a few minutes later it glimmered again, on the other side of the road, though not for long, it's true. The lights were already on. Dusk fell slowly. Occasionally we made a stop; people got off, others got on. A small square flashed by with a large low gray bush in the middle around which children were running, the railway passed by us, and overhead—the highway, where cars rushed headlong toward us in an unbroken chain, directly over the trains below, reminding me in a way of my dreams of life in the future.

Possibly others have already had ideas, lots of them,

about how to reorganize humanity. Every century—no, every quarter century—some new improvement takes a sharp right turn and new horizons open up. So it was with the eight-hour workday. Stop. Turn. Up ahead new ideals reveal themselves: free hospitalization, old age pensions. That, of course, is the least of it. Another turn, another ideal: insured burials, free dental care. Now we are anxious to lengthen time, to extend space. I am coming to the conclusion that it's time for me to put all these thoughts down on paper, to send them somewhere and apply for a patent. Yes. Apply for a patent. New perspectives are opening up. Dozens, scores, millions of cities, reconstructed, reconceptualized. The days reordered, rationalized. Special machines to calculate everything the way it should be: who lives where, who lives how, who is what, who lives when. Divisions: family, work, recreation. Subdivisions: art, child rearing, means of transport. . . . A place for everyone, even those who love solitude. Let them live!

"Solitude is no crime. There are people who long for it. Don't get in their way."

"Strange as it seems, lepers have a right to live, too."

Don't run these two slogans together, leave them separate, maybe even insert another in between:

"Leave your neighbor alone. He doesn't want your concern."

I have to be prepared for assault on two sides. Any thought, even such an ancient and now utterly meaningless thought as "There is a God" or "There is no God," is always under threat of assault on two sides: progressive humanity and the reactionaries. Especially a new thought.

Progressive humanity has been embodied for nearly seventy years in the government that controls exactly half the globe and to whose throne ascended Kuzma the Second, nephew of Sidor the Great—progressive humanity is going to be at pains to lay a trap for me not so much from the standpoint of accomplishing my spatial tasks as from that of accomplishing the tasks they entail: those two weeks a year, which, like a bonus, will fall to the working class (and all humanity), progressive humanity will immediately try to pocket, demanding that they be divided up among choral singing, atomic calculations, study of Sidor the Great's biography, and parades. Whereas the reactionaries, naturally, will rebuke me for holidays, fasts, the Gregorian calendar, the Julian calendar, reckoning time from the day of the appearance of the Star of Bethlehem and the earthquake in the Near East in the first century of our era.

But understand me, understand! I am by no means promising you an easy solution to all the world's problems. On the contrary, I'm drawing you into great difficulties: architects (above all!), stationmasters, doctors, engineers, writers, coal miners, tailors, housewives—everyone faces enormous difficulties . . . but then after! After, say, a hundred years or maybe two—what a relief! Until everything is all mixed up again in the crowd and the bustle, until some new genius appears with new ideas for reordering space and time.

A new genius. That sounds as if I considered myself a genius. That's not true at all, though. I'm a modest man, my ideal would be a job as a senior accounts clerk, maybe a junior bookkeeper, marriage—and why not to

Didi? What happiness it would be to be with her, to be with her always, and the main thing—to be loved by her. "Do you love me?" I'd ask her every day, all day long. And she would answer each time, all her life: "Yes, I love you."

It was nearly dark when we finally stopped, pulled in under thick trees and parked.

"Great Fountains," someone said behind me. We passed a caged dog with which I locked eyes for a moment. I pulled my canvas duffel bag out from under my seat, put on my hat, and suddenly the anticipation of joy descended upon me. Not asking anyone anything, I got off the bus, walked out from under the trees onto a broad square, and stopped at an ice-cream vendor's stand. I listened closely to try to work out which direction I should go—but I couldn't hear the babbling of water. Although I remembered very well that fountains are supposed to babble.

Before me was a square. Streetlamps burned all around. The wide, utterly bare place was surrounded by an even ring of small trees, beyond which rose buildings, tall, stone, with lights on in most of the windows. There must have been a traffic jam in a side street because I could hear the howl of car horns from there. When it stopped, I listened again, but there was no sound of babbling. Directly in front of me was a huge, dry, cement fountain pool, about sixty meters in diameter. It was filled with people.

"The fountains?" I asked the ice-cream vendor.

"Not working," he said.

I walked over to the pool.

I had the impression that I was still in the middle of a large city, that in fact I hadn't gone anywhere. The purple and azure signs beyond the trees burned like the windows in the buildings, on floor after floor, like offices where evening cleaning was going on. It smelled of the same dust and cigars, and if it weren't for the gold-embroidered letters *G.F.* on the ice-cream vendor's cap, I could have imagined I was somewhere not far from home—on the road to the tobacco stand, say, as I had to cross a boring square in order to get there.

A dull rumble of voices hung over the dry pool. It was full of people sitting, standing, and lying. By the light of the streetlamps you could make out faces, young and old, strange clothes; hear individual voices, voices whispering, singing, saying things; as if on that stifling summer night all these people had come out of their houses and somehow by accident, surprising even themselves, had stopped on the square, in this enormous basin, or better— on this enormous cement raft about to sail away into the expanses of the night. It's hard to say who was here; it would have been easier to name who wasn't. At first glance, there were several hundred people, a few cats, a few dogs, about a dozen children, and a large cage with a parrot that had to be taken out to breathe the night air, too.

A small group of people were standing in a circle in the middle of the pool and getting ready to sing something. A fiddle and banjo lay at their feet Turkish fashion, but it seemed as if these people were about to unfurl the sails on the raft and cast off, with everyone now gathered here after a shipwreck, me included. I sat on the edge where someone moved over to make room for me.

There were old men who had brought along folding chairs and chessboards; old ladies who had spread newspapers out under their seats and clutched fat purses against their stomachs; young girls lying in the arms of young boys and boys lying in the arms of young girls, children crawling over them, cats playing on the knees of a pregnant beauty; two tramps offering each other swigs from a flask; a lively, barely audible conversation between two people wearing sandals and Mexican belts; a bald man talking to himself; a red-lipped woman with impudent, bulging eyes, resting her arms on two young men, flashing her teeth at a third; and then a pale, middle-aged gentleman with a flushed, broad-cheeked face sitting with his back to her.

There were a bunch of housewives, fat, strong, all with the same face, in low-cut cotton print dresses, knee length, sleeveless; over them hovered the odor of kitchen fumes. Young girls with boys' haircuts, wearing trousers, others with hair loose to the waist; a sixteen-year-old mother dozing over a child's stroller; a few girl delinquents playing some wild game, collapsing onto their neighbors, toppling them from the edge of the pool, choking with silent laughter; formally dressed, in prim hats, girl twins with their mama and papa; huge blacks in vivid silk neckerchiefs and jackets over naked torsos; Spaniards with guitars; an effeminate cherub with an old, wise face; fat mother's boys holding ice-cream cones in each fist; cripples with blank faces, ranging in color from pale green to soot-black; two freckled brothers in identical Scottish caps; some others too, apparently expecting something, having come here, to the obviously long-dry fountains, to breathe this night, to watch the moon rise slowly in the black-red sky; and there it was, instead of playing in the streams of the fountain, playing on the faces of this strange, sleepless crowd. Someone struck the strings, an African- or South American–sounding song played, some people joined in, especially among those lying in each other's arms. So the cement pool was filled with song, and all it lacked was the fragrant air of summer, the swaying trees and the hushed nightingales.

We sat there until about three in the morning, dozed and sang and dozed again. It was cooler than in those stuffy houses; freer, easier, and something reminded me of the tall spray and the resilient sparkle of the water. It still smelled of dust. The ice-cream vendor was still standing at his post, but the buses were gone, the last one had sounded its horn and vanished around the corner. Like everyone else, I dozed and sang, and then I put my duffel bag under my head, perched on the pool's edge, and fell sound asleep. And certain whispers and the quiet music all around shifted into my dream, and in my dream someone kept asking me about something, some three-syllable word sounded like a question, a short, persistent question for which I had no answer.

When I awoke, the pool was nearly empty; there were no more than a dozen people still asleep in it. A stifling new day was beginning, the sun was already burning, although it wasn't yet eight o'clock. I went to find some breakfast. Streets filled with morning city life ran in all directions. People were hurrying on their way; the newsman was opening up his stand; the shoeshine man was roosting on his stools; coffeehouses were opening up; there was the smell of rolls. I drank coffee and ate eggs, and it all reminded me of my intersection, where I lived, as if after a five-hour bus race I had wound up in the place where I'd started.

But that's not what I'd wanted at all! The machine that had given me three days off hadn't done it in order to . . . and suddenly I saw a long row of yellow-green buses, the sun was blazing in their windows, their doors were wide open. On the first was written BLUE SHORE, on the second GREEN SHORE, on the third—some other shore. "They're all going to the lake, more or less," a man said to a woman as he seated her. "Only this one, you know, skirts the city gardens, and that one runs along by the river, so what do you think, will that be quicker?" From out of nowhere people started streaming in, the driver switched on the motor, and I, repeating to myself, "Blue Shore, Green Shore, blue, green, pink gardens," jumped on, too, shoved my bag under the seat, tossed my hat on the shelf, and sat down by an opened window. We howled past the empty pool, turned into a tight street, into another rather broader, into a third, and there I lost count. Hundreds of people were streaming in all directions, it seemed, a wall of people; the enormous city rumbled all around. Whether it was the same one I lived in and had hoped to break away from yesterday, or another, contiguous and similar, or yet a third—I don't know. We rolled through it now without stopping, and it seemed there would be no end to it.

I thought back to the previous evening. There had been at least two people for every square meter in the dry pool. So you see if my idea were used, then there'd be half as many because there would be, say, only Pluses relaxing, after a sultry summer day, in the square, before falling asleep until morning and, in the morning, going back to work. During this time the Minuses would have wiped their eyes, gone under the taps, gulped down some coffee after jumping up with the alarm, scurried off to their factories, plants, offices, schools. Yes, there would be half as many people in the dry fountain, on this cement raft. I must jot down my plan, commit it, finally, to paper. Only in what form? That will take some thinking. And there was no better time than the present: the bus was now rolling down the highway; buildings flashed by now and then; the passengers dozed; the road spread out endlessly, to the edge, to the very horizon. And there, as I believed, awaiting me—beyond the horizon now—were blue, green shores.

If I were to write something on the order of a novel, then at this point people would say that I'd borrowed from the great utopians of our century. Not the idea, but the device itself, and perhaps even the manner of its exposition. But generally speaking, the predictions of all these geniuses have not been borne out, and we, in our one thousand nine hundred and eighty-fourth year, have not advanced all that far from our grandfathers' times. And then, after all, I intend to apply for a patent, this being a serious business bearing no resemblance to a utopia. If I have borrowed anything from the geniuses of the first half of our age, then, after all, they too borrowed without a twinge of conscience what they could from others who had lived earlier, especially our great-great-great grandfathers, so it works out that I'm taking back what belongs to me.

But no! Let's set the novel aside. It's better and simpler—and somehow more serious—to write a report and then submit it to the senior accounts clerk. (After all, I don't manage to exchange a word with even the junior bookkeeper more than twice a year!) Ask him to pass my memo up, and up, and up, and up. . . . However, there's no need to ask: the most important people are bound to take an interest in my idea. And they can develop it without me: I'm modest and entertain no fantasies of becoming chairman of any Special Space-Time Commission. Specialists, university departments, academics— they'll develop the idea. After yesterday evening, I'm convinced that all this has to be written down. Otherwise before long there are going to be four people for every square meter on a moonlit, starry night in the municipal garden!

Despite the speed of the bus, despite the open windows, it was getting hotter and hotter. We were racing along now in the sultry trembling air of a summer's day, the sun burned, the canvas shades were lowered, and I began to doze to the monotonous, silky sound of wheels in the turbid and dusty light. "Leave your neighbor alone," I thought. "He doesn't need you at all." That's another slogan. These slogans will lend my report a certain philosophical air. "Do neither good nor bad to your neighbor; just forget all about him." And little by little I started to doze in a sudden mood of sweet certainty that the emerald gardens and azure shores were coming closer and closer and could not escape me.

I woke up with a jolt. The bus had stopped and people were filing out; I got up, too. A second later I came to: this wasn't that first bus but a second one, I told myself; this is the second day of my trip, the middle of the second day. I jumped down from the step to the ground and looked around. Whether this was Green Shore or Blue, I didn't ask. By a small lake, on a flat shore, stood an enormous brick-glass factory, which shuddered from the clanging and rumbling. The gates of the main building were wide open, and there, in the dark depths, a foundry glimmered, reminding me somehow of the terrible red sun that hung over my head. Around the lake, as far as the eye could see, in cramped rows, stood red-hot cars, all identical and of an indeterminate color.

I stretched out alongside one of them in a kind of stupor, trying to tuck myself away in its narrow shadow, on the pebbles and cigarette butts. The black smoke that obscured half the sky came from the same direction as we had but did not end either over the lake or beyond it. There, on the other shore, was a twin of the nearby factory, also brick-glass, enormous, alive somehow: even from here you could tell that it was full of people, loud noises, the mechanical might of droning and shuddering, and past it, off to one side, stood a gigantic power station, completely transparent, similar in its intricate pattern to the skeletal Eiffel Tower.

I breathed in the hot air saturated with car exhaust. Despite the shadow, the side of the car I was lying alongside, which I tried not to touch, was red-hot, there was no breeze coming from the lake, and I was starting to feel sick from the gas fumes that filled my mouth and nose, that filled my very self, from the smell of scorching tires, metal, oil. Where am I? How many towns have I passed through, towns that ran together in a blur? Where is the horizon I was promised? Where am I? What kind of lake is this, surrounded by droning factories, where's the grass, where's the forest, where's the field? Where do these streets go? To more houses, stores, signs, buses, other automobiles? And will people come here to swim as night falls, so that I can go into the water with them? But the water seemed lead-black, metallic as well, like everything around here, and about thirty steps away from me was a signpost: NO SWIMMING.

Two people were walking toward me now; one was wearing a service cap and the other—naked to the waist—was wiping his forehead and neck with a hand-kerchief and evidently looking for his car. They stepped over my hat, and I jumped up and shouted after them, louder than I should have:

"How do I get out of here?"

I wanted to ask "Where's everybody else?" but at the last second I thought the question would sound foolish.

"Turn right and the third turn will take you to the highway," said the one in the service cap slowly, having stopped and looked around at me.

"I'm on foot."

"On foot?" The other one stopped too, and they both looked at me.

"When does the bus go?" I asked again, too loudly.

"The bus goes tomorrow morning," said the first, and they walked on, farther and farther away from me. The half-naked one finally found his car, started it up, drove out, and vanished in the dust. The first, in the service cap, walked back.

"Listen," I said, quieter now. "I'm in the wrong

place, I was going to the lake. That is, I thought that this lake, well, you know how lakes can be. . . . I've been through four towns, four at the very least, there may have been five. I thought . . . I have a day and a half. Couldn't you tell me. . . ."

"Ask at Information," he said. "You're not supposed to lie down here." And he walked away.

I followed him. "You understand," I said, still trying to make him listen. "I do have a sense of humor, and yesterday I had a terrific laugh when Great Falls—that is, I mean Fountains—played a trick on me." (Did I really laugh? I have absolutely no memory of laughing!) "But today it's too much, it's not funny anymore. I'm angry, and most of all I'm angry with myself, and if you'd only listen. . . ."

"Ask at Information, they'll tell you there," he repeated, and I saw his face. It expressed nothing. Not even distaste. It simply lacked all expression, like a piece of paper or a china saucer.

My watch said a quarter to five. I was hungry, I was walking down a road between the walls of a factory that stretched to infinity. Then began the two-story houses, where evidently the workers and employees from the nearby factories lived: porch—window, window—porch, and so on, to infinity, on an utterly deserted street, without a single tree, without a bench, without a puddle, without passersby, without children. I walked for an hour and a half until I had passed through it all and seen nothing, apart from windows-porches. Then it came to a stop and I found myself, clearly, on the main street, because on the right and left was one gas station after another. Then—a square, large glass stores, three churches, a library, a school, a hotel. I walked in.

"Do you have a room?"

A room was found. I washed, changed my shirt, went downstairs, had dinner, but knew no peace. From the exhaustion, from the heat, I was overwhelmed by a feeling of distress, like when your insides are all in an uproar, and you'd like to be in an uproar yourself, but you don't have the strength, you long to lie down, but as soon as you do, the uproar inside you becomes even more powerful, and nothing you do will quiet it, unless sleep comes and crushes you completely, with your private poundings, all those pulses that beat inside you like steelworks, at an incredible depth that bears no relation whatsoever to your own manifest dimensions.

I awoke in the middle of the night and heard once again that same sound that last night in my half sleep, when I was lying on the bottom of the cement pool, gave me no rest. I could hear a brief, persistent question, perhaps a single word, with the stress on the second syllable, or three words, each one syllable long. Perhaps it wasn't a word at all but simply something striking triplets, or drops dropping—one soft, one loud, one soft, over and over, brief strokes, but no, there was some kind of word in that sound.

In the morning I went down to the restaurant where, despite the early hour, it already smelled of soup, like all cheap restaurants. I was served by the fat proprietress, who was wearing slippers on her bare feet and a clean apron. She had clean, calm hands and a motionless, once sweet face. I suddenly decided to tell her everything, then she would tell me what to do. She listened to my story and sighed heavily.

"You came to the wrong place? But why didn't you ask? And it's been so hot! I always say it's better to take your holiday when it's not so hot, otherwise you just torture yourself. On days like this it's only nice on the Gulf."

"What Gulf?"

"On the Gulf, on the sea. At the shore. At least— even if it is scorching—at least there's a breeze once in a while."

"Is it far?"

"An hour and a half. No, sorry, more. Are you in a car?"

"No, I came by bus, and then on foot."

She looked at me with disbelief, and I added faint-heartedly: "That is, I walked here from the bus stop, assuming that there'd be buses and bus stops somewhere in town." She was mollified. There was even a certain sympathy in her eyes.

"And you realize, time is passing." I couldn't hold back any longer. "And I'm still trying to get somewhere, it's just stupid, and even if I did have a sense of humor— and I do—then all this might seem very funny. Just dreadfully funny, ha ha ha!"

She displayed a row of teeth, that's how she smiled, and then went to the other tables, but already all I could think about was the Gulf.

"There's a train," she said, returning with the bill. "You'll make it. It will take you right to the Gulf, it's a passenger train, a good one. It leaves in about two hours.

You'll have a swim there, lie in the sun. Fine sand, glorious swimming. And a very broad beach, half a kilometer. The Gulf!"

I looked at her with gratitude. In that instant, I wished her, with all the heart I could muster, prosperity, for her children, her grandchildren, prosperity in this hotel, in this restaurant, the smell of which pursued me all the way to the station.

My duffel bag—under the seat. My hat—on the shelf. The train cars went from station to station, small, hot, rumbling; the passengers changed, people flitted by, but I was happy, or rather, nearly happy, because regret over the time lost descended upon me like a dark cloud; it was hot, exactly like the day before. If I tried hard I could imagine it was the day before, when I was lying in the narrow shadow of the strange car, next to the sinister lake, and then that trek, and even before that the dry reservoir, and I lost count of the buses and towns, and I was no longer completely certain how long I'd been traipsing through those towns in those buses.

Once again the white-hot sky was in the window, and the sun—fortunately, on the opposite side—was baking, burning, shimmering. I was trying not to move, since with the slightest movement I was drenched in sweat. I looked out the window, and there, in an odd, chance order, flashed: tall buildings, smaller buildings, railway tracks in between, a piece of road, a tree jammed between two churches, a factory, a gas station, another building, the trajectory of a street full of traffic, a street that seemed to have been deserted, the crisscrossing of cables over everything, a station, a plane like a silver ant crawling across the sky, an elevated road running at an angle to our train, a bridge consisting of four bridges plaited between the highway and the streets—and so it went not for two hours, or three, but almost a whole four, when the train suddenly stopped, went a little bit farther, and came to a final stop. And I looked through the window, beyond the roofs, the chimneys, the church spires and crosses, and the water towers, and I got a glimpse of the Gulf in the haze of the intense heat. It flashed for an instant and an oncoming train entering the station blocked it out. But I already knew it existed.

How is all this going to look in the future? That interests me, to be perfectly honest, much more than how it looked in the past. The past I can't change. The past is good (as we all know), twenty, thirty years back *everything* was good, anyone can tell you that. On this, I think, both the progressive thinking (as they are usually called), like that great mind Kuzma the Second, and any retrograde who believes in the evil eye will concur. So I'm not interested in the past. Whereas I can play a role in rebuilding the future, and although I feel no burning personal ambition, I have to admit that the thought comforts me in my—let's be blunt—gray life, in my utterly unremarkable fate. "Who is that man?" someone will ask, and they'll tell him: "That's the man who gained an average of one twenty-fourth of a life for each person and who doubled space." I absolutely must think everything completely through before I write my report, to say nothing of the novel. Sometimes I even find it strange that all this hasn't occurred to anyone else. After all, there are people thinking (and people of the most diverse inclinations) about how to arrange the fate of mankind.

I moved with the dense crowd toward the Gulf. The restaurants were full, people were dining under colorful umbrellas, drinking iced drinks; music rumbled from a loudspeaker, interrupted by commercials. I have nothing against advertising, but I don't understand how people can like it more than music. But after all, there are people who listen to music only reluctantly, relaxing at the commercials. Then we started down a long tunnel, where it was cool, where people on holiday, or maybe on tour, lined the walls, enjoying the cool, and a few people from our crowd stayed there, assuring us, "It's better here." But I didn't. The tunnel led us from one bend to another, finally a light appeared in the distance, that same terrible, irrevocable sun flashed, and the Gulf opened up, a watery expanse receding into the distance, into the haze, and I knew that I was going to look out at it until my eyes hurt, anything not to turn back onto the path I'd already traveled, to the six, seven, maybe even more towns I'd left behind.

Yes, everything was marvelous on that scorching, sandy shore: in long rows to the left and right, their facades facing the Gulf, rose white skyscrapers, which evidently occupied dozens of kilometers on the broad, gently sloping shore. We all took off our shoes and walked barefoot across the fine, burning sand, carefully skirting the prostrate bodies, carefully placing our feet so as not to step on anyone, stepping over strange feet, arms, sometimes even heads. The advertisements howled, interrupted by the music, sometimes more commercials howled right underfoot, from radios brought along by the swimmers.

People were settling down wherever they could find an unoccupied piece of beach, and I too quickly settled in among the bodies, hesitating for a second, trying to figure whether I was going to bump into anyone when I lay down. But someone politely shifted a little, or rather, flopped over to his other side, and I shifted, drawing my shoulders and belly in so as to take up less space. Around me I heard people breathing, conversations, snoring, children crying, for a while I didn't move, so as not to disturb anyone. Then I threw off my trousers and shirt and, dressed only in my shorts, stretched out blissfully on my stomach, rested my head on my arms, and was still. A helicopter flew over low, and its shadow brushed me for a moment. I moved a can, an empty bottle, a crumpled, half–sun-faded newspaper someone had dropped on me away from my face, and closed my eyes. It seemed to me that through the thousands of sounds—the drone of helicopters, the shrieks of swimmers, the howl, the radio, the lifeguards' whistles, I could hear the splash of waves. This was the imagination of a completely happy man— the Gulf was silent and immutable.

I must have dropped off. I came to and cautiously untangled myself from the arms and legs of my benumbed, dozing neighbors, and, once again paying attention to where I placed my feet, walked to the water's edge and stood in line to swim. Here there was perfect discipline. The Gulf was filled with swimmers as far as the eye could see, and there were long lines of them waiting at the very edge of the shore for their turn, for when there would be room for them in the water. The sun was still burning, I felt like throwing myself, hands clasped, into the blue, absolutely flat, soundless wave, but there was nowhere to throw myself, it was all full, impossible even to squeeze in on the sly. People were standing shoulder to shoulder, holding children, diving cautiously, taking turns, obeying the lifeguards' orders. "Taking turns," I said to myself. "This confirms my theory. It's interesting; what great mind thought up this idea of 'taking turns'?"

Finally it was my turn. I went in. The water was warm, but still refreshing. I went in up to my chest, the people were fewer, and I swam off. Ahead was the far shore of the Gulf—or so I surmised—and I kept watching it, the haze of the heat in which it disguised itself as an ocean. "Away, away, together, one day." I began speaking in verse suddenly from the fullness of my sense of lightness and hope. "In the end, it's not so far, there are probably steamboats, very clean, very white, as if they'd been rubbed down with cologne, and you and I will take a steamboat like that, cast off, sail away, and there won't be anyone there, or almost anyone, or only people like you and me, and you and I will stay there not two days or three but as long as the machine allows—yours and mine—the good, intelligent machine, if we wait two years or so, we'll have that shared happiness; and think how marvelous it will be: a forest, a field, a pond, birds, and flowers.

That hazy shore seemed to me like the promised land. I loved it, I dreamed of it, and it seemed to me this love was beginning to change into another, into something I had never been able to feel inside, something I had dreamed of experiencing so many times but still somehow hadn't been able to, something was missing. I turned back and half closed my eyes; ahead I saw everything I'd so wanted to leave behind. There, behind those glass-marble, pink-white skyscrapers approaching the water, lay poisoned lakes, dry fountains, towns stretched out over a grid, one emerging from another and leading into the next; there were stifling dusty nights, sultry dusty days, junior bookkeepers and senior accounts clerks, and you, you, whom I lectured so dryly and harshly, with such dispassion, for being late to work, citing as an example myself, who has never been late for anything! With half-closed eyes I swam and swam, and it seemed to me that at any moment tears would start flowing from my eyes, mixing with the salt water of the Gulf, tears of compassion and love, and tenderness, and eternity. Feeling the bottom with my feet, I stood up and walked, still remembering that behind me, across the Gulf, in the blue smoke, lay another world I had been alone with for a brief while, far from everyone, my world of silence, of our shared solitude, and of joy, also shared.

But up ahead it was the same shore, the crowd covering so much of it that if anyone asked me what color the sand was I wouldn't know what to answer, the sun swimming in the sky, already slightly slanted to one side of the buildings, and the lines of people waiting in perfect discipline for the moment a place came free in the water. And over it all that noise, when you can't hear your own voice.

I pushed through, to get out of the water, pushed through, to get to my spot, dried off as best I could, brushing my neighbors' faces with my towel and constantly begging their pardon. I couldn't find room to lie down on the cramped beach anymore, so gathering up my things, I went to eat. I waited patiently in line, ate a lot, drank a bottle of beer, wandered down the burning pavement under artificial palms, listened to the loud-speaker forecasting a clear evening and relatively cool night, and sat down on a stone bench. Evening was start-ing to fall. The sun went behind the skyscrapers.

"It would be nice to stay here till morning," said a woman's voice, and I saw two people sitting next to me, a man and a woman.

"But we've already reserved a room," he objected, "and made a deposit."

"*He* said it was going to be a clear evening and a cool night."

"Yes, *he* did."

"And we can swim again, when no one's here, and then sleep on the sand."

"If everyone thought like that, no one would ever leave, and it would be just as crowded."

"That couldn't be. Eventually almost all of them will leave. In any case, half."

I smiled but held my tongue. She said it: half. I'll soon give them what they want. They don't know it yet.

"It'll be rough sleeping," said the man, and he yawned.

"It's the air that makes you do that," said the woman. "Yes, maybe you're right." They were both silent.

"You know what"—he suddenly reached out dreamily—"let's go."

"Let's," she agreed. And they stood up, and walked away, leaving me to my thoughts.

They flowed, those thoughts, and in an unconscious but close connection with them incoherent feelings were awakening inside me, all the time pursuing my thoughts, overtaking them, exactly as if they were weaving some kind of fabric combining two threads of different colors in one design; as if two shuttles were flying inside me, and if I weren't afraid of seeming old-fashioned I would have said that one was in my mind and the other in my heart, one was related to my idea and the other to Didi. Two threads weaving together, and then suddenly the first shuttle began to leave the second behind, getting far ahead, growing dim. It didn't seem so important, so significant, so decisive; whereas at that point the second was somehow managing to deck itself out in gold, rust, autumn colors. And amid all this, suddenly, that question, that three-syllable night sound that this time didn't seem to want to wait for the night, but amid the hubbub, the shouts, the running, the crampedness, the ever-burning but now oblique sun, rustled, or flowed through:

"Where are you?" And then, about five seconds later, again: "Where are you?" and again, after a silence within me: "Where are you?"

And suddenly I realized that mankind needed nothing from me, that there was no reason to split space and give each person a time extension so that life could suddenly go on longer than it now did, so that the lines of swimmers could suddenly become half as long—that this still wouldn't fix anything. I realized that only one thing is necessary and important: the shore of the Gulf, in the rain, in the snow, in the burning heat, in storm and blizzard, where she and I together, with my one and only

forever, are going to be, as much as possible, as much as
the machine allows us to, so that, passing through the
fields and forests, like two guardian angels (she being
mine and I hers), we can feel that only she can forgive
me everything and I her, only she can protect me, and
I her, from everything in the world, past and future. That
this walk that is going to happen—there can be no living
otherwise—will be our betrothal, and wedding, which is
and can be none of anyone else's business in the world.
In those minutes despair and joy seemed to intertwine
inside me into one unbearable lump, the shuttle flew in
mad disarray, pounding loudly: "Where are you? Where
are you? Where are you?" The fabric was being woven,
the very foundation of my life, and I was hearing and
seeing her—as happens perhaps once or twice in a man's
life.

When I came to after all this the sun was gone and
the crowd at the shore had thinned. I walked along the
shore, at the water's edge, where now you could pass
without brushing anyone. I walked and walked, on the
left of me skyscrapers stood in a solid, endless wall,
sparkling now in the lights of advertisements, on the right,
barely audibly, the green-blue Gulf vacillated. In the distance, where the shore took a turn, on the background
of a darkened sky, a gigantic screen lit up and giants were
already moving around on it; the show had begun. Now
I was quiet inside; everything was silent, everything was
calm, as if some kind of decision had been reached.

Before lying down on the calm warm sand, I gazed
into the distance for a long time: the crowd was still
thinning out; someone was still splashing in the dark

water; a few people a little way away from me were getting ready to eat, spreading a cloth for a picnic; it became quieter in the air, gulls flew by slowly, one more plane droned by overhead. I stretched out—not parallel but crosswise, so that my face was to the horizon and my back to all that had been, in order to feel that this time I was lying on the edge of my former life, that right here, by this Gulf, it came to an end, and beyond it another began.

Night fell. The picnic was over. I began to doze off, my head on my duffel bag. Sleep approached so slowly, so cautiously, that it seemed as if I felt its approach with every moment, as if it were a spirit barely touching the earth, walking toward me. It seemed as though someone was placing a hand on my forehead and that the long tresses of her hair were streaming slowly and smoothly between my forehead and her palm. And then I fell asleep and must not have moved all night because when I opened my eyes in the morning I was still lying on my side, my arm stretched the length of my body.

I opened my eyes and didn't move: directly in front of me the dawn was breaking. A long, pale stripe stretched across the Gulf, and on the horizon, where yesterday the hazy smoke had wearied and tempted me, stood a huge, black city, the eighth or ninth, by my count, blocking the horizon in a concave semicircle.

I lay immobile, gazing at the black silhouette of the city. The broken line of its roofs was precisely drawn on the pink dawn; it was immense; the skyscrapers retreated in tiers; and it wasn't that this hard, black vision arose from out of the water, it wasn't that it was lowered into the water through a narrow break in the early-morning clouds that luxuriated overhead and through which the sun was already reaching out to the water and land. What amazed me about that vision was its conjunction of horror and beauty, the death of something that had scarcely arisen in me, and the return of what had always been there, of something familiar, something I had lived with, something I had grown used to, something I had made my peace with, I think. It was growing now, setting its limits before me, its laws, and there could be no question of rebelling against it or arguing with it, or of conducting any kind of dialogue with it at all. The city stood, indisputable, like that law. And above it, behind it, the sun was rising, about to be transformed from a black silhouette into something translucent, into lace made from iron, concrete, and stone, barring the way where I had thought there was a possibility of retreat—for an hour, for a day, or forever.

The day was beginning, but that scorching air I'd been breathing the days before seemed to have dispersed, and a coolness was borne in from the Gulf. The couples and solitary people who had fallen asleep on the sand had not stirred, everything was quiet, life had not yet begun, only from somewhere, probably the nearest coffeehouse, came the first broadcast of morning news. I stood up. For a minute I hesitated—take a swim? But I had no desire to go in the water. I put on my shoes, turned toward the shore, and without looking at either the Gulf or the sun shining in the heavenly glades, strode off toward the voice of the loudspeaker.

The next day I was sitting in an armchair, in a room,

and she was on a stool beside me. I was telling her that all in all there was no point going anywhere, that fountains don't gush, there's no swimming in lakes, there's no room for anyone in the gulfs, but soon all this was going to change.

"The Pill?" she asked, raising her sad eyes to me.

"Not the Pill. I've already told you, but you're so scatterbrained and you never listen to anyone and you forget everything."

Then I told her about my return trip, which was shorter than I'd expected, and how we had wound up back on Schliemann Square again.

"I bet you don't know who Schliemann was?" I asked condescendingly, sensing my superiority over her, all the seriousness, all the practicality of my nature.

"No," she said, but there was no notable regret in her voice.

"Schliemann found Troy," I said, examining my cuff links. "That's why they erected a monument to him. Do you know what Troy is?" She shook her head. No. "He made excavations, he excavated nine cities. The ninth was Troy. Vertically, you see, they were lying on top of each other."

But because she'd shaken her head, the comb had fallen out, and her hair spilled down.

A NOTE ON THE TYPE

The text of this book was set in a digitized version of Perpetua, designed by the British artist Eric Gill (1882–1940) and cut by The Monotype Corporation, London, in 1928–1930. In this contemporary typeface of original design, without any direct historical antecedents, the shapes of the roman letters derive from stonecutting, a form of lettering in which Gill was eminent. The italic is essentially an inclined roman. The general effect of the typeface in reading sizes is one of lightness and grace. The larger display sizes of the type are extremely elegant and form what is probably the most distinguished series of inscriptional letters cut in the present century.

Composed by PennSet, Inc., Bloomsburg, Pennsylvania
Printed and bound by Haddon Craftsmen, Inc.
Scranton, Pennsylvania
Designed by Iris Weinstein